4/22

D0338453

DIAMOND PARK

DIAMOND PARK

PHILLIPPE DIEDERICH

DUTTON BOOKS

DUTTON BOOKS

An imprint of Penguin Random House LLC, New York

First published in the United States of America by Dutton Books, an imprint of Penguin Random House LLC, 2021

LIBRARY OF CONGRESS CATALOGING-IN-PUBLICATION DATA

Names: Diederich, Phillippe, 1964- author.
Title: Diamond Park / Phillippe Diederich.
Description: New York : Dutton Books, an imprint of Penguin Random House LLC, [2022] | Includes bibliographical references. | Audience: Ages 14+. | Audience: Grades 10-12. | Summary: When four Mexican-American teenagers from Houston travel to Diamond Park to buy a 1959 Chevy Impala from Magaña's godfather, something goes very wrong, and one of them, Susi, ends up arrested for murder; convinced that the real killer is a drug trafficker called Anaconda, Flaco and Magaña head to Mexico hunting for him to clear Susi's name—but in the process of kidnapping Anaconda Flaco discovers how little he understands about what really happened in Diamond Park.
Identifiers: LCCN 2021029597 (print) | LCCN 2021029598 (ebook) | ISBN 9780593354254 (hardcover) | ISBN 9780593354278 (epub)
Subjects: LCSH: Mexican American teenagers—Juvenile fiction. | Drug traffic—Juvenile fiction. | Murder—Juvenile fiction. | Friendship—Juvenile fiction. | Detective and mystery stories. | Houston (Tex.)—Juvenile fiction. | CYAC: Mexican Americans—Fiction. | Drug traffic—Fiction. | Murder—Fiction. | Friendship—Fiction. | Mystery and detective stories. | Houston (Tex.)—Fiction. | LCGFT: Detective and mystery fiction.
Classification: LCC PZ7.1.D54 Di 2022 (print) | LCC PZ7.1.D54 (ebook) | DDC 813.6 [Fic]--dc23
LC record available at https://lccn.loc.gov/2021029597
LC ebook record available at https://lccn.loc.gov/2021029598

Printed in Canada

ISBN 9780593354254

1 3 5 7 9 10 8 6 4 2

FRI
Design by Anna Booth
Text set in Arno Pro

For Lorraine, con todo mi corazón

PART I.

1.

I wake up early and wait to escape. The house is small and like a hundred years old and has walls like paper. My tío Félix works with a lawn maintenance crew and leaves before dawn. Every morning it's him stomping into the bathroom, back to his room, putting his clothes on, back to the bathroom and then to the kitchen where Ana Flor's making him breakfast. The house fills with the smell of eggs and frijoles. Meat. Not bacon. Probably just carnitas or some other pork leftovers.

Ana Flor whispers like a bird, asks him if he got enough rest, asks about lunch, what he wants, offers him leftovers, a sandwich. Félix grunts, says he doesn't care. He's loud, complains like he always does, as if the whole world needs to hear how miserable he is.

The coffee smells of cinnamon and sugar. The floor creaks. He paces, probably grabbing his hat and work boots.

Ana Flor says something about a utility bill and groceries, eggs and tortillas and whatever.

Tío Félix tells her to pay the bill, but to tell my mom to buy the groceries.

Ana Flor says it isn't fair to make my mom pay for the groceries all the time. Félix is silent for a moment. The tension travels like a snake across the house and slowly fills my room, the one I used to share with my cousin Carlos before he was killed.

When Félix speaks again, his words are like grit. He says my mom's the one getting government assistance—that's what food stamps are for. I can almost see his finger inches from her face when he tells her this—when he tells her it's not her place to question his orders—que no sea metiche.

At last the screen door slams shut. The old F-150 rattles out the driveway and down the road.

I get up.

⌄

The plan is to meet Magaña and Tiny at the bus stop in half an hour. Gotta hurry, take all the money I can find in my room—twenty-three bucks and change. I stuff my backpack under my bed so Ana Flor won't see it later and get suspicious. All the while I keep thinking about the car, dreamed about it all night—'59 Impala. I don't know if I'm happy or jealous or suspicious or what. Magaña can be full of shit sometimes.

"Road trip," he said yesterday. Just walked up, dropped it like a dare. "You two up for it, o qué?"

I was sitting with Tiny at the far end of the school cafeteria, staring down at the fake taco meal the Houston Independent School District serves. Tiny was complaining like he always does, flicking the cheese off his tacos. "In Mexico they'd shoot you dead if you served this chingadera."

Tiny's Mexican. Like for real Mexican from Mexico. Mojado. He crossed over with his family six years ago and has been here ever since. No papers or nothing. So he's always going on about how things here are not like in Mexico—never stops with that.

I'm Mexican but I've never even been.

"I don't get it," he said. "What's so hard about making a real taco?"

That's when Magaña parked his ass on our table. He turned his head to the side real casual, stole a glance at Susi Taylor and the girls a couple tables away, and said, "You two cabrones up for a road trip?"

I glanced at Tiny because he knows how it is with Magaña. Fucker hovered over our trays like a vulture, picked a French fry from Tiny's and tossed it in his mouth. "Entonces, we go, no?"

"Where to," Tiny joked, "Acapulco?"

"Shut the hell up," Magaña barked. "I'm serious." Then he looked at me and spelled it out. "I found a car. No, no—I found *the* car. 1959 Chevy Impala. Con-ver-ti-ble."

Right away I figured it was bullshit. A 1959 Impala is as badass as it gets, a one-off model. The most unique Chevy ever built. Car looks like a spaceship. It was the only year it came with the teardrop lights under the folded tail fins—and convertible?

"My old man said my godfather's got one in a barn in Diamond Park."

"He's probably pulling your chain," I said.

Magaña fell quiet for a moment, just stared at us like he was waiting for something to happen. Then he leaned forward real slow and gave us that devil's grin of his. "He said he'd take a grand for it."

"A thousand bucks?" Tiny laughed. "Does it even run?"

"Just needs a little TLC."

I'm not sure what I was thinking. I didn't really believe there was a car—certainly not a '59 Impala. But a road trip to the valley sounded cool. "So when do we go?"

"Mañana."

"'Tas loco," Tiny said. "That's, like, five hours."

"Two and a half, give or take," he said and picked at Tiny's food, probably just to mess with him. "It's just south of Corpus."

"Ya!" Tiny slapped his hand. "Stop eating my fries, cabrón."

"So we good?"

"Count me out. I got a geometry test and—"

"No mames, Tiny. You have to come."

"Why does it have to be tomorrow?"

"'Cause if you snooze, you lose," he said and slid off the table. "And bring tools."

"What? No way," Tiny said. "My jefe'll kill me."

"All we need's like a few wrenches and screwdrivers and shit," Magaña said, as if he knew something about fixing cars. "We'll meet at the bus stop in the morning and take the 56 down to the Medical Center and catch the Expreso to Diamond Park. My padrino'll pick us up there. We'll drive the car back in the afternoon, be home by dinnertime. Piece of cake."

"Right," I said. "Tres leches."

Tiny laughed, his chubby cheeks jiggling like flan. "Tres. Pinches. Leches."

2.

When I walk into the kitchen, Ana Flor greets me with a kiss on the cheek and stares at my face like she's trying to see if I'm hiding something behind my eyes. That's how she is. Her eyes burrow like lasers. Sometimes I think she's taking some kind of a mental picture in case I never come back. Like Carlos.

"¿Quieres café?" she says, but she's already pouring hot water into a cup.

I grab the jar of Nescafé and drop in two heaping spoonfuls.

"It's too much," she says, complaining without really meaning it because we go through the same thing every morning. I stir the coffee until it makes a thin foam, then I lick the spoon, and almost as if on cue, she says, "Cochino."

She busies herself wiping the counter with an old jerga even though the entire kitchen, the living room, the whole house is squeaky clean. That's what she does all day. Clean, sew, cook, talk to the neighbors, pray, light candles for Carlos. Apologize to Tío Félix for whatever set him off.

I already have a text from Magaña asking if I'm up. But when I open the front door to leave, Ana Flor stops me. "What about breakfast?"

"I have to help Tiny with his homework."

"You coming back?"

"After school."

She stands in the living room, her blue-and-white-checkered apron tied at the waist, looks at me like she's trying to find me out because the sun isn't even up yet and I'm walking out the door in a hurry.

"You don't give your aunt a proper goodbye, hijo. You're just like your tío. I guess I'm just a fixture in this house."

She crosses her arms and sets a foot forward, hip to the side. "It's as if I don't exist until someone needs something. Entonces, sí."

I walk back across the living room and give her a kiss on the cheek, thank her for the coffee and for being such a nice aunt.

She purses her lips to hold back her smile. "Ándale pues. Have a good day. And remember that your mother's off on Sunday. I think you should take advantage and talk with her about this business of the art college."

Even though Ana Flor's cool with my art, I didn't tell her I sent an application to Cal Arts. She gossips too much. Not that she would tell my mom, but that she would tell one of the neighbors and then it would go around the block and come back to my mom. That's how it works around here. My mom doesn't think I can make any money as an artist. She wants me to be something she can brag about to her friends—a doctor or a lawyer or whatever.

I step out on the porch and close the screen door real easy. I see Ana Flor folded over the little shrine she put together for her dead son. It's been almost four years but she still lights a candle where she has a framed illustration of the Virgen and a photo of Carlos from before he joined the army. But not the flag. That patriotic memento is proudly displayed front and center on the mantel over the television so it's the first thing anyone'll see when they walk into the house.

Carlos was cool. He was trying to improve himself. But the fucking Taliban stopped him in his tracks. I'll never forget the two soldiers in their clean parade uniforms coming to the house to tell Félix and Ana Flor the news. I sat in my room with the door cracked open a sliver as Ana Flor bowed her head and invited them in. They were crispy-clean bolillos, stood real stiff like robots. Ana Flor gestured to the living room. The two of them sat next to each other on the plastic-covered couch where no one's allowed to sit, backs straight, hats off, eyes ahead on the wall where there's a bureau with the family pictures. Ana Flor went to the kitchen and came back with a tray with two cups with hot water and a jar of Nescafé and the plastic sugar container Carlos stole from a diner when we were little.

The soldiers sipped their coffee but I could tell it was out of politeness because they never touched their cups again. Ana Flor crossed herself twice, folded over, and wept.

I'd seen her cry before, but compared with this, it'd been just drama. This was real. She was a tough woman. Tougher than my mom and even Tío Félix for sure. But that day when she cried, and later when the soldiers left, she shuffled around the house as though she didn't know what to do with herself.

After the funeral, I was alone with Ana Flor. My mom had to work and Tío Félix went out, probably to tie one on with Julio and the neighborhood losers. I didn't know what to do. I escaped and sat in the Buick all afternoon, gave her as much space as I could. I guess I thought at any moment she would lash out, throw shit, start doing flying kicks or something. But she just moped around the house like La Llorona until she finally went into the bedroom I shared with Carlos and shut the door. When I snuck back in the house, all I could hear was her whimpering, real quiet like water.

I learned something then. Sorrow—like real, honest-to-God sadness—is so deep it doesn't let you breathe. It grabs you from the inside and squeezes like a vise and takes something away that you'll never get back. That's how I knew later, whenever Ana Flor pitched a fit about Tío Félix coming home drunk or whatever, she was probably doing it for show.

I walked over to where Tío Félix had placed the American flag the soldiers gave him at the funeral. So, you die and your family gets a piece of cloth that's supposed to mean something. It didn't seem fair.

The flag was folded into a fat triangle. It was perfect and tight and neat and smooth like something manufactured. Made me wonder who folded it, if they had, like, a factory of flags that came out in perfect triangles from some machine. I imagined an assembly plant like the one in Chicago where my mom worked in front of a big industrial sewing machine. Maybe there was a long line of Mexicans or, like us, Mexican brown but American, folding flag after flag so they could send them out to the families of the soldiers that died.

The way they're folded, you can only see the blue and the white stars. No stripes. I held my hand over the flag and thought of the time Carlos came home from basic. We sat in his '48 Buick, which had been parked on blocks in the empty lot next to the house for years. He looked different with his crew cut and uniform—taller. Like he had grown up, but his eyes were still the eyes of a kid—that teenager who'd give me a wink whenever he snuck out to meet his friends. He was my cousin but he was like my brother because I didn't have anyone else.

He said he was going to Fort something or other, and would be gone for a while. "But just 'cause I'm not gonna be here doesn't mean I won't be thinking of you," he said. "I want you to remember that."

I nodded. His sentimental goodbye kind of made me uneasy because this wasn't us. It wasn't Carlos.

"Keep drawing. Don't let anyone stop you," he said. I'd been drawing like crazy and was getting way better at it. I'd even sent him a real detailed pen-and-ink of a badass eagle attacking a bunch of bad guys. "You have talent, Flaco. Take advantage of it."

His eyebrows were all furrowed as if maybe he was gonna cry. I didn't get it then, but after he was killed, I understood. Carlos was never into being a soldier. Not that he was a coward or anything. Just that his heart wasn't into fighting or killing or following orders.

"I'll be sending some money home," he said. "I want you to take care of my mom. She's tough but she's also delicate in here." He tapped his chest with the side of his fist. "I know my old man ain't the kind of guy who understands that. So I'm entrusting her to you."

He was real serious about it. Which was scary. I had just turned fourteen and I was supposed to take care of a grown woman who scared the shit out of me because when she didn't get things the way she wanted she went batshit crazy. Whenever she threw a tantrum, the house emptied out like ICE raiding a meat plant.

Then he held up the key chain made out of an old Mexican silver peso. It had two keys. One for the front door of the house, the other for the car.

"I want you to take care of the Buick," he said. "You don't have to do anything. Just make sure no one steals it. Or breaks off any parts."

I nodded and stared at the dash, smooth clean metal with tiny rust specks. The fucking Buick. It was my place now. Some kids had tree houses. I had a rusted Buick on blocks.

I thought all this stuff about Carlos as I held my hand over the folded flag. I even started to think maybe the flag was magic. As if maybe Carlos's soul was folded into that triangle of blue and white stars. There were so many times when he said wise things. I wish I'd paid more attention. When he was real serious with me or invited me into his world, like when he called me into the bedroom and gave me my first dirty magazine, or when we sat in the back steps of the house at night and he told me he'd decided to join the army and asked me if I thought it was a good idea, it made me feel as though I was worth something.

I traced the lines of the white stars with the tip of my index finger as the memories of my dead cousin came and went. Even the bad memories were good. It was as if the flag were sucking out whatever bad feelings I might've held inside. And before I knew it, I felt a raspy pain in the pit of my throat. My hand was flat on the flag, and I swear I could almost feel Carlos's heart beating inside it when Ana Flor yelled, "Don't touch my flag!"

I bolted to my room and sat on the bed and sank my head in my hands. The room was small—two beds and a dresser—but at that moment it felt huge. The emptiness Carlos left was like in one of those Dalí paintings that have these spacious, empty brown landscapes where shit doesn't make any sense. The weird thing is, he hadn't been home in, like, forever and all that time I didn't miss him. Maybe because I knew one day he'd come back. But not anymore.

A little later Ana Flor came into the room and sat next to me. She put her arm around my shoulder and drew me close, laid her head against mine, and wept. But even then, I still didn't cry.

3.

The second I walk off the porch and step on the sidewalk, the dog next door starts barking like I'm a criminal, sets off all the other dogs in the neighborhood.

"Tuerto!" I touch the chain-link fence to shut him up. He runs up to me with a big smile and licks my fingers. He's a one-eyed black pit bull, old and gentle and kind of fat. But loves to bark like crazy.

Three houses down the old lady's sweeping her porch. At the end of the block and across the street, Susi Taylor's standing in the middle of her front yard. She's the younger of the Taylor sisters. Her mom's 100 percent Mexican. But her father's a bolillo—only one on the block. He's a reformed drug addict who found the Lord. Now they're all Catholics to the core. But Susi's cool—sometimes. She's in shorts and a tank top, has her hair in a ponytail like she's in gym class.

Across Clemens Avenue the white and greenish lights of the Lone Star Food Stop glow softly in the gray dawn. On top of the store is the big billboard JOE CÁRDENAS, ATTORNEY-AT-LAW. It's got a photo of a big Mexican-looking dude with a thick handlebar mustache, all Texas with a cowboy hat and pointing at the road. WORKING FOR YOU! SE HABLA ESPAÑOL.

Tiny's house is at the other end of the block. It looks nice now with a decent coat of white paint and a few plants growing out of cans on the porch. Before Tiny and his family moved in, the place sat abandoned forever after the bolillo who lived there died. He was an old man with a long gray beard like Santa Claus, rode a tricycle with a basket on the back. One afternoon when I came home from school there was, like, five cop cars and an ambulance in front of his place. The whole neighborhood gathered around to see them pull his body out in a gurney. Turned out he'd been dead for like a week and no one even knew.

I consider going over to Tiny's but that wasn't the plan. And he doesn't have a phone. Besides, he's probably already at the bus stop waiting.

Susi's folding over doing leg stretches in the yard. As I come level with her house on my way to Clemens Avenue, she straightens her back and waves. "Flaco! What's up?"

I jog across the street to meet her, rest my hands on top of the chain-link fence. "Nothing much. What're you doing?"

"What does it look like?"

"I didn't know you exercised."

"Just running."

"Yeah? I work out too. Sometimes." Tío Félix has an old rusted bench press and free weights on the back porch of the house. No one ever uses them. Not me, that's for sure. I just do a few push-ups and sit-ups in my bedroom. Not that I'm into getting all buff. I just don't want to be Flaco anymore.

"Yeah," she says and gives me a little smile. "I can tell."

I blush—kind of because I'm not sure if she's pulling my leg. With Susi, you never know what's up. "So you training for something or what?" I say. "It's not like you need the exercise."

"I just run," she says, no smile.

I nod, guess she didn't get the compliment. I catch a glimpse of the little gold cross on a chain that rests between her breasts. My eyes refocus behind her on the house. Her old man's real strict. He never lets Susi or her older sister, Yolanda, hang with us anymore. They're never out in the street like they used to be when we were little. It's just school, church, and home. It's like they're prisoners.

Funny thing is, before he became a disciple of the Lord, he was a bad-ass. Dude's a former marine, a veteran of one of the Gulf Wars, all muscle and grit. We call him Rambo. He's got tattoos all over, one of the Virgen de Guadalupe on his right forearm and one of a snake tangled on a .45 automatic on his left. Magaña says they hide the track marks from when he used to shoot up. But they're not the stick-and-poke tattoos of a junkie. They're cool, detailed and full of color, especially the one of the Virgen.

"So where you off to so early?" Susi says.

I glance at the road and back at her. The thing with Susi is that I never know how to take her. Like sometimes she's super nice, like right now. And then suddenly she shuts it off and it's as if we don't even know each other. Weeks'll go by and she won't even acknowledge me. Then suddenly it's "What's up Flaco, long time no see" and shit.

Anyway, it's not as if our little trip's a secret so I tell her the truth. "Diamond Park."

"What, the town?"

I nod. "We're on a mission."

"You skipping school?"

"It's not like it's the first time."

"And it probably won't be the last."

I laugh. "For real."

She stares through me as though she's reading the thoughts in the back of my head. I say, "Magaña's buying a car from his godfather. We're taking the Expreso and driving it back."

"No way."

"At least that's the plan. Tiny's coming too."

"Really? I like Tiny," she says and looks down the block toward his house. "He's nice. I babysit his sisters and the little baby. The girls are so cute."

"I heard they give you a real hard time."

"Oh yeah? You're into all that neighborhood, you know, chisme and stuff?"

"Not all of it," I say, and as much as I'd love to stay here forever, I tell her I gotta dip.

But then she lays her hand on mine. "Can I come?"

Her skin's like gold, fingernails trimmed to the skin and painted a deep red like blood. "What, to Diamond Park?"

"Yeah. Where else?" Her smile's so big and real it almost knocks me over. I imagine her sitting next to me in the Expreso. Four hours talking about anything and everything. Maybe she'll get tired and rest her head on my shoulder and I'll get to breathe in the smell of her hair all the way to the valley. Maybe.

But then there's Magaña. He's so full of shit there might not even be an Impala waiting for him in Diamond Park. Or worse. Susi's really smart. But she's sixteen. And she's a good girl. We're seniors. And we're not so good. We're not criminals or nothing, but she doesn't fit into our puzzle. Maybe it's not a good idea. Maybe.

"I don't know, Susi . . . I don't think—"

"There's room in the car, no?"

"I guess. But—"

"I'll be right back." She taps my hand and runs into the house, screen door slams behind her with a clap. I look down the road toward my house and Tiny's place. It's quiet except for the soft sound of the broom where the old lady's still sweeping her porch.

A few minutes later Susi comes out of the house wearing tight jeans, a white V-neck T-shirt and red Converse high-tops. Out of the gate she takes my arm at the bicep with both hands, squeezes gently—lovingly, leans toward me so our shoulders press together. I get a whiff of her perfume like warm rain. She laughs like an angel, tugs me toward Clemens Avenue so we're walking side by side for maybe half a block before she lets go of me and says, "Don't worry, Flaco. It's not as if I never skipped school before."

We cross the street at the Lone Star, where two big pickups are parked, beds loaded with Raza—day laborers who usually gather at the empty lot next to the Fiesta grocery up the road from where Magaña lives. We turn the corner. Seven or eight people are waiting at the bus stop—men and women, maids, cashiers, and cooks. Franchise city, McDonald's, Kroger, and a restaurant I don't recognize. If I don't get into art college, that's me right there. Carlos didn't want to be them, so he joined the army. My mother doesn't want to be them—but she is. She's them twice over and then some. I wonder how it happens, how we fall into this place where we don't want to be and can't get out.

Tiny and Magaña stand a few feet away, backs against the wall of the warehouse. When they see us coming, Tiny grabs the backpack that's resting on the ground by his feet and swings it over his shoulder. They meet us in the middle of the sidewalk. The woman in a McDonald's uniform raises her eyes from her phone and checks us out like we're trouble.

Magaña's expression twists from glad to something I can't place, then back to glad, which I know ain't real. Before either one of them say anything, I beat them to the draw. "Susi's coming."

Tiny smiles real wide. "Chingón."

Magaña puts his arm around me and pulls me to the side. "What the fuck, pinche Flaco?"

I shrug his arm off. "What's the big deal?"

"I'm not paying for her ticket."

"I have cash." I don't know if twenty-three bucks is enough for the Expreso, but otherwise I just won't go. Susi and I can just walk around downtown, maybe have breakfast at one of those hip places in the Montrose we never go to where you can sit outside and pet people's dogs as they walk by.

Magaña gives me a look. His frown tells me that somehow I've thrown a wrench into his plan. And if anything goes wrong, it's my fault.

I'm about to tell him to fuck off when I notice the people behind him stepping up to the street and reaching for their pockets and purses. The air brakes of the 56 disrupt our little moment.

"¡Ya vámonos!" Tiny says.

Susi stares at me. Her eyes are big and brown and a total mystery. I have no clue how to read them. I smile to let her know everything's cool.

We climb on the bus and go all the way to the back. Tiny sits first. Susi takes the seat beside him. An old lady shoves past me and sits across the aisle from Susi. Magaña takes the seat in front of Tiny. I have to take the only open seat in front, facing away from Susi.

The sun's rising somewhere past Baytown, rays rake across the neighborhood picking up the texture of poverty, laying it bare like the scar that is our neighborhood. We pass a line of small shotgun shacks, laundry on the line, a bench seat from a van on the porch of the last little house, then Chuy's Auto Body, a CVS, Vanessa's Beauty Shop.

When we pass under the freeway, the dental office building where Magaña's mom works appears on the corner. My eyes follow the two-story building and get a look at the mural I painted on the side of it last summer. It's the one thing I've done in my life that makes me proud. I sweated heart and soul into it and every time I see it I think, *Yeah, I did that, motherfuckers.*

It's a landscape with a big, brown Mexican dude who's all muscles like the Rock rising up from the cracked brown earth. His head is down but his shoulders are up as if he's about to stand up tall. All around him is a mix of nature—cacti and trees and butterflies and birds, quetzals and a badass-looking brown eagle. There's a long line of Aztec warriors going all the way back to the horizon. They look real strong and proud like an army. And there's a woman—my mom. I painted her wearing a traditional huipil and a rebozo so she kind of looks a little like Frida Kahlo. There's also a car exactly like the one we're on our way to buy—a '59 Impala—a clean lowrider with a badass-looking vato looks just like Machete at the wheel. It's very 3D, pops out of the building like the work of Siqueiros, the greatest of the Mexican muralists—in my very humble opinion. The entire side of the building is mine. Its color. Its history. It's a portal to our world, to our neighborhood, to the place we call home.

4.

"You know what your problem is?" Magaña says. "You're weak. When it comes to chicks, you gotta show them who's boss."

"Why, 'cause I let Susi come?"

"Yeah, bro, you let chicks walk all over you."

I ignore him and look out the window. The 56 cruises through the Heights and along a neighborhood in transition, which means rich people are moving into a poor neighborhood because they've decided it's cool. They call it gentrification.

Brand-new modern townhomes are squeezed between little wooden houses and shops that you can tell have been there forever. The wash-ateria where my mom worked when we first arrived in Houston is now a bar. It still has the red brick walls and the tall windows but now they're painted black and have neon signs advertising the craft beers you can't find at the Lone Star by my house.

As soon as we come into the Montrose we begin to lose passengers at every stop. We cross the bridge over the freeway. The neighborhood starts getting a lot nicer. Giant oak trees make a canopy over the road like a tunnel. We pass a crew of men with bandanas over their faces like bandidos in an old Western running around with leaf blowers on their backs. On the corner there's a pickup with a trailer and an industrial mower, looks just like the one my tío Félix uses for work.

The whole ride Tiny talks to Susi about his mom and the girls and the baby, how they're real precious little kids—Tiny's words. He says they're his inspiration for doing well at school. He wants to help his parents so they don't have to work so hard, feels real guilty about skipping school— which I know is bullshit—and that he's worried about missing his geometry test.

"Check it out." Magaña taps my shoulder and points across the bus. We're slowing down along the art museum. "Your future, bro." His tone's friendly now. Maybe he's making up for being an asshole earlier, or maybe he already forgot about that.

The entrance to the museum is pretty lame, but I like how the words are carved out on the side of it: MUSEUM OF FINE ARTS HOUSTON. If I ever get famous, I'm not going to forget where I come from. I'm always going to put down the shit I see, the shit I love, the shit that pisses me off. The shit that breaks my heart—like the big mural on the side of the dental office.

About ten minutes later we finally come to our stop and walk off the bus. All the other people waiting for the Expreso in the parking lot are Raza—Mexicans and Guatemalans from the countryside.

"Check it out, pinche Tiny," Magaña says, "it's like you're finally home, bro."

Susi gives Magaña a dirty look, but Tiny gets the joke and smiles because it's so true. Tiny's total Raza from some little town in Guerrero. He's short and pudgy and darker than me and Magaña put together. The men waiting for the bus look like his jefe. They wear cowboy boots and polyester pants or jeans, tight checkered shirts, and hats. The women look like his mother, short and dark-skinned with long black hair in trenzas.

"If ICE stops us," Magaña adds, "we'll have the bus to ourselves."

"Flaco . . ." Tiny says real quiet.

"He's just messing with you," I say, but I catch Susi's expression because we both know it's possible. These days anything's possible. "It's not as if any of us have papers. I know I don't." Which is not really true because I have a driver's license. But I feel Tiny—totally. I have this queasy feeling simmering in the pit of my stomach, as if at any moment the cops are going to bust us for something, skipping school, lying to someone—or just because it's us, because we're Mexican.

Susi grabs Tiny's arm, holds on to him like he's a child, like she's trying to reassure him. She's got nothing to worry about. ICE isn't going ask her shit. But if they get ahold of Tiny, they'll deport him or throw him in one of those cages. And there'd be nothing she could do to help him.

Magaña and me get the tickets and we go to the other side of the building where the big red bus is parked. Inside, it stinks of feet and too much cheap air freshener. But at least the seats are nice and plush. They even recline.

I make my move to take my place next to Susi, but Tiny's one ahead of me and sneaks it. I want to smack him on the back of the head, but Susi's looking at me with her big brown eyes like she's real sorry.

Now, if I say something to Tiny, Susi'll think I'm being an ass. Carlos told me all about that before he was shipped overseas. He was home for like a week for rest and relaxation, but spent most of his time hanging out with his friends. The night before he left, he sat me down in the Buick and gave me all this advice about chicks. I don't know if my mom put him up to it or what. It didn't even sound like Carlos. It was as if someone had turned on an educational program on PBS.

"You can't act like an asshole in front of girls," he said in a low voice, the one that was a cross between a stoned gangbanger and a gentle giant. "You need to be chill. Be in control of yourself. They like that."

He popped open a tall boy of Miller Lite in a paper bag and took a long drink, stretched his hand, and glanced out the window to see if Félix or anyone else was looking. Then he passed it to me.

I had already gotten drunk and smoked weed before, but Carlos didn't know it. I took the can from him and took a baby sip.

Carlos laughed, probably thought I was a total amateur. "I only wish we had some tunes in the car, no crees?"

I nodded and passed him the beer.

"And always wear a condom," he said, which made me think of my mom and how I might've been conceived. No one spoke of it at home—ever. She was still young when we came to Houston. She could've easily hooked up with some dude and been happy. But she didn't, still hasn't. It's as if she fucked up with some pendejo, I was born, and she just closed the book of love. End of story.

Carlos nudged me with his elbow. "Don't be sad, güey."

"I'm not."

"Cabrón." He took another long drink of beer and set the can on the dash. "You look like someone died. ¿Qué te pasa?"

"I'm fine."

"Is it a chick?"

"No!" It wasn't a chick—it was Susi.

Everyone said I was going to grow up the summer before I started high school. But no one said Susi would grow up too. When I saw her at mass at Nuestra Señora del Socorro a few weeks earlier, everything around me vanished. Even the voice of the priest and the echo of the pews creaking whenever anyone moved were all sucked away by a vacuum. It was only Susi and me. Thing is, she hadn't changed that much. It wasn't as if she'd grown big chichis or anything. She was . . . different. Gone were the long, plain childhood dresses and the shy religious aura she'd carried around since Rambo found Jesus.

I couldn't put my finger on what exactly it was about her that caught me. But the longer I looked at her across the church, sitting like a statue next to her mom, the more I sensed she'd figured something out. She seemed confident, had kind of an I-don't-need-you-or-anyone-else attitude. Maybe I wanted to feel like that too. Like I had the answer to life.

Every day after that Sunday, Susi did little more than nod at me whenever she saw me. It drove me crazy because I didn't know what to do. And all the damn comic books and lucha movies couldn't distract me from thinking of her.

I guess that shit was eating at my gut when Carlos shared that beer with me in the Buick. The booze, the conversation, it brought me down because thinking of Susi made me think of everything I wanted to be but couldn't.

Magaña bumps my arm with his elbow. "So what's the deal with la Susi?"

"Nothing," I say. "She wanted to come along."

"Can't believe the bitch is skipping school."

"Don't call her that."

He looks at me, has that devil's grin I'd love to smack off his face. "You fucking her yet, or what?"

"Fuck you. Why do you have to say that shit?"

"Don't be so damn sensitive." He laughs and crosses his arms and looks ahead as the bus lurches forward. "I's just saying. She's got you on a real short leash, cabrón."

We just started the trip and I already regretted coming. Magaña, always talking shit. Always trying to be real chingón.

Still, he's my best friend after Tiny, but from way before. We met in the second grade after he busted some kid's nose for calling him spider—said something like, "Magaña la araña." So he hammered the kid once, knuckles straight to the nose—mocos. Then he just stood there, clenched fists at his sides, waiting for the kid to come back at him.

It never happened.

That day after school, the bus dropped us off at the same street corner. I started walking home, hoping he would go another way, but he didn't. He ran after me. I thought he was gonna kick my ass. I had no idea he'd just moved into the neighborhood, that his father was in prison in Rosharon for killing a man, and that he lived with his mother, who was working as a night janitor while taking courses at HCC to become a dental hygienist.

"Ain't you the one who drew the flying car?" he said.

The drawing was a mix between the speeder Luke Skywalker drives at the beginning of *Star Wars* and the flying car from the old S.H.I.E.L.D. comics. It was hanging in the hallway with the other *best of* art projects, which was pretty much everyone in the second grade.

"That's pretty cool," he said. "What's your name, yo?"

My full name is Rafael Herrera. Everyone pretty much called me Rafa back then. But sometime in the summer when we were playing on the makeshift Slip 'N Slide we made with an old vinyl tarp in the empty lot next to our house, my cousin Carlos took to calling me skinny because I was like a calaca back then. I don't know why I said it, but I did and immediately regretted it. "Flaco."

I press the button on the armrest and push my seat back. I turn my head to the side and look at Susi in the seat behind Magaña. She smiles at me.

I swear it's always like that. One minute she's giving me this look that seems to want me there next to her, does this little nod, pushing her face forward toward me. And when I smile back or say something, she ignores me.

I turn and face the front of the bus. At the start of the school year, I had this crazy idea of joining the drama club. I didn't last a month. The only thing that was cool about it was that Susi was there. On our third meeting, the teacher said we were going to put on a Tennessee Williams play. But she said before anyone could get a part, we had to have a deep understanding of his work. Tennessee Williams—cabrón uses a ton of strange words I never even heard of. We spent the whole afternoon studying his vocabulary. Susi and I were paired up as a team. She was going down the list of words—*peculiar, perspicuous, pertinent*—and she told me she was not as religious as everyone made her out to be.

"It's my dad who's all Jesus Christ and stuff."

I said it didn't matter. "My tía's like that. Went overboard after Carlos was killed."

"I see her at church. She's really nice."

"And sad."

"I think being close to God makes people like my dad and your aunt feel better," she said. "It makes them feel like they're not alone with their pain, you know?"

"I guess." I was thinking of how much fun Ana Flor used to be before Carlos died. How she used to laugh at Tío Félix's jokes, but she also stood up to him whenever he acted like an asshole, which is most of the time.

"Whatever," Susi said. "Okay. *Precarious.*"

"What?"

"Next word," she said. "*Precarious.*"

I spelled it out: "P-r-e-c-a-r-i-o-u-s. Something delicate."

She grinned mischievously. "Precarious: dangerously close to collapse."

5.

I close my eyes to sleep and listen to Tiny and Susi talk about Mexico. Tiny says he doesn't remember much because he was so little when they left, but that's bullshit. He was about ten or eleven and is always going on about how things were in Mexico—like how the tacos were better. But he tells Susi life there was miserable. "The pueblo was nothing like here," he says. "Over there, everyone knew everyone. You couldn't get away with anything. You think our neighborhood gossips? Ni te imaginas. You don't even know. And there was nothing fun to do. We didn't have a car so we had to walk or take a micro whenever we went to Tlapa or Chilpancingo. We didn't have a big supermarket or a movie theater or anything like that. And we all had to pitch in in my apá's milpa where we grew corn. Era un chingo de trabajo."

"Did you go to school?"

"Claro." Tiny laughs. "But the teachers were real strict. And there were no computers or a media room or any technology or anything. And we always had to participate in patriotic assemblies standing in the sun at attention for hours, that kind of stuff."

"I hear it's real bad. My dad says there's a lot of crime. But my mom's family's from Reynosa and that's by the border. They say it's worse there."

"Honestly, I try not to think about it. I mean I love Mexico con todo mi corazón, but when it's on the news or someone's talking about it, it hurts real bad. I don't even recognize it. It's almost as if it doesn't exist, you know? Me queda como un sueño."

"I want to go one day."

"Me too. I just don't want to get stuck there."

Susi presses the palms of her hands together as if she's going to pray, then drops them on her lap. "Some places look real nice, no?"

"Yeah, like Cancún."

"No. I mean the old towns like Guanajuato and Oaxaca." She frowns then looks down at her hands. "But I guess it doesn't really matter. My parents won't let me go."

"'Cause of the crime?"

"Yeah, that. And my Spanish is not that good."

"Yeah." Tiny laughs. "My amá's always saying pobrecita de Susi que no habla bien el español."

"Well, Father Zamora, at Annunciation, is organizing a mission trip to San Cristóbal de las Casas next summer and I'm going for sure."

Tiny's eyes grow real wide. "For real?"

"He said I would make an excellent youth leader. I'm selling chocolate bars to pay for my trip—"

"I know." Tiny laughs. "My amá bought a ton of them."

"She just bought, like, six. She's going to spoil your sisters."

"Don't worry about that. My apá ate most of them. He loves chocolate."

"But listen," she says. "It's not that I want to convert people or anything. I just want to help the poor, and Father Zamora says the people in Chiapas are the poorest in Mexico."

"Pues, there's no shortage of poor people in Mexico, that's for sure." Tiny lowers his head a little, his eyes lock on Susi's hands. They're clenched into fists. "We were poor and all, but it wasn't so bad. At least we didn't have to beg in the streets or anything. There were people who were way poorer than us—bien, bien pobres."

Susi and he fall silent for a moment. I try to imagine her dressed like a nun, helping poor children, but I can't. All I see is the Susi from a couple years ago when she played Mary in the live Nativity at Nuestra Señora del Socorro. She was real serious about it.

"Did you know I have a tattoo?" she says, breaking the silence.

"Yeah, right." Tiny turns on his side to face her.

"It's true."

"A ver."

She nods toward her leg. "It's on my ankle."

"What's it of?"

"A dagger."

"For real?"

"Okay, so it's not real. Not yet." She sighs real deep but then waves a finger at Tiny. "But I'm gonna get it as soon as I turn eighteen."

"Why a dagger?"

"'Cause a dagger's a symbol of power. People think I'm all good and stuff. I want something that says who I really am."

"No te hagas, Susi. You're, like, the nicest person I know."

"Yeah, but not always. Besides, I hate being the good one. Everyone assumes I'm all innocent and stuff. So they don't include me in anything that's fun. Like Flaco. When I asked him if I could come along, he couldn't believe it. He was, like, 'you can't skip school.' And I'm, like, 'why not?'"

"I don't know, sounds like a good problem to have."

"I hate it. When I turn eighteen, I'm gonna go somewhere where no one knows me or my family or anything."

"No, don't say that."

"My dad's so damn strict, sometimes it feels as if I can't even breathe."

"Trust me, I know how you feel, my—"

"No, you don't." Her tone slices across the bus like a blade. "No one knows what it's like."

That shuts Tiny up real fast. People stare.

"What about you?" Susi says after a moment. Her tone's suddenly back to sugar. "What're you gonna do when you graduate?"

"Pues quién sabe. I'd like to go to college, become a mechanical engineer. But I don't know how because . . . ya sabes . . . I don't have my papers y eso."

Magaña taps my arm and whispers, "It's now or never."

I open my eyes. He's got that grin again. "What?"

"You need to make your move, bro. Tiny's gonna steal her from you."

"I don't own her."

"But you know you want to."

"Ya, no chingues."

"So, what? I'm free to put the moves on her?"

"Shut the hell up, cabrón."

"You're so uptight." He laughs like he's really enjoying his act. "You need to get laid, bro. Maybe get Susi to take care of that anger you got bottled up inside."

Magaña does that. He's an expert at fucking with your head. He prods and teases to get a rise. Then he tries to defuse or just forgets he was acting like a real pendejo. That's why I don't tell him shit. But then I forget and tell him anyway because no matter how I look at it he's my best friend. Tiny's my best friend too, but it's different with him. I think Tiny and I get each other better. I trust him.

Magaña only cares about himself. He's always had a nasty edge. But he got worse since the summer before the start of our junior year when he came back from visiting his family in Mexico and announced real proud to Tiny and me that he'd lost his virginity to a prostitute.

"Bullshit," I said. We were walking back from the Lone Star. Summer for me had been busting my ass with Tío Félix and his lawn service.

"Whatever." Magaña was all chill, as if our conversation was about what flavor Slurpee we got. "She was hot too. Kind of reminded me of a younger Daniela Castro."

"No way." Tiny was all excited. "Did you grab her chichis?"

"What do you think?"

"What were they like?"

Magaña raised a hand in front of him and brought his fingers together like he was squeezing a grapefruit. "A little soft, but nice. Just like I like them."

"Yeah, right. As if—"

"¿Y? What else did you do?"

"What do you think, pinche Tiny?"

"I know—I know. But, like, give us some details, no?"

Truth is, I was jealous. I'd never considered being with a prostitute because Carlos told me once the women who sold themselves were sad creatures. "From a distance, they look pretty good," he'd said, "but when you're close up you can see through the cracks. You get a hint of their souls and the pain. No, don't ever go there, Flaco. That shit will break your heart."

I don't know if he was talking from experience, or just trying to scare me. But what stayed with me was the way he said it. *Sad creatures*—it stuck with me like a birthmark. Who would have sex for money by choice? It sounded gross. Like, who the hell would even want to lie with a dude like Magaña?

"We did it twice," Magaña said, bragging like he always did, probably exaggerating the details. "But she only charged me for one."

"How much did it cost?" Tiny said.

But Magaña's attention shifted. Susi's older sister, Yolanda, was hanging laundry to dry in the yard. She's older. She was, like, eighteen then and real pretty like a model, looked kind of like Selena with her hair loose and tiny cutoff jean shorts and a pink T-shirt. From where we stood across the street, with the sun raking over the yard and the summer clouds all bunched up in the sky like in one of those biblical illustrations, it felt like we were walking right into a beer commercial.

Yolanda was the princess of the neighborhood. Everyone fantasized about her, even my tío Félix and Julio. Everyone stopped to check her out whenever she walked past. The women gossiped about her, said she was a tease, that attending church was a farce, something to throw everyone off to her evil ways. That she was one to watch out for.

But she never gave any of us the time of day.

Still, Magaña had just come back from Mexico. And maybe it was true that he'd lost his virginity to a soap-opera-star-looking prostitute. I don't know. There's never any way of telling if Magaña's lying. But if it was true, well, entonces sí. That kind of shit changes you. And the truth is, he came back from Mexico a little different. He seemed more confident, angrier. His hair had grown out, short on the sides and combed back in a wave at the top so you could see his bushy eyebrows when he frowned. And he dressed different too. Gone were the khaki slacks and the flannel shirts. Now he wore black like a vampire—black jeans, black sneakers, black T-shirt with a big silk screen of a silver revolver.

He gave me a wink, slapped Tiny on the shoulder, and held up the giant Icee he'd just bought at the Lone Star. "Let's see if I can get Yolanda to suck on my straw, que no?"

He crossed the street and leaned on the chain-link fence. Yolanda finished pinning a shirt on the line and walked over. They stood about two feet away, facing each other with the short fence separating them like the border.

"Pinche Magaña," Tiny said all excited. "Es bien gallo, el güey. He's got a lotta balls, no?"

I couldn't believe they were talking. Yolanda even smiled. I hated him. I hated that he got laid and that Yolanda was talking to him and that Tiny admired him. You'd think he'd done the impossible. Why did the pendejos of this world have all the luck?

I couldn't take it. I smacked Tiny on the arm to go.

"Hold up. I wanna see what happens."

I left Tiny and walked straight past my house and sat in the Buick, where I stewed over how unfair life was. But in the end nothing happened. About ten minutes later Magaña and Tiny joined me in the car, Tiny in the back seat. Magaña sat in the front and rolled a joint, lit up. He said Jesus was ruining his chances with Yolanda. "That motherfucker on the cross gets all the chicks."

"He's got her wrapped around his finger," Tiny mimicked Magaña and fell into one of his laughing fits.

"If I was a true believer, I'd marry her," Magaña said, and took a long-ass toke from the joint, spoke while holding his breath. "But that shit ain't never gonna happen."

"I don't know," Tiny said, taking the joint from Magaña and studying it real careful. The sweet smell of bud filled the car. "If it was me, I'd convert in a second."

"You're already Catholic," I said and reached back. "Toke and pass, pinche Tiny. Toke and pass."

Tiny took a drag and giggled like a little kid. "Entonces," he said to Magaña and passed me the joint. "You're not Catholic, güey?"

"I'm baptized. But that's about it." He took the joint from me. "But I sure as fuck ain't walking into no church or praying to God. I can get laid somewhere else."

"That's funny," Tiny said. "Going to church to get laid. I wish it was really like that. I'd go to church every day."

"It happens," Magaña said.

"Yeah," I said, "to little boys."

"No mames, pinche Flaco." Magaña slapped my chest. "You talk a lot of pendejadas."

———————⌣———————

The green suburbs are behind us. We're cruising Highway 59 south toward Victoria. The driver puts on an old Tin-Tan movie. No English subtitles.

I look back through the space between the seats. Susi has her eyes closed, her head comfortably against Tiny's shoulder. He's wide-awake, looking straight at me, a goofy smile on his stupid moon face.

I turn forward and try to push the image out of my mind. "I'm starving."

"Ya, no llores," Magaña says. "Just think of the Impala. We're gonna rule the hood with that ride, bro."

I can't imagine it. What I foresee is a rusted carcass half buried in the dry earth in the middle of an empty field, no tires or top or seats. Maybe no engine. Maybe no car at all.

I turn to the side and close my eyes. After Carlos was killed, no one wanted to help me fix up the Buick. The interior was presentable, but that was it. We sat inside it all the time. It was our clubhouse. I even slept in it a few times.

We could've fixed it with a little work. New engine, tires, brake work. But fucking Félix sold it from under me. Gave it away to one of his workers for a couple hundred bucks. They towed it on a weekday while I was at school.

When I got home and saw the side lot, the rectangle of dead grass where the car used to be, the four cinder blocks, the patch of grease and oil—that's when Carlos died for me. That was the one thing that kept me tied to him. Just like Ana Flor had the flag and her little shrine, I'd had the Buick. Now it was gone.

At first, I thought someone stole it. I was about to call the cops when Ana Flor told me Félix sold it.

"He what?"

"He sold it. Ignacio came and got it," she said, as if it didn't matter.

"But it was my car!"

She looked at me like I was talking in a foreign language, then she went back to sifting through the mound of rice she was cleaning on the dining room table.

"Where is he?" I said.

"I suppose he went home."

"Not Ignacio. Félix. Where's Félix?"

She raised her sad eyes and nodded to the side. "Where do you think?"

Julio. His place was a couple blocks over. "That was my car," I cried. "Carlos gave it to me. He had no right to sell it."

But Ana Flor was back in her own space, her body folded over the table, her hand moving the rice back and forth, as if she were looking for a treasure among the grains.

On my way to Julio's place, I kept thinking of Carlos and how happy he was the day they towed the car to the empty lot next to the house. He didn't talk to Félix or Ana Flor or anyone. He talked to me. "What do you think? Pretty cool, eh Flaco?"

I loved it because he loved it. It wasn't an Impala or a Lincoln. I get that. But it was his—a 1948 Buick Super with a front grille like a brooding jaguar and fat rounded fenders. Carlos used to say one day he hoped to find a woman like that. "With curves like my Buick."

I'd bet a million dollars he never said any of that to his father. Félix never sat inside that car or hung out with Carlos, listened to his dreams, his plans, his hopes. Not Félix. He just took a shit on everyone.

I found Félix and Julio and three other old-school, fat, brown gang-bangers, chilling in the backyard, drinking beer. They looked drunk and probably stoned, leaning back on plastic Walmart chairs, eyes like slits. Julio's brindled pit bull barked and yanked at its chain when I walked up to the fence.

"You sold my car!" I yelled.

"¿Qué pasó?" Félix said. "You talkin' 'bout my boy's Buick?"

"He gave it to me!"

Félix grinned. Julio and the others watched, probably hoping for some kind of drama.

"Why'd you sell it?"

"For money, what else?" he said. "It's done. Now go play."

"Fuck you!" I cried. "It was my car. You went in my room and stole the keys."

Félix staggered to his feet and waved at me with his Miller Lite. "Who do you think you are, eh? You live in my house and eat my food—"

"My mom works. We pay our share."

"Ya." Julio tapped Félix on the leg. "Leave the kid alone, homes."

"Nah . . ." He shook his head at Julio and snarled at me. "You a real smart one, eh, Flaco?"

"You sold the car!"

"Car's been rotting in my yard like old fruit. It was long overdue."

"So what? It was my . . . It was my . . ." I wanted to say hiding place, my home. I wanted to say it was my connection to Carlos. That it was our place. But they were looking at me like I was a little kid throwing a tantrum.

I stared at the space between Félix and me where the grass was dead and the weeds towered over crushed beer cans. I was crying. But my tears weren't for the car. I was crying for Carlos because I'd never cried for him.

———⌣———

When I open my eyes, the landscape's different. The green swamp is now dry with short huizache and mezquite trees and a few green fields with rows of plantings like arrows that meet at the flat horizon.

Magaña goes on and on about the Impala as if I'm listening. All I can think of is that it's not that easy. Like the Buick. Carlos thought he'd have it cruising in a couple of months but it never moved an inch.

We pass a giant Walmart and a Whataburger, Taco Bell, houses, houses, and more houses, and pretty soon we're pulling into a strip mall.

We step out into the hot, dry air of Diamond Park. Three other people get off the bus and walk away in different directions. Then the bus drives away leaving us in a cloud of diesel.

Tiny yawns and accommodates the backpack on his back. The

stores are dark, have FOR RENT signs on the windows except Mendoza's Bail Bonds at the end of the block and the Silver Spur Pawn that's got a big yellow sign on the window: WE BUY GOLD. It reminds me of our neighborhood—except it's deserted.

Magaña looks left and right. "Where the hell's that cabrón?"

I back up to where the building casts a narrow sliver of shade. Susi moves past Tiny and stands next to me.

"¿Entonces qué?" Tiny says.

Magaña shrugs and looks up and down the road. "I dunno."

"Where's your pinche primo?" Tiny says.

"He ain't my cousin," Magaña barks back. "He's my padrino."

6.

We wait. Magaña paces back and forth along the edge of the sidewalk, looks up and down the street, texts and calls, but gets no answer.

Finally, Susi points to the McDonald's two streets down. "Why don't we get something to eat?"

Tiny swings the backpack over his shoulder. "And use the bathroom."

"Yo." Magaña nods at me. "Bring me back a Big Mac and a Fanta. I'll wait here in case my padrino shows up."

It's nice and cool in the McDonald's. We take a booth by the window. Susi stands with her arms crossed, staring at me.

"What?"

She looks out the window at the strip mall. "We're eating in?"

"Yeah," I say. "It's like Africa degrees out there."

"What about Antonio?"

"He wanted to stay."

Tiny unwraps his burger. "Relax, Susi. El güey de Magaña no va pa' ningún lado. He ain't going nowhere."

"I had my doubts about the Impala," I say. "Now I'm starting to doubt he even has a godfather."

Susi slides in the booth across from me. "He has to have one, no?"

"Imagínate. All this way for nothing," Tiny says and takes a huge bite of his burger, chews with his mouth open. Susi looks away. She reminds me of my mom and how she turns away from all the bullshit Tío Félix dishes out at the dinner table. Women put up with so much crap. Ana Flor and my mom just go quietly about their lives as if Tío Félix is not an asshole to them, coming and going as he pleases, getting drunk, arguing his points as if he's the only person with an opinion—like he's right all the time. Just the sound of his voice makes the hair on the back of my neck stand.

"What if the dude doesn't show?" I say.

"Nothing," Tiny says. "We take a bus back, y ya, no?

Magaña's on the corner tapping his phone.

"You ever notice how he always convinces us to do stupid shit?" I say.

"Yeah," Tiny says. "But if we weren't here, we'd be in school."

"But still . . ."

Susi peeks at her watch. "I'd be in biology."

"Calculus."

"PE," Tiny says. "I hate that class."

"Me too."

"Pinche coach," he says. "Acts like we're playing the Super Bowl or something."

I laugh. "For real."

"I get shit from everyone. It's not my fault I suck at sports. Besides, why do they make such a big deal about it?"

"I hate basketball," I say. "And track."

"I don't hate the games. It's just that everyone makes you feel like you're a loser. Los jocks son bien cabrones. Always think they're better than everyone else."

Tiny's short and kinda chubby. He gets teased more than anyone. "You ever wonder why we never play soccer either," I say.

Tiny laughs because it's true. We used to play on our street all the time when we were little. But in all our years of high school we've never played soccer in PE.

I wipe my mouth with a napkin and nod at Susi. "What about you?"

"I like to run. But I'm not competitive about it."

"What about Coach Savino?" Tiny's thick lips are dusted with crumbs and salt.

"I block him out. I block everything out. After a few laps, I feel like I'm floating. School and my dad—it all disappears. I'm alone in my own space. If I couldn't run I don't know what I'd do. I'd probably kill myself." She dumps this on us like it's nothing—the fries on the paper.

"You should run a marathon."

"That's the thing." She dismisses me with a wave, then pops a fry in her mouth. "I don't care about that. Why does everything have to be a competition? I don't have to prove anything to anyone. When I run, it makes me feel good inside. I'm in the zone. I'm exactly who I'm supposed to be."

"And who's that?" Tiny says.

Susi lowers her head, picks up a fry, but doesn't eat it. She looks at us. Her eyes seem to grow twice the size. "Don't you ever feel like you're trapped and you're never gonna get out of the sameness of your life?"

Tiny taps the side of his head. "'Ta loquita, Flaco."

"Shut up." I slap his arm. I totally get what she's saying. "What scares me," I say, "is that I'm gonna end up like my tío, work a stupid job I hate, live in the same place, and sit around and drink beer all afternoon with Tiny and Magaña until I get old and die. But what scares me even more, is that I'll be okay with it."

Susi nods, but I can tell she's holding back. I want more. I want to hear what she has to say about life, what makes her so angry sometimes. She explains herself real well, makes perfect sense. It's almost as if she's talking about all the stuff that swirls inside my head, except I can never put it into words—even to myself.

"In the back of my mind," I say, "I have this idea that I'm gonna do something important. Like there's a promise someone made. I don't know. It's weird and it sounds kinda crazy, but it's like I know I'm setting myself up for something significant."

"Exactly." She sits up, leans forward with her arms on the table. "It's as if no one believes in you—like the real you, what you're capable of— except yourself. When I'm running, when I'm in the zone, it makes sense. It's super clear. And all the sadness goes away."

"No mames, Susi." Tiny chuckles and glances at me. "I want some of what she smoked."

I can't imagine Susi hating her life. She's pretty. She's a good student. She has both parents, an older sister, and their house is like the nicest one on the block. But she does have this other side to her that's scary and sad at the same time. It kind of reminds me of Ana Flor. You never know whether she's going to be nice or angry. Or if she's just gonna start crying.

"But you always look so . . . happy."

She gives me this stare, angry like Félix. "You don't know me, Flaco. So don't pretend. No one does."

"Even me?" Tiny says.

"Forget it."

"No, I get it." I place my hand on hers. She pulls it away quickly and stands, grabs the bag with Magaña's food. "We better get going."

"Ey, vámonos pues," Tiny says. "We don't want Magaña and his pa-drino to leave us."

"Yeah, if he even shows up," I say and follow Susi across the street to where Magaña stands at the corner as if he's waiting for the bus. She hands him the bag with the food and the Fanta, and for the first time I notice how she looks at him, like maybe she's got a thing for him. Or maybe I'm just full of it.

"We're going," Magaña says.

"Home?"

"Qué va, pinche Tiny, to my padrino's."

"Where's that?" I say.

He looks at the map on his phone and points with the bag. "That way."

"Dude." The sky's pale blue, the sun burning white. "It's hot as shit."

"Don't be a crybaby," Magaña says and starts marching like a soldier. Tiny and Susi fall in line with him. I follow.

After a while we're crossing a neighborhood that's shady with trees and green gardens and pretty houses like on TV. Then things change one block at a time—fewer trees; smaller, older houses. The sidewalk ends, the asphalt's hot and rough under my Nikes.

I'm with Tiny, walking behind Magaña and Susi. "I wonder how much longer."

"What do you think people do here?" Tiny's looking left and right. He's got the backpack with the tools on his back—doesn't complain—just walks along like a tourist.

"What people do everywhere, I guess."

"Why do they call it Diamond Park?"

"I don't know."

"You think there's diamonds somewhere?"

I laugh. "It's just a stupid name."

"Yeah, but it had to come from somewhere, no?"

"Maybe there's a park in the shape of a diamond."

He's quiet for about a block. Then he says, "We haven't passed a park. Even when we drove in. I was looking."

"Whatever."

"You don't think it's weird?"

"Maybe they called it Diamond Park 'cause it's so damn hot and flat and ugly. They needed a fancy name so people would move here."

"See, that makes sense. And all these people here came thinking there were diamonds."

I can't tell if he's being serious. "Sometimes I wonder how you manage to get straight As, cabrón."

At the corner we catch up with Magaña and Susi. Magaña looks at his phone, at the street signs. We cross and turn the corner. The houses are more spread out, pickup trucks in the driveways. Pretty soon it's mostly empty lots and small farms, a bunch of construction and farm equipment in the driveways, sheds, goats and pigs and cows.

"What's your godfather like?" Susi says.

Magaña shrugs. "Don't really know him."

"What?" Tiny takes a couple of quick steps to catch up with them. "What's so weird about that?" he says.

"I dunno," Tiny says. "It's just that . . . it's your padrino and even—"

"And nothing," Magaña barks. "We left the valley after my father went to prison. I was six years old. I haven't seen him since."

"Yeah, but the way you talk about him," Tiny says. "Pensaba que . . . pues no sé, I thought you were close. A padrino's supposed to step in when—"

"What does it matter?" Magaña says, and turns the corner where there's a line of half a dozen run-down duplexes. "I haven't seen him but he's still my padrino."

About halfway up the block, Magaña stops by a chain-link fence. There's a small farmhouse set back about thirty yards from the road. An old purple VW Beetle's parked on the side of the street. A white panel van and a brand-new-looking, totally badass red Ford King Ranch pickup are parked side by side in the gravel driveway that leads to an aluminum shed.

Magaña taps the mailbox with the palm of his hand. "This is it," he says and pulls open the gate, starts walking toward the house when someone by the shed calls out, "¿Qué fue?"

From where we stand, the van blocks our view of the shed. Magaña walks back out to the road. We follow him to the driveway. The roll-up door to the shed is all the way up. Three men sit in plastic lawn chairs in the shade. They remind me of Félix and Julio—but these guys look like the real thing, except maybe the young one. He's chubby and has a buzz cut—could be Tiny's cousin. The one in the white tank top is all muscles, has a tattoo on the front of his neck that runs around his shoulder like a spiderweb. The other one's big and tall, all Mexican, has a crisp western hat resting on his knee, wears tight jeans, pointy cowboy boots, and a checkered shirt neatly tucked in under a thick leather belt with one of those giant silver rodeo buckles. But his face is dark around the eyes and has a nasty scar that runs from his temple down to the side of his lip. Looks mean as fuck.

Their eyes move slowly from Magaña to Tiny to me, then park themselves on Susi.

7.

Magaña steps forward and tilts his head up like he's sniffing the air. "Raymundo Martínez?"

"Who's looking?" the dude with the tattoo says real calm.

"I'm Evaristo Magaña's son."

The man gestures with his hand, half waving, half pointing. "¿Toño?"

Magaña looks at us for a second to show us he wasn't full of shit after all. "That's me. I came for the Impala."

"Pero ven pa' cá," Raymundo says with a lazy hand gesture. "Come closer. I ain't seen your skinny brown ass since you were still in pañales, hijo."

Magaña walks up the driveway between the van and the pickup. We follow but stay back a couple steps.

Raymundo shakes hands with Magaña. "Call me Rayo. Only my jefa calls me Raymundo. And she's been dead and buried a hell of a long time—que en paz descanse."

"I thought you were going to pick us up at the bus stop," Magaña says.

"No, hombre, you thought wrong." Rayo leans back and kind of puckers his lips, glances at Susi for a moment that seems to stretch for a little too long.

"So, what's the deal with the car?" Under Magaña's cocky attitude I can feel a slight change in tone, as if he just got busted for something at school and is making excuses to the principal.

"What car you talking about, hijo?"

"The Impala. My father told me you said you had a—"

"Don't tell me what I said." Rayo's words strike like a hammer. He runs his hand over the lower part of his face and down his neck, his fingers stretching his skin so the tattoo seems to move on its own. "Tell me about your friends here."

Magaña introduces us.

Rayo smiles at Susi, touches his forehead like Pedro Infante tipping his hat to a lady.

Susi smiles back politely.

"¿Entonces qué?" Rayo says.

"Nada," Magaña says. "We just came for the car."

"How's your old man?"

"Fine, I guess."

"No, hombre. He ain't fine. Not in that place where they got him. That Terrell Unit's a shithole."

The Mexican cowboy sitting next Rayo chuckles, stretches his leg out, pulls at his jeans near his crotch. His dark eyes move slowly from left to right, checking us out like he's trying to choose one of us for a team or a job—or who knows what.

"Well, then I guess he's not," Magaña says. "I haven't seen him in a while."

Rayo nods real slow like he's taking it all in. "I drove up to Rosharon a couple weeks ago. He's looking old."

"He is old," Magaña says.

"No mames." Rayo laughs. "Bari and me, we're the same age, hijo. If he's old, I'm old. Shit, I'm older."

Magaña forces a chuckle, sounds like when a girl tells him to fuck off—makes light of it, pretends as if he was in on the joke the whole time.

"He said he misses you," Rayo says. "Told me you don't come around no more. Told me your visits are the one thing he's got to look forward to."

Magaña bites his lip. "I talk to him on the phone."

"Shit's disrespectful." Rayo waves a finger at Magaña. "He's your father. One day he'll be gone and then what?"

Magaña takes a breath, looks to the side like he's trying to find the answer.

"Then what, hijo?"

"I dunno," he mumbles.

Rayo nods real slow, glances at the Mexican cowboy and back at Magaña.

I hate it. Shit reminds me of Félix lecturing me, treating me like I'm a little kid. "So," I interrupt, "we really should get going, no?" I wipe the sweat from my forehead with the back of my hand and clear my throat. "I mean, if we wanna get back by the time school lets out."

Magaña glares at me, gives me this don't-butt-in look. Then looks at Rayo. "My old man said you had an Impala for sale—"

"Not me," Rayo says. "There's a gabacho I know's got one sitting in his barn."

"¿Y entonces?"

"Tell me, how's your mother?"

"She's fine."

"I know she is," Rayo says and glances at the cowboy who runs the tip of his fingers along the brim of his hat, then takes a long glance at Susi, his eyes traveling from her big brown eyes down to her Converse and back up. Rayo says, "Bari says she ain't been coming to Terrell either. What's up with that?"

"She's busy."

"Busy with some other cabrón."

"She works," Magaña barks, clenches his jaw.

"Right. She's a dentist, no?"

"Dental hygienist."

Rayo nods at the cowboy. "Así es la cosa entonces."

All I really know about Magaña's father is that he killed a man in

Brownsville. He never talked about it except to say he was defending his family. When I asked Magaña whether it was self-defense, he said it wasn't. He just narrowed his eyes and said, "It was revenge." Then he shrugged and added, "At least that's how the judge saw it and my old man was fine with that. Gave him life."

I don't have a father. Well, I do. Obviously. But I don't know him. I imagine him as a real deadbeat, a loser who got lucky and slept with my mom. Period.

Magaña told me once he felt the same way about his dad. It didn't really bother him that he wasn't around because he'd been in prison most of his life so Magaña didn't really know him. "I was in first grade when they locked him up," he said. "We moved to Houston so it'd be easier to visit him, but in my mind he's just a ghost in white coveralls."

I look at Tiny to try and read what he's thinking, but he's staring at the trash, half a dozen to-go Styrofoam containers. He's probably thinking of food.

"So, what about the Impala?" I blurt out, sounding like an idiot who can't keep his mouth shut, probably because I'm getting real nervous around these guys and how they talk, making us feel like we're nothing.

Rayo turns real slow, looks at me like I'm trash. A nasty grin grows across his face. I imagine Magaña's father looking exactly like that right before he killed that man in Brownsville.

"I mean, that's why we came, no?"

"Hold up, Flaco. I'm talking to my padrino, here. He wants to know why I don't visit my father in prison." Magaña's tone's done a total one-eighty. He sounds like he's back in our neighborhood talking to some middle school kids outside the Lone Star.

"Thing is," he goes on, "I've been visiting him for as long as I can remember. Every. Single. Saturday. Before we moved to Houston, it was like an all-day drive. I remember that real well. Hours on the road. For a little kid, that's a lifetime. I don't visit him 'cause I'm tired of wasting every weekend on him."

"That's wrong, hijo. He's your father. He's family. He deserves better from you."

"Really? 'Cause I thought a father's supposed to be there for his son, you know what I'm saying? He should be there giving him advice on life, teaching his son how to fix a car, or taking him to a ball game . . ."

Tiny and me look at Magaña—at each other. We hate baseball.

"Either way," he says real straight, "whether I visit my father or how my mom's doing ain't none of your business."

Rayo nods as if he understands. I want out, get our asses back to town, hop on the Expreso, and never come back to Diamond Park—ever.

"Cabrón tiene huevos," Rayo tells the Mexican cowboy. "¿No que no, Anaconda?" Then he looks at Magaña and laughs. "You sound just like your old man when he was your age. The thing is, hijo, my compadre's rotting away in Terrell. He feels abandoned by—"

"And how do you think I feel?"

"We all do what we can. I know he did. Shit, I would've done the same thing if I'd been in his place. But not a day goes by that I don't wish he was sitting right here, drinking a couple of cold ones with me."

Anaconda grins, his upper lip curls up like a snarling dog that's getting ready to bite. The fat guy just watches, keeps quiet. I'm starting to think he doesn't belong, like maybe he just dropped by and is now caught in the middle of it.

"Every time I see him—stooped over that metal table, looking older and older—it breaks my heart," Rayo goes on. "And when he told me he doesn't understand why you won't visit, no sé, it just hurts right here." He taps his chest with the side of his fist.

"Órale." Magaña steps forward. "I get it. But my feelings about it count too, no?"

"Simón," Rayo says with a pronounced nod. "I know how it is. But stop in and visit him. The man's losing hope."

"I can do that," Magaña says. "When I get my car, I'll be able to drive down to Rosharon whenever I want."

The tightness around Rayo's eyes fades. "As your godfather, I want you to know this car's my gift—"

"I thought it was a grand?"

Rayo raises a hand to stop him. "It is. But I talked him down from fifteen Gs for you. El gabacho and I do business together. He owes me. So we agreed on a grand. That's the deal, and that's my gift to you." Rayo gestures at the fat guy with a long sweep of his arm. "A ver, Huicho, drive them out to the Lewis farm and help them with whatever they need."

Huicho nods like a soldier and walks to where the Beetle's parked. Rayo and Anaconda stand. They're big dudes, move slowly but with purpose to where Huicho's revving the VW like he's trying to show off, the engine whining like Ana Flor's old sewing machine.

Magaña opens the door. There's no front passenger seat. Tiny steps in first, sits behind Huicho, his backpack of tools on his lap, holds it with his arms like he's hugging a baby.

Magaña rolls down the window, then follows Tiny. "We gonna have to squeeze in like sardines."

I glance at Susi, then climb in and take the place next to Magaña. I lean to the side but there's not enough room for her.

Magaña taps his thighs with the palms of hands and grins. "Ándale, Susi, you can sit right here."

"Keep dreaming," she says, and looks at me like I'm supposed to save her.

"It's the best seat in the house," Magaña says. "Trust me."

She steps back, looks pissed for real. All I can do is lean against Magaña again, but there's just no room.

"It's cool," she says seriously, but it also feels forced, like she's acting but maybe not. "I'll stay."

"Come on," I say, "you can't stay here."

"Why not?" she says defiantly, hangs her hands on the sides of her waist. "You're coming back, no?"

"Yeah, but—"

"Go." She waves us away. "I'll be fine. Just don't take forever."

Magaña leans forward and taps Huicho on the shoulder, "Ándale, bro. Let's go."

I elbow Magaña. Huicho puts the car in gear. Susi steps back—looks at me like I'm the asshole.

"Susi . . ."

Huicho pulls off the clutch. We lurch forward and start down the road.

"No!" I reach for the door handle. Huicho shifts into second, the car leaps like a rabbit. He takes a hard right and steps on the gas. A dry breeze blows in through the open windows and swirls around us like a curse.

"Stop," I cry, "let me out."

"Ya." Magaña taps my knee. "She'll be fine. We'll be right back."

"We can't just leave her, cabrón. What the fuck's wrong with you?"

"She'll be fine," he says and glances at Huicho through the rearview. "We're good, bro, keep going."

8.

The VW speeds up. Behind us the road is deserted. I'm left with this burning in my throat that swells and chokes me. I can't see Tiny, but I know he feels the same, both of us screaming on the inside for Susi—la Susi.

Huicho makes a left turn. Magaña presses against me. I shrug him off and straighten up, eyes forward. The Beetle flies. Diamond Park blurs past like a nightmare I can't wake up from.

Salsa music that even my tío Félix would call mierda comes on the stereo and Huicho turns up the volume so loud the speakers rattle. The dry air blows in like a tornado. For almost twenty minutes no one speaks. I keep telling myself we'll be back real soon.

When Yolanda and Susi were little, they used to play in the street with us. They were a big part of our universe. We were just little kids and didn't know a damn thing about what life was really like. We simply took possession of the asphalt in front of our houses and played soccer, war, hide-and-seek, tag, lucha. The street, the empty lots, the small yards with their low chain-link fences, mutts and pit-bull-mix dogs tied to trees, front and back porches crowded with junk, tiny kitchens, dark crawl spaces—this was our world.

Susi and Yolanda spent all day outside getting their knees scraped and their faces muddy. Maybe back then Rambo was still hooked on the shit.

But the day he kicked the habit, everything changed. He called the girls inside and shut the door.

No one knows what caused the change in Rambo. But the chisme that's been going around for years claims he thinks his girls are too good for the rest of us—that he's racist even though his wife's Mexican. But the thing is, Rambo and his wife never come out either. He drives a 1970s army-green Dodge pickup to work and back, goes to church and back—and that's it.

I once told Tiny I thought Rambo was paranoid that his girls might get hit by a stray bullet or mauled by a dog or something. But Tiny said it wasn't that. "La Susi says her dad's a control freak, even with his wife."

Maybe it was religion. Before Carlos left for the army he said it was probably Rambo's addictive personality. "He needs to stay busy and keep a routine so he won't stray and start with the stuff again."

"Sounds like a lame excuse to me," I said.

He looked at me real serious. "Addiction's not a joke, cabrón. That's why you wanna stay away from that shit."

"What about weed?"

"That's different."

I didn't get it then, but I could see it later by the way Rambo sat in Nuestra Señora del Socorro, his back erect like he was punishing himself. He always looks real intense. And when he shakes hands with you, he squeezes real hard as if he needs to hold on to you like a lifeline. He always has his gray hair combed back with a ton of pomade—not a hair out of place, his handlebar mustache neatly trimmed, clean shaved and smelling of Aqua Velva, and he never—ever—sits outside his house like the rest of his neighbors—even on mild April evenings. It's as if he turned into a robot—hard as a fucking brick.

Susi was a soldier in his army, at least until the last year of middle school. That's when she started dressing like a ninja—long black skirts, black T-shirts, and combat boots. She parted her hair to the side so it half covered her face and even wore black lipstick. First there was a rumor someone saw her kissing Bobby Ortiz out by where the school buses line up. Then the rumor was that she kicked his ass for no reason. The stories were totally normal if it had been anyone else. But not Susi. She was a good girl.

But then, when she started high school, she was totally different. She looked more Mexican, wore embroidered skirts like the ones they sell at Casa Ramírez, T-shirts with the Virgen or the eagle eating the serpent and stuff like that. She even told Tiny we were not Mexican enough, that we should be proud of our heritage and talked about Zapata and Dolores Huerta and stuff. But by the end of the school year she'd toned it down, kind of got the look she has now, half skater, half chola—which I guess is what she is—half gringa, half Mexican.

Still, we could tell Rambo didn't like it. Just a couple months ago she must've mouthed off to him in church because we all saw him take her by the ear and lead her out of Nuestra Señora del Socorro straight into his green pickup. It didn't look good at all. Bruised my heart for real.

But it wasn't just Susi who was changing. It was all of us—even me.

At the start of the school year all the juniors and seniors taking American History went together on a field trip to the San Jacinto Monument. Susi walked by me. All I saw was long black hair combed to the side, the smooth contour of her cheekbones, her pointy chin.

I wanted to say something nice but she'd been ignoring me all summer for no reason. And then it happened. I don't know what it was— the way she touched my arm and smiled or how she leaned into me and said, "Whassup, Flaquito. Are we going to learn about history or make history?"

That's when the sharks started swimming in the pit of my stomach. I fumbled my words like a fool. "Yeah, I guess . . . all the history Texas has to offer."

"You're too funny," she said and walked on.

I followed her like a puppy dog. We ended up hanging out, just her and me walking quietly around the monument, checking out the exhibits at the museum, the displays of uniforms, weapons, and all the military regalia from the early days of Texas.

"You know what I hate about history?" she said. "It's all about wars."

"'Cause that's how history's made."

"No, don't believe that, Flaco. That's just what they want us to remember."

At San Jacinto it was all about Sam Houston and Austin and Bowie, and how these Texans beat the Mexicans and created Texas—made the state great and all that. The way they talked about Mexico pinched a nerve. The history of Texas made the Mexicans the bad guys. It made me think of the Alamo where the Mexicans kicked some ass. That's what I told Susi. "Besides," I said, "everyone loves an underdog story."

"Yeah, but you got it backward," she said. "In the Alamo, the Americans were the underdogs. Santa Anna was the one with a huge army."

Eventually, we found a small patch of shade. We sat on a bench and she asked me about my father.

"I don't have one," I said.

"You have to have one. You've just never met him."

"Okay, technically," I said, "someone's sperm fertilized my mother's ovaries and I was born. So, yeah, I do have a father. Except he doesn't really exist in my world."

"It's eggs."

"What?"

"It's not ovaries, silly. Your father's sperm fertilized your mom's egg."

Not having a father didn't bother me. It's not as if everyone in the neighborhood had one. Still, I was feeling all weird about the conversation. But her voice was reeling me in and I didn't want the moment to end, so I just started blabbing, giving her details of life with my mom, Félix, and Ana Flor, and about my art and how I was thinking of getting serious with that, like as a career.

Then she started talking. She told me Yolanda landed a job as a cashier at the Kroger in the Heights. Her mother stayed home, never left the house except to go to church. "It's as if she's afraid of the sun," she said.

Rambo worked at some industrial yard in Baytown. Susi said he was a real hard-ass, liked everything in the house to be perfect. Said she was sick of it. "Like, you can't even leave your shoes in the living room for, like, five minutes, or a dirty spoon in the kitchen sink."

I told her how Félix is a lazy hijo de puta, and Ana Flor does all the work around the house. "I think she's real lonely since Carlos was killed."

That field trip was the only time she and I had really spent time together since we were kids. But when I saw her again in the hallway at school, she didn't even acknowledge me.

———⌣———

Huicho takes a right, then goes about three hundred yards, downshifts from fourth to third and takes a left into a long dirt driveway to a farmhouse. He pulls up in front of the big wooden barn like you see in picture books, farm machinery scattered around like a junkyard. "Ya llegamos."

On both sides it's all plowed fields—brown dirt as far as I can see. A couple of dogs come racing out of nowhere, barking like we're the mailman.

Magaña has this crazy fear of dogs, so we stay put. The dogs circle the car, bark and run around wagging their tails. They follow Huicho to the house. We finally step out. Tiny stretches. "I'm all cramped up."

The place stinks of milk and dog shit. We look around for the car. The dogs come trotting back. Magaña moves easy, places me between him and the dogs. They sniff at our pants and circle around the VW.

Tiny laughs and points to the side of the barn where the shell of a Model T Ford is half buried in the weeds. "Check it out, allí esta tu carcacha, Magaña."

I want to say something about Susi, but just then the screen door of the farmhouse slams shut like a gunshot. An old bolillo in jeans and no shirt and a big fat stomach is talking with Huicho. A moment later he goes back in the house and Huicho starts toward us.

Magaña nods at him. "So what's up?"

"He's getting the key," Huicho says. "You got the cash, right?"

"Yeah, I got it," Magaña says. "Where's the car?"

Huicho gestures toward the big barn. "It's in there."

There's a chain and lock on the doors.

I turn to Magaña. "Maybe we should go back real quick and see if Susi—"

The screen door of the house slams shut again. We turn at the same time. The farmer buttons up his blue-and-white-checkered shirt as he walks. The dogs race over to him.

He walks past us, says nothing, doesn't even lift an eye to acknowledge our presence. He mumbles something to Huicho about a couple of farmworkers who took a pair of coveralls from him. "You tell Ray it's on him. Tell'm I said so. I sure as hell ain't takin' no more workers from him if that's the kind of riffraff he's bringin' over."

The farmer pulls the lock and yanks the chain off from around the door handles. Huicho pulls it open. Magaña walks in. Then me. Then Tiny. My eyes slowly adjust to the darkness. A small green tractor. A workbench, tools.

The farmer points to the other side of the barn. "That's it right there."

It's dusty, the tires are flat, the top is torn, looks as if it's been sitting there for sixty years—a 1959 Chevrolet Impala convertible. For. Fucking. Real.

9.

We approach the car real slow as if it's the Virgen de Guadalupe or some other divine apparition. Magaña lays his hand real gentle on the fender, runs a finger over the side, picking up a layer of dust. He studies his fingers for a moment like the dust is made of gold. He wipes his hand against the side of his jeans before reaching down and opening the driver's side door. The car's a faded teal color. Blue interior. The dash is fine, like a spaceship abandoned on a distant moon. The chrome is dull, speckled with pin-pricks of rust. The seats are complete, but the back seat has a hole. Rat's nest, for sure, stinks of urine and shit.

Magaña grins. Then he turns and looks across the barn at the farmer. "Does it run?"

"Did a few years back," he says, takes a large pinch of Beech-Nut chew and sets it on the side of his mouth, a few bits of tobacco crumbs stick on his lower lip. "I done told Ray he'd have to do a little work on it, clean out the gas tank and bleed the lines before he could make a real go of it. I reckon it'll need a new battery, spark plugs, maybe belts and hoses, that sorta thing."

The car's got Texas plates from 1991, so it's been sitting for a long-ass time. It's a project, but it has solid bones, very little rust, looks totally original, complete—trim and everything.

"You got the key?" Magaña asks.

"You got the cash?"

"A grand, right?"

The farmer glances at Huicho, who nods, and the farmer says, "Cash."

Magaña leans over and pulls an envelope from the side of his big Adidas sneakers. He opens it and flips through the bills inside like he's at the bank. He strides across the barn and hands the cash to the farmer, who counts it twice, then folds the bills and shoves them in his front pant pocket. He grins and hands Magaña the title.

One of the dogs sniffs around the car, hops inside on the driver's side. Magaña yells, "Hey!"

The farmer spits to the side and whistles. The dog leaps out and runs to his side.

Magaña motions Tiny and me over to the front of the car. He pulls out his phone and we pose for a selfie. He takes a couple more pictures of himself, then leans over his phone and Snapchats.

"¿Entonces?" he says and shoves the phone back in his pocket. "What do we do first?"

I shrug and look at Tiny. "We need clean gas, no?"

Magaña taps the side of the car. "Do we take the old gas out?"

"We should, yeah."

"Hold up," Tiny says. "It's not just that, eh? You have to clean the tank and everything. The shit in there'll kill your engine."

The farmer walks back a few steps and sits on a wooden crate. I'm trying to figure if he has any clue how much the car's worth, because it's a real treasure. If Magaña can invest a few grand to clean it up, it could bring him thirty or forty grand at Barrett-Jackson—easy.

"Let's see." I pull open the hood and feel the hoses. They're cracked with age but feel solid enough. Real pressure could bust one, and they'll have to be changed eventually. But that's not a priority right now.

The wires look okay. Everything's dry and old and dusty, but these old cars didn't have computers. If the engine and transmission go, the car will go—at least get us home to Houston.

Tiny and Magaña join me and we study the engine bay. Magaña, I know for a fact, doesn't even know what he's looking at. Tiny's old man's taught him a few things. "A ver," he says, "you gonna need a battery, güey. But you're also gonna have to put air in the tires and hope they hold."

"What about the gas thing?" Magaña says, keeps an eye out across the barn at the dogs.

Tiny leans back and scratches the back of his ear. "Cleaning the gas tank's a big job."

"We can't do that here," I say.

"Flaco's right," Tiny says. "You gotta drop the tank, clean it and all that."

"Maybe we can come back," I say. "Or get a tow or something."

"No way." Magaña kicks the front tire. "We gotta figure it out. I'm not leaving it behind. No way."

Tiny leans against the back fender, shoves his hands in his pockets. Magaña glances at Huicho. He's standing at the entrance to the barn, smoking a cigarette. Then he looks at the farmer, who keeps staring at us like we're gonna steal something.

I can tell Magaña's freaking about the car. He paces back and forth a couple of times like a caged animal, doesn't know what to do.

"Maybe," I say, "if the fuel pump works we can get a container and put it in the trunk and feed it to the engine. Use it kind of like a spare gas tank."

Tiny laughs.

"Or we could push it."

Magaña looks at the farmer. "You got gas we can use?"

The farmer shakes his head, spits tobacco juice to the side.

Magaña points to the two big metal gas containers at the entrance of the barn. "What about those?"

"Diesel."

"I think you're right," Tiny says and looks at Magaña. "Aviéntate al Walmart or an AutoZone and get two of the biggest containers you can and fill them with gas—at least ten gallons. We'll do it like Flaco says."

"Why don't you go?" Magaña says.

Tiny smiles. "No hay pedo. I'll go."

"No," I say. "We still need to check the spark plugs and unplug the hose that goes from the tank to the carburetor, put air in the tires and—"

"Okay, okay. I get it, pinche Flaco. Just tell me what to get, a ten gallon gas can and what else?"

I look at Huicho. "Oye, tienes jumper cables?"

He nods.

"Just a hose," I say and look at Tiny. "What size do you think?"

Tiny leans into the engine bay and pulls a few things, fidgets. Then uses a pocketknife to cut a piece of hose, hands it to me. "Get one like this thick. Six feet, no?"

I hand it to Magaña. "And a can of Gumout."

"And fill the can with gas," Tiny adds.

Magaña clenches his jaw. His eyes travel the length of his new car, then he marches out of the barn.

I get it. He wants to be with the Impala. When Carlos first got the Buick, it was hands-off. Then, little by little he'd invite me to help with the repairs that seemed to go nowhere. It was always "get me a Phillips head" and "get me the pliers." I watched while he explained what was what. That's how I learned what little I know about cars.

Tiny's got this troubled expression, staring at the car like he's waiting for the fuse to burn and the rocket to go off—Susi. This thing with the Impala's gonna take way longer than we thought.

I glance at the farmer. "Any chance you got a compressor we can use to put air in the tires?"

He looks bothered, but he gets off his ass and walks to the side of the barn and comes back pulling an old red Craftsman compressor on wheels. I meet him halfway and roll it to the side of the Impala. We pull the top down. Tiny leans over the engine bay. I plug in the compressor. The motor breaks the silence in the barn with a loud rumbling. I fill the tires with air, then use the hose to dust off the inside of the car and the engine bay. Dirt and leaves and shit fly everywhere, fill the side of the barn with a thick cloud of dust. I stop and rub my eyes. Tiny backs away, stands where the farmer sits, faces turned away from the car and the dust.

I shut off the compressor and move it out of the way. The dust settles slowly. The tires seem to hold the air. But they're old and cracked. If we drive the car out of here, Magaña'll need to cruise easy because they look like they're on their last legs.

Tiny gets to work. He double-checks the hoses. I make sure the cables are properly connected. We clean the connections on the distributor and spark plugs, take off the air filter and expose the carburetor, check its function.

When Carlos gave me the Buick, it was as if I had my own place. And to be honest, by then I never really imagined it would ever run so I never focused on fixing it. It just gave me a place to go. Me and Tiny and Magaña spent hours in there, smoking weed, talking about girls, our dreams for the future. You'd think we were cruising all over Texas—but we never moved an inch.

Magaña does odd jobs helping a friend of his mom's, mostly carpentry and some house painting. That's how he got the money for the Impala. I only work during the summers because my mom doesn't want me to have a job. She wants me to focus on my schoolwork so I can get good grades and go to college, do something great with my life. She said so in those exact words one evening when she and Tío Félix were arguing about bills. Félix made some comment about me, that I should get a job, that I was spoiled. My mom went apeshit on him.

"What's the matter with you?" she cried. We had just finished dinner. I asked if I could have seconds. That's how it started. Ana Flor said something about how I was so skinny. My mom said the food stamps helped. That's when Tío Félix got on his high horse like he always does and started bragging about how he was the provider for everyone in the house.

"That's what I do every day for you three," he said, leaning back on his chair picking at his teeth with the corner of a playing card. "I bust my ass all day to make sure you have a roof over your heads and food on the table."

"Por favor, don't start with that," my mother said.

It wasn't the first time and it wouldn't be the last. Sometimes I wonder how they can be brother and sister, the way they argue like that. But I appreciate my mom. Unlike Ana Flor, she stands up to Félix. Fact is, she works and pays bills and gets the food stamps and everything.

"Félix . . . ," Ana Flor warned.

"What seventeen-year-old doesn't work these days?" he said.

"He has to focus on his school," my mom said. "So he can go to college. I don't want him to end up como tú y yo."

"The hell does that even mean?" Tío Félix laughed. "You think college's gonna offer something better. Truth is, they don't want us. They don't care. He'll end up mowing lawns just like me. Ya verás."

I'd worked with Félix two summers in a row. It sucked. It was real hard work, and the heat and humidity was torture. But I'd already made some money painting. I'd drawn tattoos for friends, and the dentist that owned the building where Magaña's mom worked had paid me real well for the mural I did. I was making money doing what I loved. And no one was going to take that away from me—not my mom and certainly not Tío Félix.

Ana Flor, who had been quiet, gave me a wink like she knew I was going to be okay. It's funny about Ana Flor. Ever since Carlos was killed she seemed all depressed. And maybe she was. But I think there's more to it than that. I think maybe she figured out that it's not worth it to impose your views on other people, especially teenagers. She never forces me to do anything. She's the only one who ever asks to see my drawings. For Christmas she gave me a pretty cool watercolor set. She kind of gives me this feeling like she can see I won't fuck up my life the way Félix thinks I will.

Or maybe she appreciates that I'm not causing trouble. I pretty much just go about my life listening to music, getting my homework done, and drawing. I fly below everyone's radar. I like it like that—no one giving me a hard time. She probably appreciates that. Makes her life easy.

⌣

About an hour later we hear the whine of the VW engine as Huicho downshifts on the main road, cruises up the drive almost all the way to the entrance of the barn. Magaña marches in holding two big red plastic gas cans. "Got the stuff," he says. "¿Cómo vamos?"

Tiny doesn't waste any time. He takes the coil of hose from Magaña and crawls under the car. About fifteen minutes later he pulls himself out from under the car. "It don't reach," he says.

"What the fuck?" Magaña cries. "You said six feet."

"Güey," he says, "it looked like six to me, okay?"

"Looks more like ten," I say.

Tiny glances at me and back at the car. "We can put the can in the back seat and run the hose in through the window."

"That's risky," I say. "And probably illegal."

"When did that ever stop us from doing anything?" Tiny says.

"Let's do it." Magaña claps his hands. "We can stop at the Ace later and get a longer hose."

Tiny puts the hose in the can. "We need a jump."

Magaña tells Huicho to drive his VW into the barn and give us some juice. Huicho takes a couple drags from his cigarette before making his way around the car, then drives the VW right up to the side of the Impala.

The Beetle's battery is under the back seat. It takes Huicho some work to pull the seat off. Tiny gets in and hooks up the cables.

Magaña gives me a nod. I hook the cables to the battery in the Impala and stand back. Tiny sprays some of the Gumout on the carburetor, then leans to the side and gives Magaña thumbs-up. When he turns the key, nothing happens.

"'Pérate, güey." Tiny fiddles with a lever on the carburetor. But that's not the issue. Even I know that.

I nod at Magaña. "Turn the key halfway."

We listen for the buzz of the fuel pump.

Tiny looks at me but I'm already grabbing a wrench from his backpack. I crawl under the car and find the starter, tap it a few times. "Órale, try it now."

Nothing.

I tap it again. We do this three or four times until the starter turns and the engine coughs. But it doesn't start.

Magaña slams his hand against the steering wheel and curses.

I crawl out from under the car and tell him to chill. "It'll start."

"Doesn't sound like it," he says.

"Tiny?"

"'Pérame tantito."

I come around the side. Tiny messes with the lever on the carburetor, sprays more Gumout, and calls out for Magaña to try it again. The engine turns and turns and turns—catches, backfires twice, then falls into a rough but steady idle. Even the farmer smiles.

10.

It takes us another half an hour to put everything back together, the jumper cables, the air filter, transfer the gas can onto the back seat and secure it with my belt.

Tiny sits in the back next to the gas can.

I ride shotgun. "We have to get back to Susi."

Magaña ignores me. He focuses on the car. It moves slowly, floats like a boat out of the barn and down the driveway. Huicho stays behind us even though we're not even breaking thirty. The Impala backfires a couple of times. Magaña frowns, looks at me then at the rearview.

"Did you hear me, cabrón?"

"Chill," he says. He's all giddy feeling out his new ride, turning left and right, speeding up and slowing down, checking the brakes, and speeding up again like a kid with a new toy.

"I'm serious," I say. "Susi—"

"I know," he says, doesn't take his eyes off the road.

I watch him drive, his body leaning forward like a little old lady, hands gripping the steering wheel real hard at the sides.

"How does it feel?" I say.

He lets go of the wheel.

I grab it to get a feel for it. "A little stiff, no?"

"Probably the fluid," Tiny says, looks left and right at an intersection.

"Or the line," I say. "We're gonna have to check it when we get back."
Magaña speeds up, smiles.

I smack the side of his arm. "Slow down." I hope we don't blow a hose
or a tire. We have to get home to H-town.

We cross Diamond Park, make a few turns so that pretty soon we're
back where the farms are small and unkempt. In a field to our right, about
twenty cows walk in a straight line like soldiers. Laundry flutters like flags
on a line next to a house. Large clouds of blackbirds fly overhead and land
on an electric line. We pass a small aluminum silo I hadn't noticed before
and come to the run-down duplexes.

We turn the corner on Rayo's street. Blue and red lights flash. Cop
cars. An ambulance. They're all over the street.

Tiny grips the backrest of my seat pulls himself forward. "¿Qué
chingados?"

Magaña slows down. "What—"

"It's ICE," Tiny says. "It's pinche ICE. Let me out. Let me out!"

"Be cool," I say.

"Let me out!" he yells.

Magaña pulls over across the street from the house.

Cops—bolillos in green uniforms and trooper-style hats hiked up on
the backs of their crew-cut heads, brims tilted over their brows—they're
all over the place. One is pulling yellow crime tape around the house. Two
others are checking out the shed, another is leaning into the driver's side
of the white van. Two are by a squad car, just standing around like nothing.

Then I see Susi. She comes around the ambulance with a cop at her
side, another cop follows a couple of steps behind. The whole front of her
shirt's red.

"Susi," Tiny whispers, as if he's reading my thoughts. It seems to come
from far away. Then it comes louder. "Susi!"

Magaña mouths something I don't hear over Tiny yelling, "Susi!"

Everything slows down: the cop turning to the side and pointing across the road; Magaña raising the gearshift to P; Tiny pushing and pull-ing the seat to get out of the car.

They're not walking her to the ambulance. They're walking *from* the ambulance. I pull the handle but the door won't open. I slam it with my shoulder. It swings out. I haven't taken three steps and Tiny's already out of the back seat and making his way around the car.

Susi and the cop walk to a squad car. He pulls the back door open. Susi turns and raises her eyes, sees me. Her hands are behind her back. She's had them like that the whole walk from the ambulance to the cop car—handcuffed. The officer at her side is holding her by the arm, his grip denting her bicep.

"What . . . The . . . Fuck?"

Susi's eyes are locked on mine like a laser. She slides into the back seat, the cop's hand on her head like they do in the movies. She never breaks her stare.

I'm where the first two cop cars are parked. Her eyes are screaming at me. In the distance I hear a voice, a cop, two, like an echo. "Hey! Hold up. Stop right there, son. Hey!"

They're saying all this to me, to Tiny, who's like two steps behind—and Huicho. He's out of his Beetle and running over, catching up to us. A whole platoon of cops is coming toward us.

A cop catches up to me before I make it to the car where Susi's lean-ing forward on the back seat, head turned, dark, lost eyes locked on mine. Another cop stops Tiny. Two others follow.

"Susi!" I yell.

She stares, her face distorted by the reflection in the cop car window, but I can see her eyes, cold and dead.

"Hold up." The cop that's got me by the arm pulls me back. "I said stop!"

A cop on the other side of the squad car is waving at the officer inside the car. In a second Susi travels forward, her head turning back to keep looking at me, cursing me with her stare.

When the car reaches the end of the block and takes a left, I turn. Tiny's next to me, tears all over his twisted face. Two cops are holding him, one on each side. He curses in Spanish, says, "¿No mames, la Susi . . . Susi. Chingada madre, qué pasó?"

Huicho has already handed his driver's license to one of the three cops that surround him and is telling them his full name: "José Luis Pérez Várgas." He gives them his address and says he's not a relative, says he wasn't familiar with the girl, was acquainted with one of the men, says he was just giving us a ride, says he doesn't know shit.

The cop is asking me for an ID. I reach for my wallet and hand him my license. He looks at it and asks me my name. I tell him.

I open my mouth and it comes out of me like a whimper. "What happened?"

"Brenham!" A policeman near the ambulance yells to the cop that's holding Tiny. "Take them across the street and sit them down."

My cop turns me around and leads me to the other side of the street away from Rayo's house. He points to the grass. "Hands behind your back."

"What happened?" I say.

"Sit!"

I sit on the grass, feet on the street.

"Hands behind your back."

I do what he says.

He leans his head to the side and talks to the radio handle that's latched to his shoulder. Something about the youths. Something about keeping them separate. Something about IDs.

They have Tiny sitting on the side of the road like fifteen yards away. Another cop is with Magaña next to the Impala. He leads him to the front of the car and points to the ground. Magaña sits, puts his hands behind his back, glances at me, but his expression gives me nothing.

Huicho's in the middle of the street talking to two cops. His hands move. He points to the house, to the end of the street, to the Impala, back at the house. His mouth moves so much I can only imagine he's spilling a bunch of lies.

I clear my throat. "Excuse me, officer." My mouth feels like it's full of sand. "What's going on?"

The cop standing like three feet away from me extends his hand, palm out to signal me to chill. Tiny and Magaña are the same. Each one has a cop standing in front of them. No one's talking.

Across the street they've put the yellow tape all around the property. A guy from animal control is leading a pit bull with one of those steel noose devices into his truck that's parked next to the crime scene van. Then three men and a woman in regular clothes and blue gloves walk in a line out of the house, one after the other, followed by two EMTs pushing a gurney with a body covered in a white sheet stained red with blood.

I look at Tiny. He's staring right at it, mouth open like he can't believe the shit. Rayo or Anaconda. Has to be.

My mind spins—the two hijos de puta got in a fight and Susi tried to break it up. Magaña's padrino had a temper. They both thought they were chingones. Anaconda had that scar on his face, a testament to his violent past. It started with taunting, pushing, and shoving. They were in a living room kind of like the one in my tío Félix's house, all brown wood paneled and musty and dark. Empty Miller Lite cans all over the place, cigarette butts overflowing an ashtray. A disagreement. Maybe over a girl, maybe over who drank the last beer. Tempers flared. It started with shoving and pushing. Then fists—turns into a real fight. Two men going at it like a pair of bulls, slamming against each other, punching and struggling to come out on top. One kills the other and Susi calls the cops.

No. Susi had blood all over her. And the cops took her. They. Took. Her.

And if that's Anaconda they're wheeling out and loading into the ambulance, where the hell's Rayo?

The cop's radio crackles. A voice says a few numbers and then says to bring the youths down to the station. That means us. I'm fine with that. I imagine that's where they took Susi anyway.

But the cop doesn't move.

The two cops with Tiny meet with one of the plainclothes officers. They walk slowly to where the yellow tape is, cross under it, and walk into the house. The ambulance takes off in silence, no siren, no lights. Cops pick up and pack their shit. One of the cruisers takes off.

I close my eyes and lower my head and have this stupid wish, tell myself it's a bad dream, that I'm going to open my eyes and I'll be in bed, or on the Expreso to this shithole town. That Diamond Park is not real. But when I open my eyes a few seconds later, the cop's motioning for me to stand.

One of the deputies is already leading Tiny to a squad car. Same with Magaña. I stand and follow, escorted by my own policeman.

We're in different cars. Mine's freezing cold with AC, smells of vinyl and cherry air freshener. The radio crackles once and goes quiet. I'm alone, no cuffs. Doors can't open from the inside. A thick Plexiglas separates me from the front. The cop's standing outside talking to the other cops and the woman in plainclothes.

Tiny's gotta be freaking out. We didn't do shit, but they'll find out he doesn't have any papers and he'll be done. They'll send him to one of those federal detention centers, put him in a cage, deport him back to Mexico.

Five minutes feels like an hour. Then the cop gets in the car and calls something in on his radio. A woman answers, half repeating what he said, numbers. The radio crackles. The cop presses a few buttons and we start down the road.

Huicho stands by the fence with the plainclothes cop. He gestures to the shed, then to the cars, points at the car I'm in as we pass. I crane my neck and see the white van. The red pickup's gone. A crime scene van's parked where the driveway meets the road. Neighbors stand on their porches, a man peeks over his fence—all Mexican. The cop turns the corner and we pass two kids on bikes. One points at me as the car gathers speed.

The short drive to the Diamond Park Police Department is the longest ever. I can't shake the image of Susi staring at me on her way to the police car, her shirt all bloody, the cop car pulling away. Her eyes on me like cold stones. Susi.

When we pull up to the strip mall where the police station's at, the cop barks commands: "Out . . . this way . . . over here. Move. Wait here."

He leads me inside to a small office with no windows. Everything's gray and dull. There's a desk with an office chair, a computer and a bunch of papers, three framed pictures of a bolillo family at different stages of happiness: small, medium, and large. On the other side of the desk are three metal chairs, which the cop points to and orders me to sit. Then he turns and walks out, leaves the door open.

I don't see Tiny or Magaña anywhere. And Susi. No Susi.

About twenty minutes later a plainclothes cop comes in with a Coke and sets it on the table. He closes the door and stands in front of me, nods at the Coke.

I grab the soda. It takes me a few tries to clip the can open because my hands are shaking so much. I take a sip and set the can down on the desk, take a breath. "Am I . . . like . . . under arrest?"

"Should you be?"

I have no idea how to answer that so I just shake my head, comb the floor with my eyes. "Is Susi okay?"

He moves to the end of the desk and half sits, half leans on the edge of it and looks down at me, his hands at his waist where he's got a shiny badge and a gun tucked inside a leather holster. "I'm Detective Scott," he says. "You're Rafael Herrera, that right?"

I nod.

"Good," he says. "Your friend says they call you Flaco."

I nod. I wonder which friend. Susi or Tiny or Magaña. And what the hell happened to Rayo and Anaconda?

"You mind if I call you Flaco?"

I nod.

"It appears we got quite a mess on our hands," he says. "Seems someone took a knife to Mr. Martínez. Killed him. You know anything about that?"

Martínez . . . Raymundo Martínez. The dude they took out in the gurney was Rayo.

"I could really use some help here, Flaco."

The drone of the ventilation system pounds against my ears. The air in the room seems to empty out. Feels like when you dive into the deep end of the community pool and the pressure squeezes your head and the dead silence reminds you of how alone you really are in this world.

Detective Scott eyes the Coke can for a sec, then looks back at me and does this big dramatic sigh like he's settling in for the long haul. "I need you to think very carefully and tell me everything that happened from the moment you left Houston until you drove up to the house. Don't leave anything out. You reckon you can do that for me, son?"

11.

I tell Detective Scott my side of the story, exactly as I saw it except for the part about Tiny being illegal and not even giving him his full name, which I said I didn't know, that we all just called him Tiny—even his parents. The detective and his military buzz cut leave the office again for almost an hour, leaving me alone with the photos of his family.

The man in the pictures doesn't look exactly like Detective Scott but it's him. He seems happy. They all do.

Everything's gonna be fine. I say it over and over in my head. There's no way they can arrest us for nothing. We didn't do shit. I just need to chill.

I focus on the photo of the perfect Texas family. The wife looks kind of like a chunky version of a Dallas Cowboys cheerleader, pretty face with happy blue eyes and a button nose, blond hair, wide smile, perfect white teeth. The two kids look like their father with close-cropped spiked blond hair—lots of product. They look close in age. I try and imagine what their life is like, but I can't. My mind won't slow down.

We weren't even there when it happened. This is just the cops doing the shit they do. We're cool. No problem. No fucking worries.

In one picture they're babies, then toddlers. In the latest one they're like eight and maybe ten or eleven. They're well dressed, shirts pressed and tucked in, skin shiny clean. They smile in every picture, except the baby one. That one looks genuine, just four people gazing into an uncertain future. I can't imagine what it would be like to live like them—maybe in a three-bedroom, two-bath house with a two-car garage and a playground in the backyard. Sunday grill-outs with the neighbors. The kids probably get perfect grades and play Little League football and baseball, have a shelf full of golden trophies. I tell myself not to worry. Just chill. Chill.

And church—Texas Baptist for sure. I can almost see them in one of those giant megachurches somewhere in the outskirts of Diamond Park, raising their hands in praise of the Lord, singing hymns, and then going out like a family for lunch at Applebee's, everybody very well mannered. No worries. No fucking worries.

The door flies open, and the detective gestures for me to follow him. He leads me down a hall. I'm guessing he's going to put me in a cell, but instead he opens a door to a room where Magaña sits on a metal chair, back slouched, arms resting on a long table. I go in. The detective shuts the door behind me, so it's just Magaña and me.

"What's going on?"

"Fuck if I know," he says, like he's angry with me.

I sit on a chair across from him and lean on the table. "Where's Tiny?"

He doesn't answer, just shrugs and stares at his hands.

"Did they tell you what happened?"

He looks at me like I just walked in the room. "Rayo got killed. I guess we're the suspects."

"What? We weren't even there."

"Susi was."

"Yeah, but Susi—"

"Who knows what she told the cops."

"She probably just told the truth."

"You don't know that."

The door opens and Tiny walks in, looks like a fucking zombie, eyes all round and dazed. He takes the chair next to mine, crosses his arms, hands buried in his armpits, and kind of rocks back and forth.

I pat his back. "You okay?"

He shakes his head a little and mumbles something I don't get, says, "We're fucked."

"No, we're not," Magaña says. "No one said we were under arrest. And no one read us our rights or anything. They have to do that. They're just fucking with us."

"¿Y la Susi?" Tiny says.

Magaña looks at me.

"We don't know," I say.

Tiny shakes his head. His eyes well up and his voice breaks. "We're gonna go to jail for shit we didn't do. Estamos jodidos."

"No, we're not," I say. "Magaña's right. No one's said we're under arrest."

"They're just checking us out," Magaña says and nods to the corner of the room where there's a black dome, probably houses a camera. "They wanna make sure our stories jibe. In a minute they're probably gonna bring Susi in, see if we confess or whatever."

"It was a stupid idea to come here," Tiny says.

"Why?" Magaña cries. "We didn't do shit. And I got my car."

"Chinga tu madre, pinche Magaña." Tears are running down Tiny's cheeks. "You always get us into shit. I swear—"

"What the fuck did I do?"

"Stop!" I slam my hand on the table. "You're fighting over nothing. We didn't do shit. We're not under arrest. So chill. Let's just wait for Susi and see what she says."

Magaña glances at the black dome. "See what the cops say."

Tiny wipes his tears, shivers. "Fucking cold in here."

"For real."

Magaña shakes his head like we're a couple of wimps. Then the door opens and a cop comes in. No Susi. He hands Magaña the title to the Impala. "Story checks out, son."

"Can we go?"

He looks at me but then the door opens and a plainclothes officer says, "Mattson, Chief's waitin' on you."

The cop walks to the door, nods toward us, and says something to the plainclothes one.

The plainclothes cop looks at us. "I got 'em."

Mattson leaves and the plainclothes one leans into the room and waves at us. "Let's go, gentlemen."

Magaña leads, then Tiny, then me. The cop points to the hallway. "Down to the end and make a right."

We end up at the lobby, where Detective Scott's talking with the desk officer. He turns to us and hangs his hands on his belt by the thumbs like a cowboy. "Well, I guess that's it for now, but if any of your contact information changes, you need to let us know immediately."

"What about Susi?" I say.

Magaña looks at me like I'm crazy for asking.

Detective Scott tilts his head to the side just slightly. "She's going to have to stay for now. We've contacted her parents. Her dad's on his way now."

After a moment, when no one says anything and we're all just staring at one another like the pendejos that we are—Tiny, Magaña, and me realizing the kind of shit we're in but worse for Susi—Magaña says, "So we can go, right?"

Detective Scott nods.

We move to the double glass doors. Tiny and Magaña walk out. I turn to face the detective. "Is she going to be okay?"

"Don't worry about her," he says with a sad smile, just like the one on the face of his kid in one of the photos in the office.

"Do you know what happened?"

His smile fades. "We're not sure."

"What did Susi say?"

"She's not saying much. Probably the shock. It happens. A caseworker is with her now. When her father gets here, we're hoping she'll come around."

"But is she . . . arrested?"

The detective sighs but his expression doesn't give away shit. "She was present at the scene of murder. We're hoping she can help us out."

"Can I see her?"

He lowers his head like he's checking out the shine on his boots and shakes his head just so. "I'm afraid that's not possible right now."

I walk out and join Magaña and Tiny on the sidewalk. The first words out of Magaña's mouth are "Man, we gotta walk all the way back to the Impala."

It pisses me off, but I leave it alone, tap Tiny on the arm. "You get busted for your papers?"

"Gave him fake info."

Tiny has a couple of aliases, kind of like a criminal. He figured it out all by himself. He memorized someone's name and address and all that shit and used it with a fake social security number whenever he had to do something that required documentation. Like the summer he worked at Whataburger. It took them three months to figure it out. The manager asked him if he'd given him the wrong number. Tiny said he'd check but never got back to him. It took another month for the manager to circle back around probably because he really didn't care. Everyone there had to be illegal. By then Tiny had quit and was back in school.

"I told them I didn't know your real name," I say, because I can tell he's freaking out on the inside.

"Did they tell you what happened?" he says.

I shake my head and follow Magaña, who's staring at his phone like five steps ahead of us, already at the corner waiting to cross.

"Rayo got killed," Magaña says. "He got stabbed."

"What happened to Anaconda?" I say.

"What do you think?" Magaña says. "Probably dipped in a flash."

We cross the street. He walks leaning forward, hands now deep in his pockets, eyes combing the ground like he's looking for change.

"Why would he kill him?" Tiny says.

"'Cause they're a couple of pendejos," I say. "Jesus Christ. We shouldn't have left Susi alone like that."

"She's the one who wouldn't get in the car," Magaña says.

"'Cause she knew you were gonna try and feel her up, you asshole."

"No, I wasn't," he says, his face crooked like he's about to sneeze. "I was just goofing around. It didn't mean shit."

"It did to her," I say.

"No one forced her to stay with Rayo. I sure as hell didn't."

"Where else was she gonna go, cabrón?"

"Whatever."

"This was a royal fuckup. We have to—"

"It's done," he says. "They'll probably release her to Rambo when he gets here."

"You don't know that for sure."

"What, you think she did it?"

"Hell no."

"They'll let her go just like they let us go. Ya verás, pinche Flaco. Besides, we can't turn the clock back. So let's focus on right now." He stops and looks around. We're at a major crossroads, four lanes with a traffic light. "Where's the car?"

Tiny nods at the Dollar General across the street. "I remember that place."

Magaña looks at his phone and nods. When the light changes we cross.

"We can't just leave her," I say.

"Whatcha wanna do?" Magaña barks. "You heard the cop. They called her parents. Rambo's gonna be here in a few hours. He sure as fuck don't wanna see us."

"I sure as hell don't wanna see him," Tiny says.

"But she's our friend—"

"She's *your* friend," Magaña barks. "I don't think that bitch's ever said two words to me—"

I shove him. "Don't call her that!"

"The fuck's wrong with you?" Magaña squares up against me. "You for real, cabrón?"

"Ya!" Tiny cries. "Cut the shit."

"I didn't invite her." Magaña waves a finger at me. "That was you, remember?"

"No chinguen," Tiny says. "We need to chill."

"Whatever." Magaña shrugs. "Funny how neither of you's talking about my padrino who just got killed."

"Yeah, you two were real close," I say.

"So? He's still my godfather." He taps his chest with the palm of his hand. "He's family."

That shuts us up. Dude came off like an asshole but now he's dead. I don't think anyone really deserves that. And family's family no matter what. Whether you know them or not.

We screwed up by leaving Susi with those assholes. Bad move. Bad. Bad. Bad. I just thank God that nothing happened to her. Shit. I can't even imagine.

The neighborhood changes by the block. A pretty neighborhood of two- and three-story houses. Looks like a place where all the people are happy, where they don't have any problems. Rocking chairs and wind chimes on the porches. Makes me think of the pictures of the detective and his family. I wonder if this is where they live their perfect life.

"Why do you think they let us go?" Tiny says.

"'Cause we didn't do shit," Magaña says.

"I guess our stories checked out," I say.

"It wasn't because of our stories," Magaña says. "It was the farmer. They checked with him."

"But Susi—"

"She was there," Magaña says. "Bitch had blood all over her, remember?"

"I swear, you call her that again—"

"And what?"

I keep seeing the image of Susi coming around the ambulance and getting into the cop car. It comes back to me with a vengeance. It prods me like I'm guilty of something. Her face. I keep seeing it, eyes locked on mine. That fucking look—her dark eyes like holes staring without blinking. It's as if they're screaming in silence, yelling at me, shouting, *Fucking Flaco, fuck you! This shit's on you, cabrón.*

"There's the H-E-B." Magaña points to the strip mall across the street. "We passed that on the way to Rayo's. I'm sure."

"How do you know it's the same one?" Tiny says.

"'Cause I remember, pendejo. That's how."

Tiny straightens up. "¿Qué pedo, güey?"

"There's probably just one H-E-B in Diamond Park," I say.

Tiny gives me a look. The fear in his eyes transfers to me like electricity. It's not just about Rambo, who's probably gonna kill us when we see him again, or about Susi never saying another word to me and Tiny. It's heavier. It's big and real and heavy as fuck as if something's being strapped to our backs and we'll never get to shake it off, like a big ass rock, like the dude in Mexico they call el Pípila, who carried a big rock on his back to protect him from the bullets of the Spanish during the war of independence. We're going to be lugging something massive on our backs for the rest of our lives. No. Fucking. Doubt.

We cross at the H-E-B. Three blocks later Magaña turns and smiles at us because we're coming into the shit neighborhood where the grass is brown and the weeds are tall and the street's all cracked and broken, the houses are smaller, wood and cement block, peeling paint, bars on the windows, cars on blocks in the yards—just like home.

I shake my head because I can't imagine how Magaña can smile right now. Tiny walks beside me, stares at the road as he walks, his head low, breathes with difficulty. I don't think he's ever done this much exercise in his life. In PE we never change into gym clothes. We walk around the track instead of running. Coach Savino hates that shit, but there's not much he can do about it. The only power he's got is in his grade book. If only he could see Tiny now, pushing it and keeping up with Magaña and me like it's a marathon.

About half an hour later we finally make it to the Impala. It's exactly where we left it. But I don't look at it. I stare at Rayo's house instead. It's quiet like a dead person, the yellow cordon still around it like a noose. Looking at it now, in the quiet of the late afternoon, it looks evil—looks like the place where you'd expect a crime to happen. Like in those shows on TV where they visit the sites of mass murders and shit. A creepy house that sits alone, away from the other houses in the street, belongs to some deranged person. If you saw the house, you'd know there was going to be a murder there. Only somehow we'd missed it.

"We're going to need a jump," Tiny says when we reach the car. He's panting. Leans on the tail fin and wipes the sweat from his forehead with his arm.

Magaña and I look up and down the street. "And cables," he says.

There are only a few houses spread out on the block, separated by large empty yards and the string of duplexes. I nod up the street. "You go that way and I'll go this way."

As I make my way past the first house because there's no car parked in front, I keep telling myself it's okay, it's a Mexican neighborhood—Raza. No paranoid bolillo's gonna put a bullet in me because I'm knocking on his door.

I try the second house. No one answers. I come up to the duplexes at the end of the block. There's toys, empty cans in the yard, a seat pulled from a van or pickup set on the porch. We're the same in Houston as in Diamond Park.

The next set of duplexes has a dog that barks like crazy. A Mexican woman answers the door, keeps the chain on like she's afraid. I tell her we need a jump for the car. She says she can't help me because she doesn't drive and her husband isn't home. But she tells me to go a couple of doors down and ask for Jesús.

At the other end of the block, the Impala sits like a monument. The sun's starting to set behind it. I don't see Tiny. But Magaña is up the road walking away from a house and turning toward the next one.

A few plastic chairs and a couple of gray cinder blocks are set in a circle in the driveway of the next duplex, Miller Lite empties scattered on the ground. There's an old Dodge Ram in the driveway. I can hear *Sponge-Bob* on the TV. I knock and a kid opens the door. He's Mexican, about ten or eleven years old, reminds me of Tiny when I first met him.

"¿Está Jesús?" I say.

He looks to the side. "Next door."

An older dude opens the door right away.

"I'm looking for Jesús," I say. "We need a jump and the—"

"Jesús," the dude yells into the house. "¡Que te buscan, cabrón!"

He goes back in the house that smells of wet towels. My eyes adjust to the dark interior. A couch, a small table like the ones you always see at the Salvation Army, bare walls.

A short, skinny Mexican dude stinking of booze comes to the door.

"Buenas tardes," I say. "My friends and I need a jump."

He squints. It takes him a moment. Maybe he thinks I'm speaking English. Maybe he was asleep—or drunk. He's scruffy, unshaven, hair is a mess of gray. The tattoos on his arms have no colors, just black ink, like something you get in prison: one of a skull blending into a luchador mask, says, *Viviendo el sueño*—"living the dream"—in shitty cursive and another one of a rosary wrapped around the body of naked woman that's seriously out of proportion. "Where's the car?"

"Just up the block."

"Ah, that Impala, eh?"

"Sí, señor."

He steps out, wavers a little, looks up the road to where the Impala's parked. He smiles at me. His teeth are small and brown. "I saw it when I got home," he says. "Nice ride."

"It's my friend's," I say as we walk to his pickup.

He nods toward the other side of the street. "Looks like someone finally caught up with ese Rayo."

"What do you mean?"

"Always fooling around, ese."

"What about Anaconda?"

"Pues quién sabe." He starts the truck, tilts his head to the side, and we drive slowly up the road. "Don't know about no Anaconda, ni nada. But you live like that—dealing with all kinds of people and all the coming and going—no, hombre, you're bound to end up like he did. Seguro que sí."

12.

Jesús helped us start the Impala, even gave us two quarts of motor oil. We hit the drive-through at a Whataburger and now Magaña's cruising north on Highway 77 at an even forty. We drive with the top down. The wind swirls over us and the low rumble of the engine is steady like a heartbeat. Tiny's in the seat behind me, his arms around the large plastic gas cans and looking out the side window like a zombie. It's getting dark. The sky's a deep blue, iridescent like the cloak of the Virgen in the stained glass of the Church of Nuestra Señora del Socorro.

Ever since, like, middle school, I wanted to sit near the Taylor family at mass so when the priest gave the sign of peace, I would get to shake Susi's hand. I guess puberty hit me hard and I didn't know what to do with myself. I dreamed of more, but I would've been happy even with a tiny bit of eye contact from Susi or Yolanda. I think we all would have been. Honestly, it was the only reason to go to church. Tiny and I used to joke about it. We'd sit, me with my mom if she wasn't working or with Ana Flor. Tiny sat with his whole family. We would give each other signs and steal glances at the Taylors. They sat by size, Rambo, his wife, Yolanda, and Susi, who wore her long hair loose and stared ahead like she was watching the latest Star Wars movie. When mass ended, they marched straight out without greeting anyone. Susi's mother always walked with her head down. She looked real sad, but she probably did it so she wouldn't have to catch anyone's eye and have to talk to them because all anyone ever did was ask how Rambo was holding up, or why she wouldn't come over and visit.

Yolanda and Susi walked with their backs real straight just like Rambo, who marched ahead of them all the way to his olive-green truck. He always wore a dark suit, blue or black, with a bolo tie. If you got a good look at him you'd see he was missing part of his left ear. Ana Flor said a drug addict tried to slice his throat but missed and instead took the side of his ear. She said that was when he hit rock bottom and decided to finally go to rehab. She never said whether Rambo killed the guy who tried to kill him or whether he went to jail or what. She doesn't call him Rambo either. She always calls him Mr. Taylor, real respectfully. She said he disappeared for a month or so and came back a different man. Ever since then he's been well groomed, wearing long sleeve shirts to cover the tattoos and track marks of his former life.

During the time when Rambo was away at rehab or wherever, Carlos would sometimes hang with Yolanda. They were both in high school. I was never sure if Yolanda sneaked out of her house or if she had permission from her mom. But every now and then I'd see them sitting together on the front steps of our house or walking back from the Lone Star at night.

Looking back on it now, as the breeze of the South Texas night cooled my nerves, I don't think they ever had anything going on. They just talked. Carlos never said much about her. It wasn't until Carlos was getting ready to go into the army that he said Yolanda was one of the only people who understood him. Nothing about sex or crushes or love. He just used that exact word, *understood.*

"She gets me, Flaco." We were sitting in the Buick. He stared ahead at the night, and it felt almost as if we were cruising around far in the suburbs, the Woodlands or Katy. Then he changed the subject and lectured me on drugs and addiction. "Stay away from them," he warned. "Just look at Rambo. His life is fucked."

I didn't understand it about his life being messed up. He'd gotten clean. But when I was in tenth grade some dude came to school to lecture us about drugs. He said that being addicted was like being in love and never, ever being able to shake it. He spoke real strong and loud like an actor in a play. He said that getting high for the first time was an amazing experience. Everyone in the auditorium cheered. Then he added, "But you'll be miserable for the rest of your life. Trust me, from that moment you'll spend every second trying to get that feeling back. You'll be crazy obsessed, thinking about the next high, the next hit so you can feel that way again. But you never will. You will be a slave to the drug. That's what addiction feels like. And even if you eventually kick and go straight, that feeling never goes away. Going straight means fighting that feeling every moment of your life."

That's when Carlos's words came back to me and I got it. Rambo wasn't getting high, but he sure as hell was thinking about it. And that was the shit of addiction. Rambo was never going to stop thinking about it. The way I tried to explain it to Magaña one time when he said he did coke with his cousins in Mexico the summer he lost his virginity to the prostitute, was that it was like eating Takis. "You know how you can't just have one?" I said. "You take one and right away you want another one. Imagine feeling like that all your life."

"Like you want fucking Takis?" He laughed. "'Tas loco, pinche Flaco."

That's the thing about Magaña, he never thinks deeper than what's right in front of him.

All these thoughts race through my mind as we cruise in the dark, the sky dotted with stars like dust. The rumble of the engine and the wind make me drowsy. But I can't stop thinking.

I'm surprised Magaña hasn't opened his big mouth. Tiny, I get. Like me, he's freaking out about Susi. I can't imagine how scared she must've been when Anaconda knifed Rayo. I can't imagine her sitting alone in a jail cell. I keep thinking we should've stayed, waited for Rambo to arrive.

True, none of us wants to face him. But maybe it was the thing to do, wait there. Face his wrath. Deal with it like men.

But Tiny's probably also thinking of how he doesn't have papers. I suppose he's worried they'll eventually find out the social he gave them doesn't match the name and they'll come looking for him.

I turn around. Tiny's face is serious—sad, even. He turns his eyes to me, doesn't smile, then looks back outside at the night.

"You okay?" I say.

He doesn't answer, doesn't even move his eyes. Yeah, Tiny's freaking out about a lot more than I can imagine.

"What's that?" Magaña calls out over the noise of the wind.

"Nothing," I say.

"The fuck's the matter with you? You been crying like a couple of girls since we left."

"Fuck you," I say.

"It's 'cause of Susi, no?"

"What do you think?" I say.

"She'll be fine. By now her old man's picking her up. Probably taking her out for a nice dinner at the Olive Garden."

"That's not the point," I say. "This whole thing's fucked up, man. Think. Where's Anaconda now?"

"Not our problem."

"He doesn't get it," Tiny says from the back, first words out of his mouth since we left Diamond Park.

"I don't get what?"

"Susi's a witness," I cry out. "She saw the shit go down. She knows Anaconda did it."

"So?"

Tiny leans forward between the two of us. "No seas pendejo. Anaconda's gonna wanna get to her."

Magaña grins at Tiny in the rearview. "This ain't no movie, pinche

Tiny. This is real life. Fucking Anaconda's probably hiding under a rock somewhere."

"You don't know that."

"I know one thing," Magaña says. "That fucker killed my godfather—"

"You didn't even know the guy," Tiny cried.

"He knows Susi," I say. "And he knows she knows what he did."

"The cops'll get him," Magaña says. His tone is low and quiet, as if he's verbalizing his thoughts. "They'll do their job. They'll get him."

We leave it there, ride in silence, each one of us alone with our nightmares.

"Look." Magaña breaks the silence after a long while. "Tomorrow morning we're gonna wake up and it's gonna be like nothing happened." He taps the steering wheel with the palm of his hand and smiles. "Except I'll have a new car."

Tiny shakes his head, leans back on the seat, and turns away, looks out the window at the lights of Sugar Land.

I think of all the bullshit we've put up with from Magaña. This isn't the worst. At least I tell myself that. Anaconda's killing Rayo had nothing to do with him. I can't blame him for that. And what happened to Susi, I'll take part of the blame, no doubt.

Right there and then I resolve to go over and knock on Rambo's door and apologize first thing in the morning. I'll take the blame. I'll tell him I was the one who invited her to Diamond Park. She was my responsibility and I fucked up. I'm sorry. My. Fucking. Bad.

13.

The next morning I don't go to Rambo's. I go to school. Tiny and I sit together in the back of the bus. Magaña's skipping the first couple periods so he can get new plates and registration for the Impala.

Tiny and I don't talk about Diamond Park. Not a word about Susi or Rayo or Anaconda. But I can tell Tiny's thinking about it. I can see he's worried to the point of panic—like ICE is waiting for him around the next corner. Still, he says nothing. All day he goes on as if nothing happened, as if Diamond Park were just a bad dream. I think of Susi's father going down to the police station and Anaconda catching up with them on the road back, cutting them up into pieces like he did Rayo. I wonder whether Anaconda ever killed other people. That maybe he's serial—the Diamond Park killer. He had that scar. He had the look for sure. I keep trying to imagine how it went down. Rayo and Anaconda.

What happened?

My brain is so cluttered with worry and fear, that by the end of class I don't understand the stupid calculus lesson and we're supposed to have a test on Monday.

We meet Magaña at lunch. He parks his ass on the table where Tiny and I sit. He starts about the Impala. I swear, he can't say a single word without me thinking back to the image of Susi, bloodied, walking around that ambulance and getting in the cop car, staring at me like the devil.

But Tiny interrupts him. "Jimmy Archuleta said Susi's old man's still in Diamond Park."

"The fuck does he know about it?" Magaña says.

"He just said."

"I didn't see his truck this morning," I say.

"'Cause he was probably at work," Magaña says.

"Or maybe they're still down there," I say, trying to reason, make excuses. "I mean, he probably got there late at night and didn't wanna drive back, no?"

Magaña chuckles and stretches his leg, runs his hand over the top of his thigh like he's wiping something gross off it. "So, here's the deal . . . I need your help pulling out the gas tank."

Magaña's so pissing me off, I wanna deck him. I turn back to Tiny. "Yeah, like, maybe they spent the night in a hotel and are making their way back now, sabes?"

"That's what I think," he says. "Seguro que sí."

"So?" Magaña says. "This weekend, que no?"

I'm still talking to Tiny. "I bet you anything they'll be home tonight."

He gives me an uneasy smile because either way it's a lose-lose because we're going to get reamed by Rambo. Never mind that Susi will probably never talk to us ever again.

"About the gas tank?" Magaña says.

"You worried about Anaconda, güey?"

I nod. "I keep thinking it's okay 'cause Rambo'll be with her. He's a tough mother, no, ex-marine and all?"

"True," he says. "Besides, Anaconda doesn't know where we live, no?"

"Puta madre," Magaña cusses. "Ya, leave it alone. It's over."

Nothing changes with this hijo de puta. I look at Tiny but I'm also addressing Magaña when I say, "This shit isn't going away just like that." I snap my fingers. "We need to do right by Susi."

Tiny nods. "For real."

"Whatever." Magaña slides off the table and stands. "I didn't do shit."

"You're the reason she stayed behind!" I cry.

"True," Tiny says real calm. "You always do that, cabrón. Always trying to be real chingón and you don't care who it hurts."

"The fuck do you know about me?"

"Too much," he says.

Magaña pauses like he's suspended between slapping Tiny or apologizing to us for all the bullshit he's put us through. But then he just blinks and says, "I'll be at home working on my car."

We watch him walk away, pause at a table crowded with girls. I turn to Tiny. "Pinche cabrón gets worse with age, no?"

Tiny shakes his head. "Must run in the family."

But I don't know if he means his father, who is in prison, or Rayo, who's probably not even his stupid godfather.

By the time we walk out of school, just about everyone we know is gossiping about Susi. The rumors are all over the place—a drug deal, a murder, the cowards who left her there to rot—meaning Magaña, Tiny, and me.

"I don't know where you get your information," I tell Sawyer Bickman, one of the popular bolillos, star of the basketball team, dates a hot white chick who's besties with Susi. "The shit didn't go down like that. The cops said her parents were picking her up."

"Not what I heard, bro," he says, trying to sound all gangster and shit. "Word is you all ran out of town real fast and left her behind."

"We couldn't get her out."

He gets in my face. "I wouldn't have left her in jail like that."

"She's not in jail, pendejo."

"Then where the fuck is she?"

That's when Magaña comes around the corner and steps in, gets in Sawyer's face. "You fucking with my boy, Bickman?"

"I'm asking about my girlfriend's friend." Sawyer steps back. "She heard she's in jail 'cause y'all did some fucked-up shit and left her in Diamond Park."

Magaña grins like he does when he smells a fight coming his way. "We did a lot of shit that ain't none of your fucking business, cabrón."

"Not like I give a shit what you do, but you left her. What kind of a-hole does that?"

"What'd you call me?" Magaña's about to pounce on the hijo de puta when Coach Savino moves in like a ghost. He doesn't touch either of them, just looks at them like a cop, which he used to be before he injured his knee and took early retirement, was put out to pasture at HISD. "There a problem, gentlemen?"

Sawyer and Magaña ignore him, stare at each other.

"Bickman!" Coach says. "Walk it off."

"Coach—"

"I said walk it off!"

Sawyer glances at Coach and walks away, swinging his shoulders the way jocks do when they walk off the field, like they got a lot of attitude—a big fucking show.

Coach turns to Magaña. "Problem?"

"No, Coach."

"You touch any of my players and I'll have your ass expelled in a New York minute. That clear, son?"

"He started it with my boy Flaco."

Coach looks at me, back at Magaña. "I don't give a damn who started what. It's finished. You got that?"

Magaña shrugs.

"Got it?"

"Yessir," he says and breaks away. We walk to the bus. He says, "No thanks needed, bro."

"I didn't ask for your help," I say.

"Guy was gonna kick your ass, pinche Flaco. But that's cool. I got your back."

I hate it when he calls me his boy, like I'm his kid or his slave or something. Whatever. We climb into the bus. Everyone's eyes are on me. We join Tiny, who's sitting way in the back—alone.

"Addison said she talked to Susi's sister," Tiny says. "She said Yolanda said she's still down there."

"Did she say why?" I say.

"I guess they're not letting her out."

"For real?"

"That's what she said."

"But why?"

"I don't know."

"Maybe 'cause she's a witness," Magaña says. "Cops do that. They hold you for evidence."

"No they don't," I say. "They can't just hold her against her will unless she's arrested."

"You don't know that for sure," Magaña says.

"I saw it on *America's Most Wanted*. They can't do that."

"They can if you're Mexican," Tiny says.

"She's not Mexican like you," I say, then add a quick apology because it sounded bad. "I mean, she's like half and half, no?"

"Maybe they're still holding her for questioning," Magaña says. "Or maybe they're putting her in like a witness protection program or something."

"Why the fuck would they do that?" I say.

"'Cause Anaconda, pendejo," Magaña cries and looks at Tiny. "That's who they wanna catch, no?"

"Yeah, but—"

"They need to protect her so she can testify when they catch him."

"I think they're holding her 'cause she's Mexican," Tiny says. "It don't matter if you got papers or if your jefe's a gringo. She's brown. That makes her a suspect."

"Did Addison say if Rambo's with her?" I'm thinking it's gotta be real shitty to be alone in a holding cell at the police station, not knowing your family is there trying to help out. And I also wonder if I'm thinking this to convince myself that we didn't fuck up as bad as I think we did. That she's not scared. That everything's going to work out in the end.

"You think," Tiny says after a moment, "maybe she . . . like, maybe she had something to do with it?"

"What, that she killed Rayo?" I say. "You're crazy."

Magaña laughs. "Right, and Anaconda just ran away 'cause he was afraid of a teenage girl."

"I guess," Tiny says all chill, but I can tell from the sound of his voice and the way he moves his eyes, from left to right like he's checking out his shoes, that he has no idea what's going on.

The school bus drops us off at the corner and the whole walk home I feel as if everyone's checking us out. The women at the beauty salon glance out the window; the people at Tacos Rapido and Mariscos Merida look at us as if we don't belong. Even the lady putting laundry out to dry despite the rain clouds turns to stare. Or maybe it's normal, it's always been this way, and it's just that I'm noticing it for the first time—or it's my guilty conscience working overtime. Maybe I'm just paranoid, like when you smoke too much weed and you start thinking everything's about you when it's really not.

The people at the washateria look up from where they sit and turn back to their work except for the two women folding clothes at the front. I recognize them from the neighborhood. They keep their eyes on us as we cross the street away from the strip mall. Maybe they're friends of Yolanda and Susi. Maybe they know Rambo or his wife. Maybe they heard the rumors. Maybe they know more than we do about what happened. Or maybe . . . maybe we look like three teenage pendejos walking with our heads low like we're guilty of being who we are.

I try not to think about it. I try to forget the look Susi gave me. I try to erase Sawyer's words.

At the next corner, the one where the Taylor house is right across the street from us, everything looks the same. Their house is clean, white, statuette of the Virgen on the front porch, neat green lawn, edges of the grass perfectly trimmed up to the walkway, chain-link fence tight and straight, laundry hanging on the line to dry. The blinds on every window drawn shut. The only thing that's missing is Rambo's green pickup.

We stand there like it's any other day. Magaña says, "Mañana, no?"

"Tomorrow what?" Tiny says.

"The gas tank. I told you at lunch. We pull it out and clean it. Or get a new one."

"I don't know," I say. "I have a calculus test coming up—"

"No se rajen," he says. "I need your help. I don't want my car to sit in the driveway like your cousin's Buick."

"What's that supposed to mean?"

"Just help me fix the Impala. Then we can ride all over town."

"We'll see."

"Ten o'clock," he says. "Tiny, you bring the tools."

"Yeah, whatever."

Tiny and I take a left and go home. Magaña crosses and goes two more blocks to his house, a duplex on a street of Section 8 housing and a couple of halfway houses.

"I don't feel right about this," I say when we're down our street a bit. Tuerto the pit bull is up against the fence barking like he does. "Susi should've been home by now."

"I know," Tiny says. "I just hope she's with her dad."

"If they're not back by tomorrow, maybe we should ask, no?"

He nods.

"We go together," I say. "We knock and ask if Susi's home, see what her mom says."

I turn toward my house. Tiny keeps walking to the end of the block and crosses the street to his place. His father's outside, under the hood of his van.

My mom's at work. Félix is probably at Julio's drinking beer. Ana Flor's standing in the kitchen making meatballs with ground beef and breadcrumbs and egg. I give her a kiss on the cheek and get a glass of cold water.

"How was school?" she says.

"Fine. Why?"

"Why what?"

"Nothing."

She stops her work and squints. "¿Y a ti qué te pasa?"

"Nothing, I just have a lot of homework."

"That's good, no?"

"Not for me," I say with a little humor. I set my glass down. She smiles at me and goes back to the meatballs, taking a pinch of meat from a bowl and rolling it into a ball between the palms of her hands.

I know I should say something but I don't know what. Finally, before I walk out of the kitchen, I say, "So, Italian tonight?"

She shrugs and half smiles. "Ni que Italian ni que nada. Albondigas are Mexican."

"With spaghetti?"

She holds back a smile and nods.

I spend the next couple of hours shut up in my room doing calculus homework, but it's not sinking in. I go through the motions, do the problems without thinking, as if I'm on automatic pilot, because all I can think about is Susi.

I run everything through my head for like the hundredth time and it's all the same, just like calculus. It doesn't add up any different. I close my eyes and think of tomorrow. Tiny and Magaña and me working on the Impala. I guess it'll take my mind off things.

At dinner, Tío Félix chomps down on his meatballs and spaghetti like it's his last meal. He takes a sip of his Miller Lite, keeps chewing, and looks at me and Ana Flor and says, "Julio says Taylor's youngest got in some kind of trouble down in Diamond Park."

He doesn't wait for an answer, looks down at his plate, manages another forkful of food into his mouth, and chews with half a smile. "Funny how the mighty will fall, que no?"

Ana Flor agrees. "Se cree mucho ese."

Tío Félix points at her with his fork. "That's what I say. Acts like his shit don't stink."

"Félix!"

He looks at me and grins. "He's old enough."

"But not at the table," she says. "Pero de verdad, mi amor."

"You know those girls?" he asks.

"Not really," I say real quick like we're talking about skipping school or something. "But yeah, Susi," I add to soften the guilt, "I see her around school. We talk every now and then. She's nice."

"She the youngest, no?"

I nod.

"That's the one they're holding."

"Like in jail?"

"Ey, that's what Julio said."

I push my plate away. "Why?"

"Quien sabe," he says with a shrug, takes a long drink of Miller Lite. "Probably ran off with some pendejo. Taylor better hope it's not drugs.

They have little tolerance for that kind of thing in those small towns in the valley."

I open my mouth to explain, but I can't. Félix wouldn't get it. If Carlos was here, yes. Maybe. But I'm alone.

I'm lying on my bed and staring at the cracks in the ceiling when I hear a knock on my window. I lift it open halfway, as far as it will go. It's Tiny.

"What's up?"

"My jefe says he heard la Susi's in real trouble."

"Félix says they're holding her in jail."

"No, güey, not holding her. She's under arrest," he says. "Es en serio."

"For what?"

"For killing Rayo."

"But why? No way she could kill someone like that—and Rayo? Dude was more than twice her size."

"I don't believe it either," Tiny says, but his words trail off like maybe he's not so sure.

"You think—"

"All I know is that she's under arrest. That's why Rambo hasn't come back. Güey, the shit's gonna hit the fan. We have to do something."

"Like what?"

"I don't know," he says. "But we left her there. We have to help her."

"No mames. Maybe it's just chisme. You know how everybody loves to talk shit. Let's knock on their door tomorrow like we agreed and ask them straight up."

"But what if it's the truth?" he says and looks down, runs his fingers across the windowsill.

I'm caught up in the word *truth*. The way he said it, I can't tell if he meant if it's true she's under arrest or if it's true she killed Rayo.

"I'm gonna have to tell my parents what happened, Flaco. I have to.

If the cops see the name I gave doesn't match the social . . . me van a chingar."

"They don't know where you live."

"But they know where you and Susi and Magaña live. Doesn't take a genius to figure it out."

"Okay, okay. Chill," I say. "Don't tell them anything. Not yet. Let's talk to Susi's mom and see."

"We're so fucked."

"No. We didn't do anything wrong. Don't freak. We'll talk to Susi's mom. We need to find out the truth."

14.

All night I toss and turn. I can't stop thinking of Susi sitting in a cell in Diamond Park, of the look she gave me, her eyes, the gurney being wheeled out, the white sheet. The blood.

Anaconda. I can see his face as clear as if he were in the room with me. His black eyes and the deep, permanent frown, the scar, the way the side of his lip curled like a snarling dog, his rotten teeth. I see him fighting with Rayo over something I don't get, but the knife appears and Anaconda stabs him seventeen times. I actually count them in my dream. I see each one with amazing clarity, the steel blade sinking into the skin seventeen times, one after another like the needle in a sewing machine moving in slow motion. Rayo's hands get cut as he tries to stop the blade. He's on the floor, helpless. Anaconda stabs him over and over even though he's already dead. And in the other room is Susi. She's got that look she gave me, stunned, angry, freaked out beyond anything I can imagine.

Then Anaconda sees her. She slams the door shut. He kicks it. She screams, calls 911. Anaconda hears the cops coming and takes off, out the window. He runs between the houses, a dark figure scurrying between the empty lots and the short chain-link fences. He runs and runs and runs.

In the morning Tiny shows up at my house. I'm in my room getting dressed. I hear Ana Flor tell him to come in. She offers him a seat in the kitchen and some coffee and pan dulce—"fresh from Arandas Bakery."

"No," he says. "Muchas gracias. I had a real big breakfast. My amá made tacos with eggs and chorizo."

I rush out before the conversation gets too involved or Ana Flor gets suspicious about Tiny saying no to food. When she sees me, she offers me the plate of sweet bread.

"No thanks," I say and nod at Tiny. "Magaña's waiting for us."

"Take a concha or something," she says. "Estás hecho un palillo."

"Yeah." Tiny chuckles. "That's why we call him Flaco."

I kiss Ana Flor on the cheek and lead Tiny out of the house as fast as I can. The second the door closes behind us, he says, "I didn't sleep a wink last night."

"Me neither."

We walk across the street to the end of the block and stop in front of the Taylor house. A little dog is barking inside. The blinds are drawn like they always are. The house looks dead.

"You think they're home?"

I shrug. Thing is, I don't know why we're so scared of walking up and knocking on the door. It's just the Taylors. We've known them for years. We used to play when we were kids. We say hello every now and then. But Tiny and I are frozen standing on the sidewalk, hands on the chain-link fence staring at the house.

"So what," I say, "we just ask if Susi's home?"

"Pues no sé. They know she was with us in Diamond Park, no?"

"I guess. If Rambo talked to her, they know everything."

"He must've talked to her by now if he went down there."

"We can't take ourselves out of it," I say. "We can't lie. It'll come out eventually and then we'll have more shit to face."

Tiny nods. He looks so scared it makes me scared. After a long silence,

I pull the latch and open the gate and we walk in and up the steps to the door. I knock. I step back and rub the palm of my hand against my jeans.

The dog keeps barking. A moment later we hear the lock unlatch and the door opens. It's Susi's mom. We never see her outside except at church. She looks older than I remember from last week. Her hair is up in a bun and her face is caked with makeup and pink lipstick. Despite the soft blue eye shadow, you can see the dark circles under her eyes. She's got this faraway look like she just woke up or something—and skinny like a skeleton, reminds me of Posada's Catrina, just needs the big hat with the flowers.

"Buenos días, señora," I say in my friendliest tone. "We were wondering if there's any news of Susi?"

Mrs. Taylor frowns just slightly. Her mouth sort of shuts tight making a straight line across her face. "My husband is with her."

She doesn't say anything more. I'm suddenly tongue-tied, don't know what to say. But Tiny steps up to the plate. "Do you know when she's coming back?"

She shakes her head, no. Her hands are on the door, she's kind of leaning into it, or holding it for support. She tilts her head to the side and mumbles something I don't catch. I glance at Tiny. He shrugs. I look at Mrs. Taylor again. She's looking past us at the street, her eyes squinting like the sunlight is hurting her eyes.

"She's in good hands. El Señor will look after her," she says with a sad smile and nods knowingly. "Que Dios los bendiga, muchachos."

She closes the door in our faces, but slowly. There is no anger in her gesture, just resignation. It's as if she's saying it's none of our business. Period.

We walk back to the gate. Tiny shrugs. "What does that even mean?"

"Señor," I say. "Could be Rambo."

"Or God. Like, that she's dead?" Tiny says all freaked. "Like the Lord is looking after her now. That's what you say when someone's dead. Susi's dead."

"No mames." I smack him on the chest with the back of my hand. "Pinche Tiny, you need to chill, man. How could she be dead? She's in the jail with the cops."

"You heard her. When someone says el Señor is looking after her, that's what it means. The person's dead."

"That's not what she meant." I push him onto the sidewalk. The gate slams shut behind us. The dog's still barking at us from somewhere inside the house as we start toward Magaña's. "She said 'el Señor is looking after her.' That means God is keeping an eye on her."

"Well, that's not good, güey. It means she's in trouble and she's relying on God for help. Eso nunca sale bien."

"What else can she do?" I say. At the end of the yard Yolanda's hanging laundry to dry, big white sheets that dance in the breeze.

I look at Tiny. He looks at me.

"Yolanda?" I call.

She glances over the line. She grabs the pins she's holding between her lips and tosses them in the plastic laundry basket on the ground by her bare feet. She takes a quick look at the house, then walks over to us.

"What's up?" she says, which is an odd greeting from someone we don't talk to. Or who doesn't talk to us. She's wearing skintight jeans, looks wider at the hips and thighs. Her hair is in a ponytail but kind of messy. Looks like her mom, but pretty. Her eyes are big, brown, and bright, her skin's smooth, lips thick with lipstick.

"Nada," Tiny says. "We were just wondering about Susi. She okay?"

Yolanda looks back at the house again. My eyes follow. The blinds are closed. Door closed. A big tanker truck rumbles past behind us on Clemens Avenue.

Yolanda leans forward, hands resting on the sides of her hips. "I don't want you all spreading rumors about my sister, you get that?"

"No, of course not," I say. "We just wanna know if she's okay."

The words come out of Yolanda's mouth in super slow motion. "They say she's in trouble."

I grab on to the fence real tight. I know I heard her right, but still. I glance at Tiny and back at Yolanda. "Like . . . what kind of trouble?"

She nods as if to reaffirm her statement. "Serious trouble down in Diamond Park. My father's there right now. He even hired Joe Cárdenas to help him."

Tiny and I turn at the same time to look at the big billboard across the street. "Joe Cárdenas from the billboard?" Tiny's voice is pinched and real high like he's about to cry.

"The one and only," she says kind of proud, showing off her brush with a celebrity, because in our world Joe Cárdenas is big-time. The shit's for real.

Yolanda takes her sweet time, turns her eyes to the side, moistens her lips, then adds, "They say she's involved in a murder."

"No, no." I can't believe it—don't want to. "Who's they?"

"The cops," she says with a nod.

"She's still in jail?" Tiny asks.

She bows her head and looks at her toes, speaks real slow. "I'm only telling you this because your cousin Carlos was my friend." She stops and lets that hang for a moment like she's being all mysterious. "My mom says Susi deserves whatever she gets. She says that's what happens when you stray from the righteous path." Then she raises her eyes and stares at me, as if to tell me she knows way more than we think. "They say she went off with some boys to Diamond Park. What did she expect?"

Tiny stutters. "B-b-but—"

"Involved doesn't mean she did it, right?"

"Susi's always rebelling. She says she hates it here, in this house, in this neighborhood. I was like that when I was her age, I guess. Maybe not as impetuous as her, but your cousin Carlos—"

"What does that have to do with anything?" I glance at Tiny and back at Yolanda. "Besides, you're still here. And Carlos—"

"If the Lord hadn't taken Carlos away from us, who knows what our lives would be like right now."

"That doesn't make Susi a killer," Tiny says.

"Besides," I say, "she didn't do it."

"Oh yeah? Then why is she in jail?"

"'Cause . . . 'cause . . . she just didn't."

Then Tiny spits it out. "It was Anaconda."

Yolanda frowns, but she kind of grins like she knows more than she's letting on. "I told you not to start any crazy rumors. My mom can't take it anymore. She has a nervous condition. All the gossip gets to her. It's gross. It's disgusting how you all talk about us."

"It's not chisme," Tiny says and kisses his thumb crossed over his index finger. "La neta—I swear."

Yolanda takes a moment before she speaks again. "Well, like my mother says, it's in the hands of the Lord." Then she glances to the side toward the Lone Star. "And Joe Cárdenas."

"So when's your dad coming back?" I say.

She shifts her weight onto her other leg and tilts her head to the side. "Late tonight, I think. He has one of his church meetings in the morning."

I nod real slow and lean back. I want to get away, not just from Yolanda but from this whole mess.

"Una cosita," Tiny says before we start off. "Do you know if she's okay?"

Yolanda takes a step back. "She won't talk to my dad. They say it's the shock. Maybe Joe Cárdenas will help her out." Then she squints. "I have a different idea."

"What's that?" I say.

"Maybe she had enough and just snapped," she says.

"Enough what?"

"Or maybe," she says with a shrug and brings her hands to the sides of her head, her fingers pointing at the sky like a pair of horns, and grins, "it's the devil."

"Qué diablo ni que nada," Tiny cries. "She didn't do it."

"Don't be spreading no rumors, you hear?" Yolanda says flatly, then turns and walks slowly back to the laundry. She moves real deliberate, tossing her head to the side, leaning down to pick up a sheet from the basket as if hanging laundry is the most important job in the universe. I know Magaña would make a comment about how she looks for sure. We watch her for a second, how she leans over, stretches, arms up, hip to the side. It's as if she knows we're checking out her curves. I'm thinking maybe that's her thing, to stand out here looking real nice and pretty and letting everyone see her. Or maybe it's how she does things. All I know is that when we see her in church, she sure as hell doesn't dress or move like that.

"She's lying," Tiny says. "En serio, Flaco. She has to be lying. No way did Susi do it."

I tell Tiny about my dream but he dismisses me with a shrug. His eyes are all bloodshot like he's stoned. "That's just un pinche sueño. We don't even know how many times Rayo got stabbed. Or with what."

"It was a knife," I say.

"You don't know that, güey. We just saw him wheeled out. There's no way Susi could've done it. She's, like, half his size."

"Less."

"What're we gonna do, cabrón?"

"I don't know."

I keep my head bowed as we walk, watch my feet move, one step in front of the other. One of my old Nikes is starting to rip at the toes.

We turn the corner. Two blocks later we're facing the row of duplexes— ten buildings, twenty units—we jokingly call the projects. Two units before the last one has a convertible Impala parked in the driveway with the hood open. Magaña's leaning into it, half his body inside the engine bay so it looks like the car's eating him alive.

He steps out as we arrive, wipes his hands on a rag, and tosses it back into the engine bay. "¿No que no, cabrones?"

I spit and peek under the hood as if maybe the answer to our problem's right there between the carburetor and the alternator. But all there is is a dirty, big block engine.

"So what's the plan?" Tiny says. I can tell he's not in the mood for Magaña's shit. Across the street, a pair of drunks sit together on the porch of the halfway house staring at us.

"Gas tank," Magaña says. "I think it's in good shape, we just need to clean it out real good. I got new spark plugs and cables and a new air filter."

"So we taking out the tank to clean it?" I say.

Magaña slaps Tiny on the back. "What do you think? You're my chief mechanic, bro."

"Better to do it right the first time. It's not such a big deal."

We both look at Magaña moving around the car like a kid. Even Carlos didn't act that stupid and proud when he got the Buick. But whatever. Magaña ain't Carlos, that's for sure.

Tiny and I peek into the trunk, look at the gas tank. "We're gonna have to jack up the back," Tiny says. "It comes off through the bottom."

We get to work, avoid talking about Susi. All day under the hot sun and the swampy humidity with Tiny leading us, Magaña doing what Tiny tells him to. It's almost funny to watch. Magaña empties the tank of the old rusted-out gasoline right there on the sidewalk. It runs down the driveway like an orange creek to the street and down the storm drain.

We wash the thing with a hose and spray the special detergent Magaña bought at the AutoZone. Then we set it aside to dry in the sun.

"And that's it?" he says.

"Simón." Tiny scratches the back of his head. "When it's dry we put it back on, hook up the sending unit, and we're good."

Magaña stretches.

"I'm starving," I say. "¿Tortas Perronas, no?"

"I'll stay," Magaña says. "Just bring me one, de milanesa con queso. Extra chiles. And a Jarritos de mandarina."

We walk to the store. I get ham and cheese, Tiny a Hawaiana. I pay. Then I look at Tiny and tell him what's been bothering us the whole time we were cleaning that stupid gas tank but didn't talk about. "We have to do something."

He nods. He knows what I'm talking about.

"We need to talk to Susi and find out the truth."

"¿Y?" he says and takes the bag with the tortas. "How we gonna do that?"

"We have to go back to Diamond Park."

15.

On Sunday morning my mom's at the foot of my bed. She shakes my leg real gently. "Rafa . . . Rafa, wake up, mijo."

It's as if I'm still dreaming. She's dressed in a plain gray skirt and jacket she probably bought at the Marshalls on Northline, looks like the secretary at school. Her eyes are bright but puffy and tired. Before I can smile at her, I remember everything from the last few days.

"What's the matter?" she says.

"Nothing." I shake off the sleep and try to put aside reality if only for this moment. But Diamond Park won't go away. It's at the front of my brain. I can't stop thinking of Susi. "What are you doing here?"

"¿Pero qué, ni buenos días ni nada? What kind of greeting is that?" She gives me a gentle slap on the thigh. "It's nice to see you too."

"I'm just . . . surprised."

"Hopefully a good surprise. Ándale pues, get up and get dressed. You're coming to church and—"

"But, Ma—"

"But, Ma, nothing. You're coming. And after, we're going out to lunch together."

"For real?"

"Yes, just you and me. And then some shopping. ¿Cómo ves?"

"You win the lottery or what?"

"No. But I've been working a lot of hours and I would like to enjoy my day off with my favorite man." She stands and ruffles my hair, looks at her watch. "Pero apúrate. We have twenty minutes."

———⌄———

At church my mom takes my hand and holds it real tight like she's afraid I'll float away like a balloon. And with everything that's going on, maybe I would. Yeah, maybe that would be better, to go far away and disappear into the blue like smoke.

We sit all the way in the back. The Taylors are missing. And Tiny and his family too. And those guys never miss church. It's just too weird. Pretty soon my mind's going crazy thinking they all went down to Diamond Park together. All during mass, I picture different scenarios. Maybe Tiny confessed and they're all over at Joe Cárdenas's office testifying about what happened, that I invited Susi when I shouldn't have. Or worse—maybe Anaconda got to them.

I go over the plan Tiny and I made after we bought the tortas yesterday: drive the Impala down to Diamond Park; see Susi; find out what's going on; find out why she won't talk. Tell the cops. They need to know Susi was just there by accident. That she didn't do anything. If we leave early tomorrow morning, we can be back in the afternoon before school lets out. I need to talk with Magaña after church.

———⌄———

Tío Félix gives us a ride to Las Islitas after mass. Before we go inside I ask my mom what's going on, because this whole morning's been way too weird. She hasn't forced me to go to church in forever, and the holding hands thing is not our style at all. And we never go out to eat unless we're celebrating something important like my santo or something. Mariscos on Sundays is not something we do. Seafood ain't cheap—even at Las Islitas.

"It's a surprise," she says, real tender like I'm a little kid.

"Really?" I can't imagine what it is, except it has to be something good, otherwise we wouldn't be here. It's probably some guy. She's going to tell me she met some dude and now they're dating and wants my blessing so she can introduce me to him. I've been wanting this for her for a long time. As long as he's not a pendejo like her brother, I'm good. She deserves to be happy.

But she says nothing more, just smiles like she's hiding something fun and leads me into the restaurant, which is packed and loud with banda music blaring, kids screaming. You'd think there was a party going on.

We find a table near the very back. She orders a cóctel, some kind of vuelve a la vida gross octopus-tentacle thing that comes in one of those parfaits like a milkshake. I have the filete de mojarra empanizado. Always delicious with a little lime and Tapatío sauce.

"So," she says at last, "Ana Flor tells me you're doing pretty well in school."

"Just not so good with calculus."

"You know I feel terrible for not being home."

"I know." The last thing I want is for her to feel guilty. She works too much as it is. "It's fine. It's just Tío Félix—you know how he is."

She nods and unfolds the paper napkin, places it on her lap like a lady. "It's not easy, mijo. I know he can be bien menso, but we have to be grateful for his help."

She's right. But I'd rather we lived in our own place even if it was one of the Section 8 duplexes where Magaña lives.

"Look"—she reaches across the table and takes my hand—"I know it's not easy. Sometimes it can feel as if everything is working against you, but that's how life can be. You have to take the good with the bad."

I bite my lip and keep quiet because I know she wants to be a mom— act like one, share her wisdom and all that. It's important to her. So I smile and nod like I care. After a while, I just see her mouth moving as she goes on and on and on about life. But all I can think of is Magaña. If he cleaned the carburetor like Tiny told him to and got the new distributor cap and drained and refilled the power-steering fluid, the Impala should be able to make it back to Diamond Park. The only problem's the tires. Sergio over at Hidalgo Used Tires might give us a break on some used ones, but even then we'd be talking a couple hundred for sure. None of us has that kind of cash.

"...look at a house," my mom says.

"What?"

"We're going to go look at a house," she says with a big smile across her face. She's glowing, actually. And for the first time in, like, forever, I think of how beautiful she must've been when she was young and hooked up with the man who is my father.

"Okay," I say, my enthusiasm tempered by confusion. "Look at a house for what?"

"To buy it, what else?"

"For real?"

"Claro, mi amor."

"But how?"

She leans over the table and whispers, "I've been saving. All these years I've been putting away un poquito a la vez. I found a place. It's small, two bedrooms, but for you and me, no necesitamos más, no?"

"Wow. That's . . . that's like the last thing I expected."

She makes a face. "You can get my brother off your back."

"Yeah." I shrug. "He's not that bad."

"I know," she says. "Pero estamos bien amontonados in his place. It would be nice to have our own home. Besides it's near the University of Houston."

"But, Ma, what if I don't wanna go there."

"Listen to me, Rafa." Her tone's like needles. "The University of Houston is a good school. You can study something you can make a decent living with and you can do your art on the side."

What does it even mean, on the side? As if art's a plate of French fries or cole slaw. "Ma. I wanna be an artist."

"Rafael—"

"Ma, please."

"You have to think of your future, mijo."

"I am. I'm thinking of it all the time. As a matter of fact, sometimes I feel that's all I think about. It's driving me crazy."

"But art is just a phase. You—"

"It's not a phase. And I'm pretty good at it too. It's what I love doing. Doesn't that count for anything?"

"Of course it does. But you don't know what it's like out there. How're you going to find a good job?"

"There're lots of jobs in art, Ma. Mr. Edens, my counselor, says it's a great career choice for me 'cause I got talent."

She sighs and turns away like I've killed her dream. I don't want this. We don't spend enough time together as it is, and now we're arguing. But it's my future, not hers.

I reach across the table and touch her hand. "I'm sorry, Ma. Maybe we can talk about it another time, okay?"

She shrugs and looks at her watch again. "We have an appointment to see the house."

"Now?"

She waves to the waitress for the check. Then she dumps her purse on the table and finds her phone and calls Ulises Taxi to pick us up. She says nothing else about school. She just pays the bill, leaves less than a ten percent tip, and marches out of the restaurant like she hated the food.

"Ma, don't be mad at me."

"I've worked very hard. All my life I've been working, Rafael. I don't want you to throw away your future."

"Ma . . ."

"You're a smart boy. You can be anything you set your mind to, a doctor, a lawyer—or an engineer. You like machines."

"I wanna be an artist."

"Rafael . . ."

"It's my life. Why can't I do what I want with it?"

She doesn't answer. It's a battle neither one of us is going to win. As far as I know, no one in our family's been to college. I'm sure my mom wants this so she can throw it in her father's face. Whatever. There's really no point in fighting about it right now anyway. And if she wants to buy a house, fine. She worked hard for it. It's her money. It's not as if I ever expected her to pay for my college anyway. She can do whatever she wants. I just envisioned her living with Félix and Ana Flor for the rest of her life.

The taxi takes us to a neighborhood I've never been to just outside the 610 loop. Looks way better than where we live, but it's nothing like River Oaks or the Heights. The houses are small, single story, nice green lawns, a couple of basketball hoops, no bars on the windows.

We pull up to a yellow house with flowers and a welcome mat at the front. A Volvo SUV is parked in the driveway. A woman in a navy skirt and a pink blouse and a scarf around her neck comes around the side and waits for us between the driveway and the front entrance. When my mom and I get out of the taxi, her face kind of falls. Her cheeks sink in like she's out of air. Then she smiles real wide as if for a picture. But she doesn't say cheese. Instead she says, "Miss Herrera?"

"Yes." My mom offers her hand.

The Realtor's light brown hair bounces with the perky movement of her head. She juggles her clipboard, places it under her arm, and takes my mom's hand in hers and shakes it.

"I'm Wendy Ross, we spoke on the phone." She's all syrupy Texas in her manner, gives my mom a brochure. "It's a lovely home. An absolute dollhouse if I ever saw one. And a real find in this neighborhood. Absolutely no flood damage, and it just got a brand-new roof last year. Such gorgeous curb appeal, don't you think?"

My mom glances at the brochure as we follow Wendy the Realtor into the house that smells like my closet.

"It hasn't been lived in for a while," she says. "I opened a couple windows in the back by the kitchen to air it out. Which by the way has all new stainless-steel appliances and a premier granite countertop."

We tour the house one room at a time. My mom peeks in, looks up and down as if the carpet and the ceiling were the most important parts, acts very thorough, examines everything, even the linen closet. To me, the house is like the one we live in now. The bedrooms are small and there's only one bathroom and a small concrete patio out back. But it doesn't have wood paneling and has no furniture. That's it.

My mom glances at the brochure. "It says central air and heat."

"Absolutely. The unit is four years old and still under warranty."

My mom looks around the living area like she's trying to find something that isn't there.

"It's a very family friendly neighborhood," Wendy adds. "And with property values shootin' up the way they are, you can't go wrong for the price. Not in this area. No, ma'am."

My mom smiles at me. "What do you think, Rafa?"

"I kind of like our neighborhood."

"But do you like the house?" she says.

"I guess."

"Is it just the two of you?" the Realtor asks.

My mom nods. Then she wanders off for another tour of the house on her own. Wendy the Realtor and I stay in the living room. I stare at the fake fireplace and mantel. I can feel Wendy's eyes looking me up and down like she's trying to decide if I'm trouble. "So, you're still in school?" she says.

"I'm a senior."

"Awesome. Best year of high school. You play sports at all?"

"I'm an artist."

"Oh, really? That's terrific. You plan on going to school for it? You people are so talented," she says, just as my mom makes it back to the living room.

"We should go," my mom says.

I kind of got the same drift she did. It might have been the "you people" comment. But I'm so used to hearing shit like that I automatically dismiss it. I'm not even sure my mom got it. Maybe she's seen all she wants to see. Or maybe it was the Realtor encouraging my art.

"Any thoughts on the house, Mrs. Herrera?"

My mom stops by the door and frowns. "It's Miss."

"Oh, I'm so sorry," Wendy Ross says. "But just a little FYI, I don't think the house will last long on the market at this price."

My mom gives me a nod. "Vámonos, Rafael."

"Is there anything I can tell the seller?"

"No, thank you." She forces a polite smile just like the one she gives people at the Walmart when she's working the register, and we're out the door and back in the taxi in less than ten seconds.

As we take off down the street, she crosses her arms and huffs. "I don't like it."

"Why, 'cause she said 'you people'?"

"Because I don't like it, Rafael. It's a very small house for the two of us. And we don't know anyone in this neighborhood. No me gusta."

True. But it's not as if we didn't know this before we came. I say nothing. I know she's pissed at something but I'll never know what. Stuff just sets her off. She's tough and stubborn. Never cracks. She will never— ever—tell me something she doesn't want to tell me. Like about my father. It's as if he doesn't exist, never did. I was just born out of nothing and she's my mom by some miracle from God and that's it. Period.

Thing is, she's too proud. She'll never admit people look at her as something less. But they do. They do it all the time. People cross the street to avoid walking by me all the time. And when you walk into a store they look at you like maybe you're going to steal something. It happens at the Lone Star despite the fact that I've been going into that stupid store since I was five years old and never stole a damn thing.

***

When we get home, she doesn't go inside right away. I can see the hurt in her eyes.

I clear my throat so my voice won't crack. "Ma . . ."

"There are things I want for you, mijo, so you can have a better life."

"Ma . . ."

"Por una vez . . . just once I would like to be appreciated. I would like my wish to be appreciated. That is all, Rafael."

With that, she turns and marches up the steps and into the house, the screen door slamming shut behind her with a solitary clap. I don't get a chance to speak. And then it hits me. This was her thing. She wasn't planning on buying the house. She has no money saved up. Today was just her day to go out and feel like someone important, like someone who could actually go out and buy a house in a decent neighborhood.

I didn't see it at first because we've never been to look at a house before. Usually we just go to the Galleria Mall and browse the stores. She'll go into Nordstrom or Armani or whatever fancy store and have the people there treat her like royalty. That's her thing. Once we even went to the Infinity dealership off Memorial, had the sales guy take her for rides, serve her coffee and everything. She doesn't even know how to drive. She does this every now and then. She does it so she can feel human.

***

I walk over to Tiny's house. There's a big pile of junk on the sidewalk in front—a broken chair, a ripped love seat, old toys, and a bicycle without a wheel. The driveway's empty. I knock on the front door. No kids crying or little dog barking or Tiny's jefe watching fútbol on TV. Nothing.

I knock again, hard.

I don't get an answer. I peek in the window. The house is empty—no furniture or rugs or paintings or plates or TV or toys. I go to the next window and the next and the next. Every room, even the little shed where Tiny's jefe kept his tools, is empty.

16.

He told his parents. Tiny fucking told them what happened in Diamond Park and they got the hell out in case ICE decided to come looking. Better safe than sorry. I can't blame them—but shit. He could've waited. He could've told me. I would never tell anyone, even if they tortured me.

It's my own fault. This whole thing. If I hadn't walked across the street to talk to Susi, none of this would've happened. I should've just kept walking. Now Tiny's gone.

I run over to Magaña's house. He's sitting in the Impala, hands on the wheel like he's driving. I get in the passenger side, slam the door.

"Easy on the ride, cabrón."

"Tiny's gone," I say.

"Gone where?"

"Gone—gone. He left with his family."

"What the hell?"

"They packed all their shit and left. Didn't tell anyone. He didn't even tell me."

"Where'd they go?"

"Who knows. Tiny probably told his parents what happened and about the fake name and social he gave the cops."

"They got scared."

"Yeah, they got scared. They thought ICE was gonna come looking for them. Shit, man, wouldn't you take off?"

"Bro, I'm legit."

I'm pretty sure Magaña can see my rage because his demeanor changes real quick. He raises his eyebrows and tells me to take it easy. "He probably just moved across town. I bet you we see him tomorrow at school. Or he'll get in touch on WhatsApp or something."

"He doesn't have a phone." Magaña means well, but he doesn't get it. I don't think we'll see Tiny at school or anywhere else ever again.

"He ain't gonna just disappear like that," he says.

I shake my head, tell myself to give it time. Maybe he'll prove me wrong and show up one day like he did when he first arrived in the neighborhood a few years ago. Still, the way the house looked, Tiny's fear of getting busted by ICE, the loyalty to his family. I admire and hate it at the same time. Why him? Why us? Why Susi?

I have this real shitty feeling about Diamond Park. But what Tiny did—telling his family what went down—it was the right thing. I would've done the same if I'd been in his shoes, although I wouldn't tell Félix. No, I would. I just don't imagine we'd split like that—or maybe we would if we were illegal.

I lean back on the seat that smells of Armor All. The sun is setting somewhere far to the west and lighting up the edges of the chrome in the car like it's made of silver. In the side-view mirror I see the halfway house across the street like a picture in a round frame. An old bolillo steps out to the porch, looks left and right, then lights up a cigarette. He leans against the column and stares at the Impala as he sucks down the smoke like it's oxygen.

When I first met Tiny he came to me at school because he'd heard I'd drawn a few tattoos. He told me he wanted to get one, but it had to be unique, a mix of the Mexican eagle eating the serpent, the Virgen, and a badass-looking bull with el Popo and Ixta in the background. I was, like, "No offense, but it's way too much for a tattoo."

I told him simple was better. Half the time I can't even tell what people's tattoos are. But I made the drawing for him anyway. I even added a banner across the bottom that read: *México Lindo y Querido.* He loved it. He didn't get the tattoo. I don't know if his parents wouldn't let him or if Jaime who runs the Hernández tattoo studio on Airline wouldn't do it because Tiny was underage. Or maybe he chickened out. But he did frame the drawing and hung it in his bedroom.

He probably took it with him. Maybe it'll remind him of me wherever he goes—Kansas or Florida or wherever. And maybe one day he'll get the tattoo, and then he'll never forget me.

Magaña pulls out a joint from his breast pocket and waves it back and forth between us. "So you wanna light up, o qué?"

"Did you clean the carburetor?"

"All done, bro. I even got a new battery with a thirty-percent-off coupon." He reaches for the ignition and turns the key. The starter whines, the engine turns, and the car rumbles and settles into a steady idle.

I can't help but smile. Magaña's got himself a real running car. Feels good. One good thing out of Diamond Park. The Buick never ran. Magaña's done wonders with the Impala in just a weekend—with Tiny's help.

He revs the car a couple of times and turns the key. The engine knocks and shakes a couple of times before falling silent. He punches the lighter in and we both stare at it and wait. But it doesn't pop out. So he takes a Bic lighter from his pocket and lights the joint, takes a couple of drags, and hands it to me.

I take a deep toke and let the smoke cover me. I close my eyes. The scent of the weed lifts me to the sky. The gravity of my problems slowly fades—but only slightly. I take another drag and hold the smoke and pass the joint back to Magaña, who's got this maniac smile on his face, and I think, yeah, we're smoking dope in his car.

"Man," he says, "I wish we had some tunes, no?"

"Stereo doesn't work?"

"It's a 1959." He laughs. "FM hadn't even been invented."

I turn on the radio and move the tuner up and down. It crackles with static. All I get is talk radio, sports, a classical station. Then I find an old Mexican song. It's one of those old crooners, Pedro Infante or Jorge Negrete or Vicénte Fernández. Ana Flor could call it for sure, but they all sound the same to me. Still, it sounds cool, small and tinny through the speakers that are probably torn and frayed—feels as if we've gone back in time.

We smoke half the joint, then Magaña crushes the lit end of it and sets it in the ashtray. "When I get some bucks, I'm gonna redo the whole interior, Flaco. It's gonna be lit as fuck. I'm checking out these badass rims I saw in a magazine, una chingonería—"

"No, man. Keep it original."

"Original's for old people."

"The car's badass as it is. Why fuck it up?"

"You know what your problem is? You got no vision."

"I could see pimping out the Buick. But this car?" I tap the curve of the dash. "It's way too cool to screw it up."

"Close your eyes," he says. "Close them. Now, try to visualize the car in a shiny red metallic paint. No chrome. Imagine it lowered to the ground with these fine low-profile Goodyears and rims that look like stars."

"Nah, man. That does nothing for me. I see a restored spaceship." I run my hand over the backrest like it's made of fur. "They don't make shit like this anymore."

"But the color—"

"Original."

He looks around as if he never noticed the bluish green like something out of an old Elvis Presley flick. "Green?"

"Teal."

"It's a chick color, bro."

"It's original."

"It's like that *Thelma and Louise* movie."

"So?"

"Es de viejas, pinche Flaco. Red. Deep metallic red like blood. Sangre."

That word hits me hard. I sink back in my seat, my body like lead, and think of the moment Susi came around the ambulance, her shirt all bloody.

"Doesn't matter anyway," he says. "No money, no paint."

A different song comes on the radio. Angélica María singing a ranchera-style song I've never heard before.

Magaña reaches for the tuner. I slap his hand.

"This country shit sucks," he says.

"I like it."

"You're weird."

I turn in my seat and face him. "We have to go back."

"What, to Diamond Park?"

"We have to talk to Susi. We have to find out what's going on."

"What's going on about what?"

"She's still in jail. Yolanda says they're pinning Rayo's murder on her 'cause she won't talk."

"That's bullshit."

"No, it's not. She said Susi's involved in a murder. She told me to my face."

He looks at me like he's trying to find out if it's a lie or a joke. "We don't even know . . . like maybe she did."

"What?"

"Maybe Susi did do it."

"Fuck you. You think she stabbed a two-hundred-pound gangbanger?"

"Rayo's not in a gang."

"Whatever."

"No mames, Flaco. Let her old man take care of it. He's there, no?"

"Yolanda said he hired Joe Cárdenas."

"From the billboard?"

"Except Susi's not talking to him."

"And you think she's gonna talk to us?"

"She's our friend. She trusts us."

"Yeah, you think?"

"We have to try."

"You're crazy, bro." He glances at the ashtray, back at me. "The weed's twisting your brain."

"Tiny and I talked about it all day yesterday."

"¿Y qué? You weren't gonna bring me in on it?"

"I'm bringing you in now."

He leans back, moves his hand over the steering wheel. "So, what do we do?"

"We drive down there—"

"In my car . . ."

"No, in mine."

"No chingues, Flaco."

"I'm serious. We drive down there and talk to Susi. We find out what happened and tell Joe Cárdenas. He'll straighten everything out."

"What if they won't let us see her?"

"Why wouldn't they?"

"'Cause they didn't let us before."

"Cárdenas'll help us. She has rights."

He gives me a look that tells me he's not convinced.

"You get to visit your father in prison, no?" I say. "How's this any different?"

Magaña picks at a crack in the steering wheel with his thumbnail. The sun's down and the lights in the street and the houses are glowing in warm colors like stars. Inside the car Magaña looks almost delicate; his expression's sad and worried at the same time. It makes me wonder about when he was a little kid, before I met him, before he was Magaña, when he was just little Antonio Magaña, before his father went to prison, before he got the mean streak he's got that makes him do stupid shit that gets him in trouble all the time. I wonder whether there was once a boy, just an innocent, good little kid like all the other little kids. Or was he born like this?

He takes a deep breath and says, "When do we go?"

PART II

17.

We drive out of the neighborhood at around the same time as the school bus and hit major rush-hour traffic on 59.

We're driving with the windows open and the top down. Magaña's acting all smug, laughing at the cars. "Look at them all. Commuting to their lame-ass jobs like worker ants."

"That's us one day."

"Not me, bro."

I stick my hand out and take in the slow-moving air. "You're full of it."

"For real, Flaco, I ain't doing this." He flips his hand over the steering wheel. "I'm gonna figure something out, something different. Maybe I'll sell vintage cars like this, or I'll invent something. But I'm never gonna fall into laboring like a slave. No fucking way." Then he glances at me and adds, "And neither are you, cabrón."

"You don't know that."

"You're an artist, bro. I can see it."

"'Tas loco."

"No, no. I do. I can see your future. You're gonna be a big deal, bro."

"Thanks. I'll be happy with a decent job, even if it's inking at Hernández's Tattoo or some other kind of work—"

"Don't say that. Don't kill the dream before it even starts."

"I'm just being real."

"You're an artist, Flaco. You got the talent. You can do great things. That mural at the dentist office ain't shit compared to what you'll do in the future. Ya verás, cabrón. It's gonna get real for you. I see it as clear as I can see that truck in front of us."

That's the difference between Magaña and me. He kind of goes by the gut, always acts on his feelings. Sometimes he's right. But most of the time he's full of shit.

As soon as we pass the Bissonnet exit, the traffic loosens up slowly and the Impala gathers speed. The radio goes to commercial. I turn it down so we don't have to listen to a loud Mexican salesman telling us about some new bus service to Ciudad Victoria.

⌄

We pull over at a truck stop and check the fluids and the tires. The Impala's holding up real nice. We get some beef jerky from the bolillo selling it from a little stand next to the coin-operated air compressor. When we hit the road again, we drive in silence for a long time, the sun burning bright and hot, the wind rushing over us, the rips on the convertible top flapping behind us like little flags.

One Saturday near the end of my sophomore year, we went to a party at Violet Mejía's. She lived with her parents in a huge house in River Oaks. She'd told us she wanted guys to come because she attended Incarnate Word Academy downtown, which is only for girls.

Magaña stole his mother's Toyota and we went there thinking we'd hang for an hour or two, then go cruising, but it was all girls and they had a real bar with serious booze set out by the pool—so we stayed.

Then Susi showed up. Turns out she was good friends with one of Violet's friends from the youth group at church. It was Susi like we'd never seen her before. She looked real pretty in a red-and-orange sundress that showed off her shoulders and back. She even had makeup on and everything. She looked totally different from when we saw her in the neighborhood.

Magaña said something about how it was a miracle that Rambo let her out of her cage. Tiny sucked in his gut and stood real straight, raised his chin, and ran his hand over his buzz cut. Back then that's how we all wore our hair, buzz cuts and thin mustaches that looked like smudges of dirt. We thought we were the coolest.

There was something about Susi that night, the way she talked, how she made us feel, like everything we said was important. I would've loved to make a move, but I guess I was more interested in drinking. Not Tiny, though. He hung out with her, at first talking quietly by the snacks, then slowly receding to their own quiet spot in the garden away from the ruckus of the party.

Magaña and I played bartender, getting hammered and chatting up the chicks who came to get drinks at the bar. At one point we danced to some old Red Hot Chili Peppers tune, just Magaña and me surrounded by like ten drunk chicks raising their hands in the air and shaking their heads, hair all over the sky.

Meanwhile, Susi and Tiny sat on a pair of swings that hung from an oak tree in the corner of the yard and talked. They didn't kiss or touch or anything you'd expect. I don't think they even drank because the next morning Tiny was up early mowing the lawn in front of his house.

A couple of days later, when we were smoking a joint in the Buick, he confessed it had been totally innocent.

"No pasó nada," he said out of the blue like he was talking to himself, just tossing a rock in the water to see where the ripples led.

"You guys talked all night," I said.

"She's like a real sad person, sabes? Bien, bien triste."

"Why?"

"All kinds of heavy stuff. Rambo has all these expectations. He's always pushing for more, you know? And she doesn't like her friends. She says they're selfish and judgmental, but they've been her friends for so long she doesn't know how to change it. She feels like she's living someone else's life."

Until that moment, I hadn't really thought of her as a chick, as some-one to date or anything. Yolanda, yes. She was older and had real curves. Besides, everyone talked about her like she was special. Not Susi. Up until then I guess she'd been a kid I played with when we were little. But hearing Tiny tell me this about her life woke something in me, so that pretty soon I found myself staring at the dark, empty lot trying to figure out a way to get close to her. I wanted to save her.

Then Tiny said, "She told me she hates her life."

"Dude, we all hate our lives."

"No. En serio, güey. She was real serious. She said she lays in bed at night wondering whether she should just . . . you know . . . end it."

"That's fucked up."

"Flaco . . ." he whispered, "I don't want her to die."

"She won't do it," I said to appease him, but what the hell did I know? "She's super Catholic. It goes against everything." But the truth was, I got it. I totally understood how she felt. Sometimes, when I argued with Félix, I thought about doing it myself. Like if they found me hanging dead on the back porch or drowned in the tub, Félix would feel like shit for the rest of his miserable life. Everyone would blame him. But I'd be dead so what would be the point of that?

Tiny nodded and looked out the side window. "It's weird. You know, she grabbed my hand and held it, but it didn't feel like . . . like sexual or like boyfriend-girlfriend or anything like that. It was just . . . friendly. Cosa de amigos, na' más."

I took a long toke of the joint and leaned my head back against the seat and tried thinking of what it would really be like to take your own life. And Susi. How would she do it? Like when she lies there at night thinking about it, does she think of different ways, like jumping off the bridge onto I-10 or taking a razor blade to her wrists?

I didn't want to believe that Susi was being real. Félix was an asshole and talked a lot of shit, but Rambo was damn strict. He ruled over Susi and Yolanda like he was God. I couldn't imagine living with that.

"Why would she tell me all this?"

I didn't have an answer for him. As far as I was concerned, we were all kind of fucked up. I was confused about so many things. I was still trying to figure out why my mother and I had to leave Chicago and come live with her brother and his wife, and why she worked so much, why she had this anger—this permanent resentment toward something that was no longer a part of her life.

"You think she likes me?" he said.

"Shit, you have to ask her."

He looked at me and took the joint and set it in the ashtray. "I don't know how."

"Just ask her, no?"

He shrugged and settled sideways on the seat so if he focused past me he could see the Taylor house at the end of the block. "She probably just wants a friend."

"What about you?" I said.

"What about me?"

"You like her like that, o qué?"

He smiled like a little kid, kind of blushed. "I guess . . . It's just . . . she's got all that sadness inside."

We're all sad sometimes. I was sad when Carlos got killed. When Tiny said she was sad, I just figured something made her sad. I didn't get it then—Susi's sadness was constant.

At noon, we pull into a Sonic outside Diamond Park and order. The girl who brings our burgers is a plump Mexican-looking girl with a big smile and a gap between her teeth.

"Aren't you supposed to be wearing roller skates?" Magaña starts.

"Not anymore," she says, sounding real Texan but kind of tired, as if she's asked that same question ten times a day. "It's a liability thing."

"You from here?"

"Where else am I gonna be from?" she says and hands him the drinks.

He squints at her name tag. "So . . . Laura, you ever take a ride in a vintage automobile?"

She glances down at her name tag, then passes the bag with the burgers to Magaña, who passes it to me. I grab a handful of fries.

"I sure have," she says. "But it broke down in the middle of nowhere and I had to walk home."

"Híjole, that sucks. My car might not look too good on the outside, but it's what's inside that counts."

"Fourteen fifty-five," she says.

He hands her three fives. "Keep the change, corazón."

She puts the money in the pocket of her apron. "You need anything else?"

"Yeah. Why don't you give me your number so I can call later and we can hang."

"Sure," she says and steps back. "I only have one number." Then she raises her hand level with Magaña's face and lifts her middle finger at him.

Magaña cracks up. Laura glances over the car for a second, and then walks back to the restaurant. A big-ass pickup pulls into the spot next to us, blaring Toby Keith or some other redneck shit music.

Magaña looks over. "There goes the neighborhood."

I grab my burger and fries and hand him the bag. I avoid looking next to me at the driver. When he doesn't turn his music down, I put my window up as if it might help because we have the top down.

Magaña takes a bite of his burger, looks past me at the truck.

"Let's get out of here," I say.

"You want me to tell that pendejo to turn it down?"

"No. I wanna see Susi. That's why we came."

"Can we eat first?"

"You can't eat and drive?"

He's chewing with his mouth open. Takes another bite of the burger, sets it on his lap and starts the car, pulls out of the spot. "You shouldn't be scared of confronting people," he says.

"I'm not."

"Shit. I've known you since forever and you do that. Don't be such a pussy, bro."

"Look, I don't want to get in a fight with some redneck."

"It's not that." He takes another bite of his burger, steers the car with his knee. "But you do that. You choose to live in the shadows."

"What the fuck does that even mean?"

"You don't stand up for yourself."

"Yes I do." But there's some truth to that. My tío Félix says I'm like that, always trying to defuse shit and make peace.

"You never speak up," he says. "You don't argue ni nada."

"It's 'cause I'm a Virgo."

"Qué chingaos does that have to do with anything?"

"Virgos don't like confrontation."

"What are you, Walter Mercado?"

"It's a fact," I say real firm so he knows I don't want to have this conversation because we've had it a million times. And yes, I'm shy. Kind of. Maybe that's why I hang with Magaña in the first place. He balances me. And Tiny too. Magaña'll take the bullet while we run.

"Whatever," he says. "But one day you're going to have to stand up and be counted, cabrón."

I point to the corner. "It's that way."

"I know where it is."

Two blocks later we pull up to the Diamond Park police station where we were interrogated. I gather the wrappers and stuff it all in the bag. I drink my Dr Pepper until it gurgles and toss it in the trash on our way into the station where a woman in uniform sitting behind a desk studies us up and down like we don't belong. "Can I help you, boys?"

"We'd like to see Susi Taylor," I say sharply to prove to Magaña that I'm not a wimp. Then I let my words trail off. "She's being held—"

"Taylor . . ." The cop turns to the computer and taps a few keys. Then looks up. "You family?"

"No. We're friends," I say. "We just want to talk—"

"Family only," she said and looks at the computer. "Or her attorney."

"Joe Cárdenas," I say. "That's her attorney."

"Hispanic?" She touches her lip. "Has a mustache?"

We nod.

"He went to get some grub at the Ranch."

The Ranch is across the town square. Parked right in front of the restaurant is a big black Cadillac Escalade.

"That's gotta be his, no?"

"You can always spot a lawyer by the car he drives," Magaña says. "It's just missing a pair of longhorns on the front of the hood."

The restaurant is all country, wood-paneled walls with a few mounted deer heads, pieces of old barbed wire, spurs, and other western shit, and red-and-white-checkered tablecloths. It smells like garlic and grease and sugar all mixed up.

A waitress gives us a big smile—just like Laura at the Sonic. "Take a seat anywhere you like, boys."

In a booth by the window we spot Joe Cárdenas hunched over a giant steak. He's kind of a short dude, fat, looks like anyone from the neighborhood except he wears a brown suit jacket and a cowboy hat despite sitting at the table.

"Mr. Cárdenas?" I say.

He doesn't look up. Shoves a forkful of meat and mashed potatoes into his mouth. "That's my name."

"Can we talk to you a sec?"

"What's this about?" He battles the steak with his knife and fork, slicing a big chunk. Plate's all blood and grease.

"Susi Taylor."

He looks up. His thick handlebar mustache is as gray as his sideburns. He's got mashed potatoes on the ends of it, keeps chewing, offers us the seats across from him with his fork.

We slide in.

He's got a napkin tucked into his neck like people do in the movies. His phone's set down beside his plate. He glances out the window to where his fancy ride is parked and says, "A ver, muchachos. Díganme, what's goin' on?"

I look at Magaña. He looks at me. I say, "We're friends of Susi from Houston."

He stops chewing, turns his head to the side, and seems to look at us for the first time, rolls his hand a couple of time like he's reeling in a fish. "Go on."

"We wanna talk to her," Magaña says flatly. He's leaning back, arm stretched out over the backrest of the booth, looking real comfortable.

Cárdenas shakes his head. "Ain't gonna happen. Girl's in a heap of trouble. Pero de veras. DA ain't being very cooperative. I'm afraid he might just charge her with murder one."

My stomach sinks, feels as if I'm gonna topple over. "But . . . she didn't do it."

"Your friend refuses to open her mouth." He points at me with his knife. "DA's hell-bent on pinning it on her for lack of another suspect. La pobre don't start talking soon, the judge's gonna put her away for a long time."

"They can't do that. She's sixteen."

"This is Texas, amigo."

"Why won't she talk?" Magaña asks.

Cárdenas shrugs and starts cutting steak again. He has five gold rings, two on his right hand, three on his left. One's a wedding band, another looks like those high school rings you're supposed to get when you graduate, the one I didn't order because it's, like, three hundred bucks.

"Look," I say, "maybe if she sees us, she'll talk. We're friends."

"Girl wouldn't talk to her own father," he says and shoves more food into his mouth. Then his phone rings. He sets his utensils down and takes the call, speaks with his mouth full. "Yup . . . Dígame."

"..."

"'Ta bien," he says in a real thick norteño accent. "Dígale que se deje de payasadas y pague la multa. El jueves hablo con el juez y lo arreglamos todo."

"..."

"No se preocupe. Aquí estamos pa' servirle." He ends the call, sets his phone down, and picks up his fork.

"Susi didn't kill Rayo," I say.

"Here's the thing." Cárdenas pushes his plate away. "She's the only suspect. She's got the victim's blood all over her clothes. Her prints are on the knife. Everything points to her. There's no one else. And to complicate matters further, Mr. Martínez's property where the incident occurred was a stash house."

"What's a stash house?"

"Where the coyotes hide the migrants they bring over the border. They keep 'em there until they can move 'em, take 'em to their final destination."

I glance at Magaña. "Anaconda."

Cárdenas frowns. "What?"

"Rayo's friend."

"Rayo, you mean Raymundo Martínez?"

I tell him everything we know, to the last detail—even about Tiny leaving Houston.

Cárdenas pulls the napkin from his chest, dabs his mouth and mustache, then drops it on his plate. "I saw that name on the police report. Thought it was puro cuento. But if you're telling the truth, we might have something there to help us. But Anaconda's obviously a nickname. What we need is a real name and hopefully an address. Phone would be nice too. We need to find this hijo de la chingada and see what he's got to say." Then he points at both of us, his hand like the horns of a bull. "You two stay in touch. As it stands now, all the prosecutor's got is circumstantial. But for lack of another suspect, they'll hang this on her and lock her up por diez años—mínimo."

The image of Susi's look that day—her eyes—comes back to me in a flash. "What about her father?"

He shrugs and signals the waitress for the check. "He hired me. Paid me a retainer. Y se desapareció. Así na' mas. Maybe he went back to work. Quién sabe."

"No, we didn't seen him in Houston," I say.

"Well, la niña wouldn't talk to me," Cárdenas says. "But not talking ain't gonna fly as a defense, I can guarantee you that much."

The waitress drops the check, looks at Magaña and me, and says, "I'm sorry, were y'all gonna order?"

"No," Magaña says. "We're good."

She waits for Cárdenas to count his money. He smiles at her. "Keep the change, darlin'."

Cárdenas watches her walk away, then he turns to us. "Listen up. You see Mr. Taylor, tell him I have paperwork I need to file with the court, which he needs to sign, otherwise my hands are tied. And I need a check from him if he wants me to stay with the case." He pulls a couple of business cards from his wallet and sets them down on the table like a pair of aces. "If you talk to the girl or you find more on this character Anaconda, give me a holler. But be real careful. If that was a stash house de verdad, you could be dealing with some real cabrones. These people don't work alone. You find out where he is, alert the authorities immediately. Don't be heroes. You got it?"

"Yessir."

"Con mucho cuidado," he says and struggles to slide out of the booth. He stands and tucks in his shirt and adjusts the collar of his jacket, then tips his hat at us and marches out of the restaurant.

We watch through the window. Turns out he doesn't get into the Escalade. He gets in a '90s Buick with a dented fender and drives off.

"Oye," Magaña says. "I imagined him much bigger. He's nothing like the dude in the billboard, que no?"

18.

We drive back to the police station. Somewhere in the building there's a holding cell with a sixteen-year-old girl who refuses to talk even to her dad. But to see the cops go about their business, you'd think everything in the world was fine.

When I ask the desk officer if we can see Susi, she tilts her head to the side just slightly and asks, "Weren't you just here?"

"Please," I say, "we're best friends."

She shakes her head. "Only family or counsel."

Down the hallway some redneck kid is arguing with a woman about someone named Robert, saying Robert was the one who done the shit and it ain't his fault his father went to Corpus and didn't know the shit was in the car.

"Drugs," Magaña whispers.

The guy down the hallway yells, "Wasn't him, you goddamn bitch!"

"Travis," the desk officer yells, "control your subject!"

I lean over the counter and smile politely. "Can you tell her it's us, Magaña and Flaco . . . please?"

The desk officer half rolls her eyes like she's tired of the back-and-forth with us. "It ain't gonna happen, son. Only family."

On the wall of the lobby there's a photograph of the force, like twenty or thirty cops all lined up like in a school photo. They're surrounded by a dozen or so shiny squad cars, four SUVs, and a helicopter in the background. Looks like the photo was taken in the parking lot of a Walmart or Target. The officers are half smiling, looking friendly but tough—the Diamond Park warriors. Like twenty in uniform, six plainclothes detectives, and six other dudes in all black tactical gear like they're in *Mission Impossible*. All that firepower for a little cow town that's no more than a dot south of Corpus Christi.

This real shitty feeling about what Joe Cárdenas said creeps around my gut. If he's not enthusiastic about Susi's situation, it's gotta mean things are not looking good for her. And then that bit about the stash house.

The officer ignores us. After a moment I open my mouth to tell her what we discussed about Anaconda, but Magaña grabs my arm as if he knows exactly what I'm about to say and leads me out of the station. It's already midafternoon and the sun's leaning over the buildings on the other side of the street and burning down on our side with a vengeance.

"What's the point?" he says. "We already told them everything we know about Rayo and Anaconda."

"Yeah, but they need to find him. Susi—"

"Joe Cárdenas said we need his real name."

"Let the cops do it. That's their job."

"Don't believe it, bro. They have Susi. And how do we even know the cops aren't in on it?"

"In on what?"

"Think. They're the ones who won't let us see Susi."

"No. No way they're on Anaconda's side," I say. "They're cops. This isn't Mexico."

"Don't fool yourself, Flaco. I know how cops operate, here and in Mexico."

"I don't believe it."

"Okay, so maybe it's not like that. But what if it is? Or maybe they just don't care who the real killer is."

"But she's innocent."

"I know," he says and gives me the devil's grin.

"What?"

"We find Anaconda and hand him over to the cops."

"What? You're crazy."

"No. Listen to me."

"Déjate de pendejadas, Magaña. We're not cops. Think. Anaconda killed your godfather. And you heard Cárdenas—he's some kind of a coyote. He could be with a cartel or a gang or something. He'll kill us just as easy."

"Listen to me, Flaco. These gabacho cops don't give a shit about us or Susi. They might not be in on it with Anaconda, but as far as they're concerned, they got their killer. To them we're all the same—just Mexicans. They ain't gonna move a finger for us. I guarantee it. My old man told me all about how the cops operate. They just wanna win cases. It looks good on their résumé. It ain't about justice, it's about putting people away. And if you're brown or black, no one gives a fuck whether you're guilty or not."

"That's bullshit."

"No, that's reality."

"We're kids, cabrón. We don't even know where to start looking for this guy."

"Look," he says real serious. "Let's try and find out who he is and where he's hiding. Then we call the cops and let them nab him. That's what Cárdenas told us to do. Otherwise we'll never know shit. They won't let us see Susi; they won't tell us shit. For all we know they're not even trying, meanwhile Susi stays behind bars."

"That's not how it works."

"I thought you wanted to help Susi."

I force a laugh. It's crazy. And I'm scared. It's not a game. I have this image in my head of Anaconda when we met him in the driveway of the house, how chill he acted, his grin, the scar on the side of his face. Dude had criminal written all over him.

"We shouldn't have left her like we did."

"It's done," he says. "There's nothing we can do about that now."

Magaña always said his father pleaded guilty in order to avoid death row. The judge gives you two choices and they both suck, only one is worse than the other. Magaña knows a hell of a lot more about the Texas criminal justice system than anyone I know. And he got it all from real firsthand experience.

When we get to the car, I lean against the door. "So, how're we gonna find him?"

"Huicho."

"And how we gonna find him?"

"We start at the beginning."

"The beginning of what?"

"Rayo's house, dummy."

We don't talk the whole way to Rayo's. Magaña's focused on the drive. I'm looking out the side at how the sun paints Diamond Park with its warm afternoon light. It's different from the light in Houston, warmer, turns everything more three-dimensional. I've never taken an art history class—our school doesn't even offer something like that—but I've looked at a lot of books. The impressionists were obsessed with light. People like to focus on Van Gogh's colors because they're real bright. They say it had to do with his mental state. That he was nuts and all that. But I don't think that's true. I think he was really affected by light. It must've been a real change for him in the south of France. I used to think I wanted to live in a place like that, paint sunflowers and haystacks and shit. But right now, in this light, even Diamond Park looks beautiful. Feels as if we're driving into a painting or a movie. It makes you wish you lived here—until Magaña takes a left and we see the sad, lone house where Rayo was killed. I blink, and in that millisecond of darkness, I see Susi. I see her T-shirt covered in Rayo's blood, her dark eyes staring at me, telling me it's my fault.

But that's nothing compared with what it must be like to sit in a cell by yourself. I can't blame her for shutting down like she has. Shit. I didn't even witness the murder, and the whole thing has me wigged out.

Right now, if none of this had happened, we'd be hanging out. Tiny would be making stupid jokes or telling Magaña and me how something's not how it was in Mexico. Maybe we'd stop at the Lone Star for a drink or some Takis. Maybe we'd sit in the empty lot by the house and smoke a joint and laugh our asses off about nothing.

As we pull up across the street from Rayo's house, I think maybe Magaña's right. I can spend the rest of my life blaming myself for what happened to Susi or I can do something about it. We got a fifty-fifty chance that things'll work out the way we think they'll work out. The other fifty, I don't know what lies there. Hopefully, I'll never find out. Rayo was hiding migrants. Maybe that's why he had the van, to move people back and forth from the border to Diamond Park. Anaconda had to be part of that for sure.

Magaña kills the engine, but we stay in the car. The house is dark and alone in the big empty lot. The yellow crime-scene tape cuts across the building like someone took a crayon and drew lines and Xs all over it as a warning.

Magaña stares at the house, the windows reflecting the sun behind us. It's as if he's under a spell, just stares and stares and says nothing.

"Entonces," I say to break the eerie silence, "you gonna tell me about Rayo or what?"

He doesn't turn away from the house. "What do you mean?"

"I mean everything."

"Nothing. I only met him once when I was little, before they sent my father to prison."

"What else?"

"All I know's that my old man and him grew up in the same town in Mexico, came over together when they were teenagers, worked la pisca in the fields and all that shit. That's all."

When Magaña says that's all, it means there's a whole lot he's not telling. "Come on," I say. "I need to know."

"Know what, pinche Flaco?"

"About the house."

Finally, he turns to face me. "I don't know shit about the house."

"Who was he?"

"He was my father's best friend."

"Who told you about the Impala?"

"My father did. I told you."

"What, he called you and said, 'Hey, son, we got your dream car in a farm down in Diamond Park.'"

Magaña sighs, his tone turns soft. "So, like, three months ago, right? When my mom and I went to see my old man, I mentioned I had about a grand saved up for a car. He seemed proud, no? It was the first time in forever that we kind of connected and talked about something that mattered to both of us. I told him I was looking into getting some wheels, something cool and vintage I could customize into a solid ride. He knew my dream was a '59 Impala. All he said was that he'd talk to my godfather 'cause there were all kinds of old cars in the valley."

"Weird how he found an Impala, no?"

"But that's exactly what happened. I swear. Last week he calls and says my compadre knows of a farmer's got an old Impala sitting in his barn."

Maybe it's the truth, maybe not. But he still doesn't tell me about Rayo and the stash house and the coyotes and migrants.

"What about his business?"

"My old man said he managed crews for the farms. That's how he made the deal with the gabacho for the car."

"Crews of migrant workers."

"Yeah, para la pisca. He finds them work."

"So he *was* a coyote."

"No, bro. That's different. He's a niclero. He managed the labor. Or used to."

"That's a fucking coyote."

"No, cabrón. A coyote brings them over from Mexico. Rayo puts crews together and drives them to the farm. That shit's legit. Like, if you have a farm and you need pickers, you go to him. He didn't bring anyone over. He's got nothing to do with that as far as I know."

"What about the house? Cárdenas said—"

"I heard what he said. I don't know shit about that."

"This is so fucked up, man."

"Chill, cabrón."

"No. Tiny had to run away and Susi's in jail. She might go to prison for killing this pendejo."

"Hey! Maybe I didn't know Rayo, but he's like family. You think I don't give a shit about that? Think." He taps the side of his head with his finger. "What Rayo did for a living has nothing to do with Susi."

"What about Anaconda?"

"I don't know shit about him."

"Right. And that's the asshole we need to find."

I lean back in my seat. The sun is setting. It's gonna be getting dark and we don't even know what we're doing, what we're waiting for. I should've asked Magaña about all this before we left Houston last week. But it all seemed so simple, so straightforward. If Susi hadn't been stretching in her yard that morning . . .

"I feel like I'm digging a hole," I say. "And the more I dig the more shit I find."

"The fuck's that supposed to mean?"

"Tell me about Anaconda."

"I. Don't. Know. I never met him or heard his name. I swear."

I'm not sure I can trust Magaña. I mean I trust him, but I don't. All these years we've been friends there's always been an edge to him, something sharp and dangerous that I felt could turn on me at any moment. Yet it never has. Yeah, he's a selfish pendejo for sure, but he's loyal. I mean we're here trying to help Susi. That has to count for something. Maybe he's telling the truth. When we came to pick up the car, Anaconda did seem different from Rayo. Maybe he had just crossed over and Rayo was setting him up for a job. Or maybe *he's* the coyote.

"I don't think this is such a good idea," I say.

"What the fuck?"

"How long are we gonna wait?"

"Seriously, pinche Flaco, stop asking so many stupid questions. Maybe Huicho or Anaconda'll come back, or drive by or something."

Maybe.

The sky's a deep blue, almost black. I count two stars. Some of the lights on the street are flickering weakly as they warm up, so the street has this faded look like an old oil painting. But there's nothing beautiful about the house. It's dark and alone and spooky. For all we know Anaconda could be inside. Maybe he knows the cops won't come around again. Maybe he works for a cartel, for real. Maybe he's watching the house, watching us, waiting for it to get darker. Waiting for his chance to kill us.

A loud knock on the back of the car—*toc-toc*.

19.

"¿Ya están de regreso?" Jesús—the guy who gave us the jump the day everything went down—walks slowly to my side of the car, has a tall boy in a brown paper bag. Reeks of booze. "¿Eh, amigos?"

I smile nervously at Magaña. "Scared the shit out of me."

Magaña nods to Jesús, who's holding on to the side of the car to keep his balance. "¿Entonces qué, agarrando la jarra?"

Jesús laughs, holds up his paper bag. "Un poquitito na' más, pues." He leans forward, resting his arm against the top of the windshield. "You checking out the house, eh?"

"I'm looking for my friend," Magaña says. "The big guy that drives that red King Ranch."

"No." Jesús shakes his head. "Ya no. They all gone away. Ain't nobody been back."

"Doesn't sound good," I say.

Jesús waves a finger in the air. "Se fueron toditos. Everyone. They just abandon the house. That's how they go."

"We should go in," Magaña says.

"What?"

He gives me that devil's grin again. "Maybe we can find a clue or something."

"No way. We came to look for Huicho or Anaconda. They're not here. Let's go."

"No, no. Remember the big lecture you gave me about Susi being our responsibility and shit. Well, this is it."

Behind Magaña, on the other side of the road, the house sits like a dark tomb on an empty lot. "Let's do it in the morning."

"Ni madres." Magaña gets out of the car. "I'm gonna check it out. You can stay if you want, bro. But I'll tell Susi all about it when I get her out of jail."

I get out of the car, almost crashing against Jesús.

I catch up with Magaña and we fast-walk to the front door. "Locked."

He nods to the side. I follow. We pause by a window. He tries it and moves on. I peek inside but can't see a damn thing.

The backyard's a mess, junk everywhere, a thousand times worse than Julio's place. Three plastic trash cans overflowing with scrap wood, clothes, plastic bottles, Styrofoam food containers, plastic bags with a purple grasshopper printed on the side, wrappers, paper plates, plastic utensils everywhere.

Magaña tries the back door. It's locked, but he gives me this look like he's got an idea.

"Let's just go," I whisper, "we're gonna get busted."

"I got this." He fiddles with the handle.

The house is wood frame with vinyl siding and vinyl windows. The door looks just like the one in my tío Félix's place. Cheap Home Depot shit that's been rigged so it can be padlocked from the outside.

Magaña does the credit card slide between the jamb and the lock with his driver's license, just like on TV, but it doesn't work. After a few tries, he steps back. He picks up a plastic knife from the trash and runs it down the jamb, fiddles it back and forth. He turns the knob and pulls the door a crack, looks at me.

He opens the door real slow. It's darker inside than outside. I can't see a thing. And it stinks like shit. Worse. I gag and cover my nose with my arm.

Magaña coughs and spits, takes a couple steps forward. I'm like a foot behind him. I can see the outline of his hand as he reaches for the wall.

He flicks the switch. The room floods with light. Magaña's standing by a door looking at me, a big smile on his face. Then his focus shifts. His smile fades real fast.

"¡No veo nada!"

I jump.

It's Jesús. He stumbles in, puts his finger to his lips. "Shh, calladitos. You gonna wake up los chamacos."

I turn back to Magaña. "What is it with this guy?"

We're in a utility room, but it's empty. No washer and dryer, nothing on the shelves. Just the horrible stink like the sewer backed up.

We walk into the next room. Jesús stays a couple of steps behind, giggling.

The living room has a couch and one of those old tube TVs. There's two mattresses and a bunch of blankets on the floor. Magaña looks at me and shrugs, points to the side, one door. Points to the other side—another door.

He opens the door closest to us, switches the light on. A single bulb hangs from a wire, a few mattresses on the floor lined up one next to the other, sheets and blankets. The walls are bare and dirty. Looks like a homeless camp.

We back out, cross the living room and go into the other room. He flicks the switch. Same thing—old mattresses, clothes everywhere. A poster of Mexico's World Cup team from a few years back—Chicharito's not even on it.

It takes me a moment to realize the brown stain on one of the mattresses is blood—and on the floor and part of the wall—blood everywhere.

My stomach spasms. Before I can turn away, I puke like the girl in *The Exorcist*. I double over and it comes out my mouth and nose like a faucet.

"You okay?"

"It's the stink."

"Yeah," he says. "And the blood's not helping either."

I lean against the door and spit. He walks around the room, steps on the mattresses, looks in the drawers of a side table like a thief searching for valuables.

Someone yells in Spanish, "¡ . . . fue sin querer queriendo!"

I jump. Fucking Jesús is standing in the middle of the living room, staring at the TV. *El Chavo del Ocho*.

"Let's get out of here," I tell Magaña. "This is useless."

He gestures with his hand, wants me to wait, but I can't take the stink. And the blood. I make my way back outside and take a long, deep breath, let the dry air enter my lungs, cleanse me of all the shit in the house. I snort and spit a couple of times. The sour taste of puke lingers in my mouth. I walk across the street to the Impala and lie back on the hood, my arms extended. I stare at the dark sky and all the tiny stars we never see in Houston.

Susi. That horrible, horrible stink. I can't imagine her in there with Rayo and Anaconda fighting. But I can see her screaming, telling them to stop. Maybe they heard her. Maybe Rayo stopped but Anaconda didn't. Or maybe she wasn't even in the house. Maybe she was outside the whole time. I keep seeing the same thing, kind of like in my dream—Anaconda pulling the knife, stabbing Rayo again and again, then running away. Susi goes to Rayo, tries to help him, tries to save him. That's how she is. She has a huge heart. Maybe she tries CPR. Maybe she calls the cops. Someone had to do that.

I sit up. Across the street, the house is dark, which is weird because Magaña turned on the lights. Jesús was watching TV. But all I can see is a weak glow at the back, probably from the open door.

A moment later, Magaña appears around the house, passes the gate. Jesús follows, his steps wavering.

"I know where we can find Huicho," Magaña says.

"Where?"

"Did you see the trash?"

"Ese pinche Don Ramón." Jesús chuckles. "He's a real piece of work, ese." He laughs by himself, tilts the bag of beer, then looks at it and tosses it on the sidewalk, empty.

"What about the trash?" I say.

Magaña taps me on the chest with the back of his hand. "The Purple Grasshopper, bro."

"What about it?"

"It's a restaurant."

"So?"

"No mames, Flaco. You really don't get it?"

"Tell me."

"Someone obviously liked their food." He smiles at me and taps the side of his head with his index finger. "¿Eh?"

He gets in the car. I go to my side and open the door. Jesús stands there waiting for me to pull the seat forward and let him in. I don't. I glance at Magaña and back at Jesús. "Where's the Purple Grasshopper?"

20.

The Purple Grasshopper's all pink and red and purple and covered with a ton of neon. And it's huge, like a converted warehouse, with a gravel parking lot surrounded by farmland.

We park in the back between a pickup and a dumpster. Magaña runs his hand over his hair like he's about to go talk to a chick. "Busy place, que no?"

"Must be Margarita Monday."

"Two for one." He taps my arm. "Check it out."

Huicho's VW is parked at the end of a row of pickups.

Inside, the place looks half Mexican, half gringo. It's all fiesta with little plastic triangular flags with the Corona logo strewn across the ceiling, serapes, and flashy charro hats and piñatas everywhere. It's as if they've taken every Mexican cliché and stuffed it into a warehouse. The music's overproduced country, loud and redundant and shiny. A big crowd's gathered along the bar, standing room only, cowboy hats, ponytails, and denim. Everyone's having a good ol' time.

The hostess, a pretty teenager in shorts and a T-shirt tied up tight below her breasts greets us at the entrance with all the joy in the world and leads us to a table.

"I can already hear Tiny complaining," I say as we slide into the booth. "He'd say it's not Mexican."

"'Cause it's not. It's Texan."

The menus are heavy plastic, six pages with fuzzy pictures of the food, lots of red sauce and melted cheese.

"I'm starving."

"You puked everything out, cabrón."

"It was the stink."

Magaña doesn't look up from the menu. "And the blood."

"I guess that's where he kept the migrants, no?"

"Imagine having to live in that shit?"

"Pinche Jesús scared the shit out of me."

He laughs. "Fucking borracho checking out *El Chavo*."

The waitress is older, dressed like the hostess, and speaks with a thick drawl. "Can I get y'all anything to drink?"

"Two margaritas," Magaña says before I can even open my mouth.

"I'll need to see some IDs."

"You a cop?"

She doesn't bat an eye. "It's the law, dear."

"I left it in the car," he says and makes a sad face. "And it's parked way in the back."

She shifts her weight to one leg.

"Dr Pepper," I say.

Magaña frowns at her. "You're serious."

She taps her notebook with the back of her pen.

"Orange Fanta."

After she leaves, I text Ana Flor and tell her I'm at Magaña's working on the car and that I'll be home late. Magaña leans over the table and reads the menu like it's the Bible, his index finger moving along slowly as he mouths the words to himself.

"You got any cash?" I say.

He smiles kind of smug and pulls out his wallet, shows me a credit card.

"For real?"

"My mom's ATM," he says. "Lifted it from her purse this morning."

"That's not cool."

"You hungry, o qué?"

The waitress comes back with our drinks, a basket of chips, and a little plastic bowl looks like a miniature molcajete of red salsa.

"So, what's good here?" Magaña says.

"It's all good. Most people order the combination plates. You get to taste some of everything."

"I'll have the taco plate. Chicken, corn tortillas," I say.

Magaña orders combination number 6, with extra cream on the enchiladas. The waitress writes it down and walks away. I dig into the chips and salsa, and cough.

"Spicy?"

"It's all tomato. Tiny would have a field day with this shit."

Magaña dips a chip. "Yeah, cabrón would complain, but he wouldn't stop eating."

"For real."

We laugh, then fall silent. I picture Tiny in a drab flat place like Kansas, no friends, no life. Starting over from nothing like when he first came to the neighborhood. I wonder if that's why he's so tight with his family. Their secrets belong to them and no one else. Even as best friends, he never talked about his journey to the US or how he was always having to twist things around to hide the truth. He lied to everyone, even though he didn't want to. I guess, when you have a secret like that, when your whole family's at risk, you do what you have to. I can't blame him. No one can.

Across from me, Magaña looks small and skinny behind the big booth, leaning over the table, munching chips mechanically, his eyes darting left and right like a squirrel.

"He probably works in the back," I say.

"Yeah, washing dishes with the rest of the Raza."

I take a long drink of Dr Pepper and lean back, look at the bolillos at the bar. No Raza. No Mexicans. We're always in the back doing the work while everyone else is having a good time.

When we were in middle school and Tiny first showed up, we all made fun of him because he was all Mexican. He got shit from us and he got shit from the white kids and even from the teachers because he hardly spoke any English. I guess we were real pendejos back then. We didn't know how it felt to be him.

About two years ago, Susi and me were walking back from the bus stop after school. I was a sophomore. She had just started high school and was going through her Mexican activist phase. She wore jeans and a red bandana on her head so she looked like a brown Rosie the Riveter.

"Flaco, I heard you did the welcome-back-to-school banner," she said as she caught up to me at the corner. "That's pretty cool."

"Thanks."

"It could've been a little more Mexican, no?"

The banner was just supposed to say *Welcome Back, Students* and have a painting of our mascot—a tough-looking armadillo.

"Well, the teacher didn't give me any artistic license," I said. "She said use the school colors, y ya."

"What's that, like permission?"

"Yeah, kinda." I wasn't sure whether she was giving me shit or not, so I tried to change the subject. "I heard your sister graduated with good grades. She going to college?"

"No. My dad won't let her move out."

"Still, she could go to UH or HCC."

"I guess."

"What's the point of getting good grades in high school if you're not gonna go to college?"

"Maybe she liked learning. I mean that's the reason we go to school, no?"

"Yeah, but—"

"Geez, Flaco, why does it have to be the way you say?"

"What?"

"Guys think they know everything."

"I was just saying—"

"Well, don't. No one asked for your opinion anyway. You ever think maybe Yolanda liked studying? Maybe it was easy for her to get good grades. It's not like it's that hard to do well in school."

"Never mind," I said.

"I won't," she said and pressed her books against her chest and marched ahead of me. But when she got to the corner where she had to cross the street to her house, she turned and apologized. "I guess I'm just in a mood. Everyone's always telling me how things should be, pushing their opinion on me. It's like I have a bunch of noise in my head and it drives me crazy."

My point was about ambition. If you work hard and then stop, it all goes to waste in the end. I don't know. But I understood what she meant about the noise in her head. Tío Félix and Magaña and everyone were always talking all the time, telling everyone else how things are—or how they should be. Never shut up about it.

"Don't worry," I said. "I mean, we're all trying to figure life out, no?"

She smiled. "That's what I'm saying. We each have our own heart. And it's worse when you're Mexican 'cause it makes everything more intense."

With that, she skipped off across the street.

I watched her disappear into the house, wondering what one thing had to do with the other. I thought we were talking about people telling us what to do and about ambition. Who said anything about hearts?

When I told Magaña what happened with Susi, he said I had a crush on her but it was only because she was the forbidden fruit. "I think Rambo knows exactly what he's doing keeping his girls clean and pure for the right guy. It makes us want to marry them instead of just fucking them."

"I don't have a crush," I said. I was pretty sure I didn't.

But Tiny agreed with Magaña. "Te trae de nalgas, pinche Flaco. But what's worse is that first loves are the ones that stay with you forever. Estas jodido, güey."

"I get it," I said, "but it can't be first love if she doesn't love me."

Tiny wasn't so sure. "Maybe you'll get over it, maybe you won't. But you'll suffer. Seguro que sí. You're fifteen, and you're Mexican. Good luck with that."

We eat like a pair of stray dogs, no manners or care, wolf it down like it's our last meal, don't speak a word to each other, lick the plates clean. I even eat the shitty salad of chopped lettuce and diced tomato they serve on the side. The chips and the salsa and the ice in our drinks are all gone by the time the waitress comes back to check on us.

"Y'all were hun-gree!" she says all happy and takes our plates. "Left any room for dessert?"

Magaña nods toward the double swinging doors to the kitchen. "When's Huicho getting off?"

"Y'all know Huicho?"

"We're cousins."

"Kitchen closes at ten," she says with a shrug. "He's usually out by eleven."

It's just after nine. "Does he get a break before that?" I say.

"Sure. He takes breaks all the time." She grimaces and whispers, "Goes out back to smoke."

"Do I pay you or up front?" Magaña says.

"Either's fine." She sets our bill on the table. "You want me to tell Huicho you're here?"

"Yeah," Magaña says, "tell him his cousins from Chiapas are here. We'll meet him in the back."

She smiles and says "Chiapas" to herself as if to remember it or to try it out and see how it feels in her mouth. "Well, thanks. Hope y'all have a real nice evening," she says and picks up the plates. Then she locks eyes with Magaña for a second. "And next time don't forget your ID. Mondays is two-for-one margaritas. We're famous for our margaritas."

"So what's the plan?" I say as we make our way back to the car.

"No plan. We ask Huicho what he knows about Anaconda. That's it."

The back door to the kitchen is open. People talk in Spanish. Norteño music plays from a radio inside, sad with lots of accordion. We lean against the tailgate of a big pickup and face the back door and wait.

About ten minutes later, a short Mexican dude walks out carrying two black trash bags, one in each hand. He wears a baseball cap and a long vinyl apron. He walks past, avoids looking at us. He tosses the bags into the green dumpster next to the Impala and starts back.

"¡Oye, compa!" Magaña calls to him. "Can you tell Huicho his primo from Chiapas is out here? Que lo estamos esperando."

He looks at Magaña kind of weird, nods, and walks back into the kitchen.

About five minutes later Huicho walks slowly out the door, looks left and right. He wears a dirty white apron around the waist and a hairnet even though he doesn't have any hair to speak of.

"My primo from Chiapas," he says, and we shake hands, first Magaña, then me. "I didn't think I'd see you again, qué pasó, pues, how's that Impala?"

He takes out a pack of Marlboro Reds from his pocket, offers it real fast like a habit, picks one out, and then looks at it for a moment as if he's trying to decide whether to smoke it.

"Our friend's in jail," I say.

"I heard." He places the cigarette in his mouth and lights up, takes a long drag, and exhales. "Who woulda thought it, que no? And fucking Rayo. Cabrón's really dead."

"Thing is," Magaña says, "we know la Susi didn't chop up my padrino."

"Pinche Rayo."

"He was your friend, que no?

"Not really," Huicho says. "He was just un güey. I worked for him running food and stuff to the . . . to the house and . . . shit like that."

"From here?"

"Ey. From here to there. He helped my boss get workers, you know, like under the table. That kind of shit."

I'm thinking of the Mexican dude that just came out with the trash bags. I had to ask. "Illegals?"

"Pues, a güevo," he says. "That's how it is, no? Win-win for everyone."

"What about Anaconda?" I say.

Huicho takes another long drag from his cigarette and waves. "Ese hijo de puta es un coyote. I don't know him too well. He brings people to Rayo's place. Pays Rayo to keep them undercover until his people here can move them again." He shrugs and gestures with his cigarette from left to right. "They take them all over the country."

"What do you mean, his people?" I say.

"His partners."

"Partners, or like a gang?" I add.

"Gang, cartel, whatever you wanna call it. Same shit. That ain't the kind of thing you go around announcing, no?"

"We need to find him," Magaña says.

"Anaconda?" Huicho laughs. "Pues ni madres. That fucker's gotta be back in Mexico by now. I'm sure he don't wanna be found after what went down at Rayo's. I can guarantee you that."

I look at Magaña and back at Huicho. He shakes his head and takes a smoke, flicks the butt. It flies like a little red spark over the pickup and into the bush. "You ain't gonna find him. And if you did, I don't think you'd know what to do with him. Es bien cabrón."

"He killed Rayo," I say, "and Susi's gonna go to prison for it."

"No, hijo. Take my advice and leave it alone. You don't wanna fuck with Anaconda and his people. Just look at what happened to Rayo."

"We need your help, Huicho. For real," I say. "Susi didn't do shit, and you know it. It's not fair."

"But I don't *know* shit."

"She's a good person. She'd never hurt anyone," I say. "She doesn't deserve this."

"None of us deserve the shit we got. But we sure as hell got it, no?"

"Va en serio," Magaña says. I'm surprised at his tone, honest and heartfelt. Doesn't even sound like him. "We need your help. We need to do this for her 'cause no one else will."

Huicho shakes his head. "I don't know where he went, other than that I'm pretty sure he ain't in this country no more. Ese cabrón lives in an underworld. If he doesn't wanna be found, no one can find him."

"We have to try," I say. "At least . . . Please, Huicho."

He steps back and seems to size us up, like he's about to give us a job shoveling horseshit or something. He adjusts the strap of his hairnet. "I can ask around."

"It's better than nothing," I say.

"It don't guarantee shit." He pulls out his phone and taps the screen.

The small Mexican guy who took out the trash earlier comes out of the kitchen and looks around. "Huicho, te anda buscando el patrón."

Huicho nods at him, then at us. "Where you staying?"

Magaña looks at me.

"No mamen," Huicho says.

"We just drove down," Magaña says.

"I don't get out for at least another hour," he says.

"No problem," Magaña says and nods to the side where we parked the Impala. "We'll chill in the car."

21.

We sit in the Impala with the top down and look up at the stars. The air stinks of old fryer grease and trash. The thump of the country music in the Purple Grasshopper feels like a sad heartbeat against our chests. Every now and then people come out of the restaurant in groups laughing at nothing.

"I guess Huicho's thing was feeding Rayo's workers?" I say to break the silence.

"We got a way to go to find this pendejo."

"But we're getting close, no?"

He doesn't answer, probably because he knows if Anaconda's hiding in Mexico, we'll never find him. Huicho's right about that. I know it, and Magaña knows it.

"I saw a show once," I say. "They hypnotized people from the audience and made them do things, act like chickens and stuff like that. But they also made them talk about their past lives."

"Like when they were kids?"

"Like when they were different people from the past."

"And you believe that shit?"

"I don't know. But maybe if we hypnotize Susi, she can go back to that day and she can tell the cops exactly what happened."

"That's a crazy-ass thought."

I look at the stars shining over Diamond Park and think of Susi alone in a dark, run-down cell without windows. "I wonder if she can see the stars."

Magaña looks up. "I wonder that about my old man. All those years in prison and never seeing the sky at night. I can't imagine that shit."

The sky's like a film, a layer between us with the whole universe, so many tiny sparks against the dark.

"How come you never talk about him?"

"Who, my old man?" he says with a shrug. "I dunno. I guess 'cause I don't really know him." He turns and looks at me real serious. "Maybe that's why you and me get along, no? We ain't got fathers."

"They're overrated."

"No, they're not," he says flatly. "I wish I had one to give me shit. Sometimes I feel like he's the reason I'm such a fuckup. You don't have a dad but at least you got Félix."

"Yeah." I laugh. "He's been a real good influence too."

"He's not that bad, bro. He does what he can."

"Yeah, well, Carlos did more for me than Félix ever did."

"Pobre Carlos," he says with a deep breath. "He was cool. He didn't have to die."

"He shouldn't have joined," I say. "If it was now, I'd tell him not to."

"He'd still do it. I know I would. Guys like Carlos make up their mind and go through with their shit."

True. Carlos pulled through more than any other person I ever knew. Even my mom. Whenever he said he was going to do something, he stuck with it. Except fixing the Buick.

"He was doing it for the GI Bill," I say.

"I don't think Mexicans should join the army or anything . . . the way they treat us here, como pinches perros."

I don't want to have that conversation, get all political because we're Mexican. We're also American. I'd fight for my country if there was a real war, like against the Nazis or something. "You know how you told me your dad pleaded guilty to murder?" I say.

"So?"

"You never told me what happened."

"I don't know ... It's private, I guess."

"Oye." I sit up. "You still got that roach?"

He smiles and flicks open the ashtray and fishes for the roach. Almost half a joint, really. He lights it with his Bic, takes a toke, and passes it to me.

The dope pulls me closer to the stars, makes me feel easy, like I'm home in my room but the ceiling is the universe. I imagine Susi looking up at the stars from her cell. Maybe it'll make her feel better, less afraid— remind her of everything that lives beyond our reach, outside her cell, the house, the neighborhood, Houston.

"So what happened," Magaña says real quiet, "if you really care to know, is that when I was little and we lived in Brownsville, my old man's sister worked as a maid at a La Quinta. It was right there where the University Inn Motel is now, right on the border by the bridge. She was fifteen and didn't have any papers and was working under the table, no? So one day some fucking gabacho that was staying there forced himself on her ... raped her ... messed her up real bad. The manager was a real hijo de puta and refused to call the cops or do anything 'cause he didn't wanna get busted for hiring undocumented workers."

He swallows hard and stares at the stars as if the story's unfolding somewhere up there. "So when my father got wind of it, he went nuts. He found the gabacho that raped her and beat him to a fucking pulp."

"Killed him?"

"No. But he slammed a car door on his face, messed the guy's brain real bad, put him in a coma. At first he was charged with aggravated assault. But a few months later the guy's family pulled the plug on him and the charge went to murder one."

"No mames."

"He says he doesn't regret it. He told me he'd do it again every time."

"And his sister?"

"Back in Mexico. She married some guy there runs the only movie theater in town."

"She gets to see free movies?"

"Who the fuck cares about that?"

"I'm just saying."

"Pinche Flaco. I tell you this and that's what you say?"

"Ya, it's just something to say. I'm sorry, okay?"

"Well, don't say it."

"I said I was sorry."

"Hijo de puta raped her and now she's stuck down there in Limones. Her life sucks. You don't get it 'cause you ain't never been down there."

"But better Mexico than in prison, no?"

He takes a deep breath and closes his eyes like he's meditating. The music from the Purple Grasshopper's lower, the rhythm's slower like a last dance.

"You know, this time next year you'll be gone like Tiny," he says. "I'll be the only one left."

"If I get accepted."

"You will."

"At least you have the Impala."

"So?"

"You can cruise anywhere you want. You said it yourself."

"Nah," he says like he's taking a shit on his own dream. "The neighborhood's all I know. I actually like it there. I can't imagine being anywhere else."

"Me too."

"You're full of it."

"It's true," I say. "My mom talks of moving to a different neighborhood, but I'm not into it."

"She wants better for you, bro. That's what parents do. When my old man went to prison, my mom went to school and became a dental hygienist so I could have it better."

"That makes sense, but moving just to move?"

"It's gotta suck for your mom to have to live with Félix and Ana Flor."

"True."

"Having your own place has to be pretty cool. As long as it's not like Rayo's."

"What a fucking mess, no?"

"Like a pig."

"You know what's weird?" I say. "When I got back to the car, I was looking at the house and it was dark."

"So?"

"You had the lights on and Jesús was watching TV, no?"

"It's 'cause of the boards. The windows had plywood boards on the inside."

I think of the house, the room, the poster of the Mexican national team, the dirty mattresses, the stink. That's how they lived. The poor people who came over were stuffed in there like sardines waiting for their rides to wherever they were going. Tiny must've gone through it. I can almost see him, little kid all crowded in there after crossing the river, watching cartoons or Chabelo on that TV, eating food from the Purple Grasshopper.

Magaña sits up straight. "Here he comes."

Huicho walks up to Magaña's side, waves his phone. "I asked around about Anaconda. We'll see what happens."

"¿Y ahora?" Magaña says.

"No plan," he says. "Follow me to my uncle's chicken farm. You can crash there."

We follow Huicho's VW to the other side of Diamond Park. The country seems darker, the houses more sparse. About five miles out, he pulls into a driveway, gets out, opens a gate, and drives in. We follow him to a long barn and kill the engine. Huicho leaves his car running, lights shining directly on the wooden barn, peeling white and gray paint, big square windows open along the sides covered with mosquito screen and chicken wire.

We wait for him to pull open the door to the barn before getting out of the car. "My uncle's got a bunch of laying hens."

Magaña spits and rubs his nose with the back of his hand. "It fucking stinks."

Huicho turns on the light. Both sides of the barn are lined up with cages stacked one over the other—two hens in each cage. Flies buzzing all over the place.

The grumbling from the chickens gets louder when we walk in. I cover my nose with the side of my arm. "No way I'm gonna sleep with this stink."

"It helps when there's a breeze."

Magaña makes his way between the cages. "Look at all your relatives, Flaco."

"A hundred and twenty," Huicho says. "Organic eggs. Makes out pretty good at the farmer's market in Corpus."

Magaña walks back to where Huicho stands by the entrance. "So what's the deal with Anaconda?"

"I told you. But if no one gets back to me on WhatsApp, there's this one guy I know. Pulga. Ese cabrón might help."

Magaña grins. "The flea."

"Dude knows his shit." Huicho scratches the back of his neck and spits to the side. "Got involved with Anaconda and his people when he was a kid—"

"You mean his cartel?" I say.

He frowns. "Okay, yeah, his cartel. Whatever."

"No." I wave off the flies buzzing around my face and nod at Magaña. "We gotta tell the cops."

"Let's hear him out," Magaña says.

"Listen to your buddy," Huicho says. "You're not messing with amateurs here. Estos cabrones—"

"Just tell us about Pulga," Magaña says.

"He had a fight with Anaconda over some chick," he says. "Pulga still holds a grudge."

"And you think he'll help us?" Magaña says.

Huicho shrugs and pulls out the Marlboros, lights one up. "Maybe. You gotta talk to him. He works at the Flying J in Combes."

"Fuck it," I say. "That's almost all the way to the border. And cartels? No way. No. Fucking. Way."

"Maybe we should tell the cops about Pulga," Magaña says.

"Ni madres." Huicho shakes his head and flicks the ashes from his cigarette. "Pulga's no dummy. He ain't gonna talk to no cops."

"Right," I say. "But he'll talk to us."

"I doubt it." Huicho exhales a cloud of blue smoke, gestures with his cigarette as he talks just like my tío Félix does when he's drunk. "But it's all you got. Unless someone comes through on WhatsApp. Either way, you gotta be real careful. I don't know what all you know or what you imagine, but guys like Anaconda don't work alone. You're messing with some real hijos de puta."

"Yeah?" Magaña grins. "We're pretty badass ourselves. ¿Que no, Flaco?"

I shake my head because I'm thinking no. No. And no. We should get the hell out, tell the cops, or go back to Houston. The shit's way over our heads.

"Órale." Huicho laughs and points to the back of the barn. "We'll deal with it tomorrow. There's some horse blankets over there, just shake them out real good. And turn the light off. I'll be back first thing in the morn-ing." He gets in the VW and drives down the long stretch of dark road.

We stare at the barn, the dust, the sacks of feed—the chickens. I turn to Magaña just as he turns to me. "I ain't sleeping in here," he says. We both look at the Impala at the same time.

I stretch out on the back seat. Magaña in the front. It's a nice, clear night, stars everywhere. After a while, the chickens quiet down. A light breeze blows over us. But the flies are relentless.

I can make out the outline of the roof of the barn, and way past it, the lights from a couple of houses out on the other side of the field.

I can't decide if this is good or bad—Huicho, messaging on WhatsApp. Like, who's he messaging? Maybe we're getting close. But maybe it's not a good thing. And Magaña's been strangely quiet about it. Finally, I ask, "So what do you think?"

"I don't know," he says slowly. After like a minute he adds, "I just hope Huicho's not playing us."

"How do you mean?"

"We don't know him."

"We know him some," I say. "He gave us a place to crash, no?"

"Yeah, nice place. Doesn't mean he's not on his way to rat us out to Anaconda."

It sinks in slowly like a blade—we're in the middle of nowhere Dia-mond Park. No one knows we're here. And yeah, Huicho could return with Anaconda and his people—kill us in our sleep.

22.

A rooster brings me slowly out of dreamland. The sun isn't up yet, but the sky's starting to turn blue to the east of us.

I close my eyes and try to fall asleep again. All night I kept waking up in spurts, worrying about Anaconda coming to kill us. I had these crazy dreams about sitting in the barn with Tiny and Magaña, making plans, living in a stash house. And always, Anaconda looms in the background, like the smell of chicken shit.

I open my eyes again and yawn. My mouth is dry and nasty. The flies are all over. I sit up. I think of waking Magaña but we're going to have to wait for Huicho anyway. I hop out of the car and rub my arms to get rid of the morning chill. The land is flat and green. Two lanes of asphalt separate us from another field that's planted with rows of frijoles or zucchini or something. The field ends at a line of small trees and another field starts after it, then the thin orange line of the sunrise.

I glance at my phone. No message from Huicho or anyone. I take a leak on the side of the barn and sit on a stack of wood pallets. As blurry as my head feels from lack of sleep, I'm optimistic. I mean, at least Anaconda didn't kill us last night. It's stupid to think about but so far so good. Maybe Magaña's right. If we find out where he's hiding, we can tell the cops and they can arrest him. I can almost see Susi walking out of the police station with a big smile on her face. I imagine her running up and putting her arms around me, thanking me. We'll be friends again. Maybe her father would respect me, let us hang out like normal people.

Magaña finally sits up and looks around, stretches. He steps out of the car, takes two steps to the side and pees by the front tire. He shrugs and moves his right arm in a circle and cranes his neck to the side. "Man." He massages his shoulder. "I slept all crooked."

"I wonder when Huicho's coming."

He looks at his phone.

"Anything?"

He shoves it back in his pocket. "Dead battery." He looks left and right. "Oye, it's kind of nice here, que no?"

The sun's raking across the fields with a sharp warm light. Feels like a scene on one of those butter packages. All it needs are the words *from our farm to your table*, or something like that. A white school bus drives down the road. My first thought is that it's carrying prisoners—Susi. But it's run-down and dirty, has a sign that says M. FLORES over the front windshield. It turns off the asphalt onto a narrow dirt road that cuts the field across from us in half, rows of vegetables on both sides.

Magaña nods at the Impala. "It's done pretty well so far, eh?"

"So far."

"It's a good sign."

He walks over to the car. I hop off the pallets and join him. "I have to admit, man, it's much cooler than the Buick."

"Anything's cooler than the Buick."

When the bus reaches the middle of the field, it stops and out come thirty or forty men and women covered with bandanas and hats so only their eyes and hands are visible.

I glance at my phone. Still no message from Huicho. "I had a dream about Tiny. It was like he never left. We were sitting in the Impala, kind of the way we used to do with the Buick, remember?"

Magaña shrugs and looks across the road at the field. A couple of flatbed trucks are parked at the end of the first rows. The workers that were gathered around the bus are spreading out along the fields, bent over whatever crop they're harvesting.

I tell Magaña about my dream and how Tiny was sitting in the driver's seat and talking like it was his car. But I keep some details out, like the part where Tiny bragged about getting it on with Susi like she was una puta or something. It had pissed me off. Even now, standing by the Impala and looking out at the migrants working the field, I'm still angry—except I'm not sure with who: Tiny or Susi. Or maybe I'm just angry with myself for getting into this stupid mess.

"What do you think's going on with Huicho?"

"I dunno," I say. "Maybe he's got a lead."

"I don't like it," he says, his eyes focused on the workers. "He said he'd be here first thing in the morning."

"You think it's a trick?"

"I don't know," he says. "You trust him?"

"He's been cool so far, no?"

"I guess," he says and nods toward the workers. "You think they're illegal?"

"Probably."

"My old man said that's how he started when he came to this country. Him and Rayo and a couple other guys from his pueblo."

"Everyone starts somewhere, no?"

My phone chimes. WhatsApp. A message from Huicho: *Where are you?*

"It's him," I say and answer: *Where do u think?*

Magaña peeks over my shoulder. "Ask him if he got any news?"

I send the message.

He answers: *Tell me where you are.*

Chicken farm. When u coming?

There's no response. I look at Magaña. I send it again: *When u coming?*

After a moment he answers: *What chicken farm?*

Magaña frowns. "What the fuck's he on?"

"Maybe something's up," I say. "You think he's trying to tell us something?"

"Or . . . maybe it's not him."

"Should we go to the cops?"

"Fuck the police."

Anaconda, his gang, a cartel—it all buzzes around me like flies. Something's definitely up. And Magaña could be right on. Maybe Huicho's one of them.

"The cops," I say. "For real. We should tell them. Something's going on—"

"No. If they did their job right, Susi wouldn't be in jail."

I take his words where they end because I know he's talking about his father. That the bolillo who raped his aunt should've been the one sent to prison. I get it.

"Let's get outta here," he says and gets in the car. I've known Magaña for most of my life. But this is the first time I ever heard him sound so determined about doing the right thing.

"Where we going?"

"Combes. To find Pulga. Para la Susi."

23.

First thing we do is fuel up the Impala, top off the oil, and check the tire pressure. So far so good.

A small beat-up truck with a trailer pulls up next to us. A cowboy-looking dude gets out, says something to the dogs in the bed, and goes into the convenience store.

When Magaña and I walk in, he goes straight for the ATM.

"Nope," the woman behind the counter says. "Machine's broke."

"Just get cash back from the register," I say.

"I need to check the balance. I don't want to empty my mom's account. The electric bill's due Friday."

I go straight to the aisle with the auto supplies and grab a can of Fix-a-Flat, just in case. Magaña gives me a look and shakes his head like I'm a fool. "That shit don't work."

"Right," I say. "You'll thank me later."

We browse the selection of warm food: pizza; hot dogs; little rolled taquitos that look more like skinny egg rolls; fat burritos wrapped in foil.

Magaña pulls the lid and grabs two of the burritos, hands me one. We get a large Dr Pepper and an orange Fanta from the fountain.

When we're back in the car, he sets his burrito on the dash and the drink between his legs, drives out of the station nice and slow. "We need to find a bank."

I toss the Fix-a-Flat on the back seat, unwrap my burrito, and dig in.

He turns on the main road south. "How is it?"

"Mucho bueno," I joke. It's all bean, very little meat.

He doesn't even crack a smile, just takes a drink of his Fanta and looks left and right as he drives. We're coming out of town. There's another gas station, a couple of fast-food places, industrial warehouses, a John Deere dealership, an abandoned drive-in theater that has a sign for a flea market at the end of the month. Then a giant Walmart with a huge parking lot—maybe it's where they took the photograph I saw at the police station. We pull in and park at the end near the garden section.

At the ATM by the registers, Magaña checks the balance. Doesn't tell me, but takes out a hundred and twenty bucks, folds the twenties, and places them in his front pocket.

I follow him into the store, straight to sporting goods.

"What're we doing?"

"We're being careful," he says and peers into a slowly turning tower of Plexiglas that's got five levels of knives, blades of all sizes and colors. He points to a steel folding knife with a five-inch blade painted in camouflage—nineteen bucks. He pays for the knife with his mom's card and tells me that's it for the card. "She'll probably notice it's missing and report it stolen."

When we get back in the car, Magaña takes a sip of Fanta, then opens the knife and feels the sharpness of the blade against his thumb, checks how secure it locks up, how fast he can open it. He does this like four or five times. Then he reaches across the car and tosses it in the glove compartment with his dead phone.

"Combes or bust," he says with a grin.

We pull out of the parking spot and drive to the end of the row and turn left. Construction's blocking the feeder, so he keeps going to the rear entrance at the far end of the garden section where they have pallets with sacks of mulch and dirt and pavers stacked one over the other. He turns.

There's a single oak tree in the farthest corner where a green pickup is parked.

"Check it out." I nod. "Isn't that Rambo's truck?"

"Looks like it." He stops, backs up, and makes a U-turn, then approaches real slow.

"It's gotta be, no?" We pull up in front of the pickup. "Who else drives a military-green truck with a Jesus sticker."

Magaña leaves the car running. The windows of the pickup are half-open. A man's inside, sleeping.

We approach slowly from the driver's side. Rambo doesn't move. He sits with his head back and slightly tilted to the side, mouth half-open—totally zonked.

Magaña looks at me and laughs. "'Ta jetón."

I wonder whether it's a good idea to wake him. Guy's gotta hate us. But we're here to help his daughter. Maybe he'll get that. I tap on the front hood a couple times. "Mr. Taylor?"

He doesn't move.

"Flaco . . . ," Magaña says real slow. Rambo's complexion is a pale, whitish blue. He looks sad and relaxed at once.

We reach his door. His skin looks as if it's made of plastic. His eyes are slits, not closed all the way, eyeballs rolled back.

"You think . . . Anaconda?"

Magaña points to the center console. Rambo's right arm rests on it like he's asleep. On the passenger seat is a spoon and a lighter, a hypodermic on the mat. His forearm's kind of twisted weird so the tattoo of the Virgen de Guadalupe faces up, her eyes downcast, like she's praying for him.

"What the fuck?"

"OD," Magaña says matter-of-fact. "He overdosed on the shit."

"On what shit?" I've never seen a dead person before. Even when they sent Carlos home, we had a closed casket funeral. Tío Félix and Ana Flor and my mom all saw him—or the pieces of him. But not me. They went to the funeral home after the army sent him back but wouldn't let me come.

"So is he . . . ? For real?"

Magaña nods. "Pretty sure."

I take out my phone to call an ambulance. It's dead. We're alone at the farthest corner of the Walmart parking lot. The beep of a forklift backing up startles me. I point to the store, don't wait for Magaña, and start walking fast.

"Flaco!"

I go from a walk to a jog to running as fast as I can. I bust into the garden section. Everyone stares at me.

"Ambulance. Call an ambulance!" It shoots out of me like bullets. "Please. A man overdosed." I point to the side. The three people in line all turn to look at the shelves of ceramic pots.

"In the back of the parking lot," I cry. "Under the oak tree."

They pull out their phones and start tapping screens. The cashier picks up the phone that hangs on a pole by her register and starts talking.

Maybe thirty seconds later a security guard appears through the sliding doors that connect the garden section with the rest of the Walmart.

I shake my head, step back, as the guard comes closer. "It's not me," I cry. "He's outside, a guy in a truck."

I run out of the garden section and cross the drive. From there, I can see the green truck across the parking lot and point. The Impala's gone. It's just the green pickup and Rambo's dead body and la Virgen de Guadalupe.

The security guard sees the truck and stops, doesn't touch me, just stares, hands down at his sides. The people that were in line are out in the parking lot, staring at the truck for what feels like forever. The guard holds his radio to the side of his face. "Leslie," he says in a raspy voice, "call nine-one-one right away. We need an ambulance at the southwest corner of the parking lot. Now."

The radio crackles and he starts walking fast toward the pickup. The customers follow him.

The cashier's staring at me like I did something wrong, probably thinks I'm an addict. For a moment I think she's being nice. That she's, like, look at this poor kid who's hooked and just saw his friend overdose. But that's not it. She's frowning, accusing me, thinks it's my fault.

A car horn startles me—two short beeps. Magaña's sitting in the Impala about twenty yards away. I get to the car just as the ambulance comes speeding down the highway, turns at the construction, and makes its way to the back of the parking lot where the security guard and the customers crowd around Rambo's pickup.

"Pinche Flaco." Magaña drives to the exit on the opposite side of the Walmart. "Why'd you have to go screaming like that? Rambo's dead."

"You don't know that."

"Bro, the fucker's blue and not breathing. He's probably been dead for a day or two."

I take in a deep breath, lean my head to the side and let the air cool my face. My hands are shaking. "Why?"

"Why what?"

"Why would he do that?"

"It's not like he did it on purpose," Magaña says. "Maybe the shit was cut with something. Who knows?"

"But he was okay. He was clean."

"He was an addict. He fell off the wagon and fucked up."

We're headed south. The breeze smells like earth and manure. Farms all around. I breathe deep and slow, shake my head, trying to put things together like a puzzle—Magaña buys a car and our world goes to shit. When Susi gets out, she won't have a dad. I know how that is. Magaña knows how that is. But for her it'll be worse because she knew her father. I'm sure she loved him despite his faults. She has memories with him, dreams. She'll have a lot to regret. She'll mourn. I don't mourn my father because I never knew him.

I breathe and breathe and breathe. The country, the valley, the light reminds me of paintings by Thomas Hart Benton except this isn't all curvy and funky. It's flat, and the pretty farms on both sides of the road are dotted with workers, migrants, Mexicans folded over like they're bowing to God—it's all closing in on me, pressing on my shoulders, turning my stomach. I lean over the door, but I don't puke. I breathe.

I hear Magaña's voice from far away: "You okay?"

I shudder.

"You want me to pull over, bro?"

I shake my head and tell him to keep going, but he probably doesn't hear me because I'm talking to the wind. "Let's just find Pulga and finish this."

24.

We drive in silence for about an hour and a half, pass a bunch of cotton fields. Migrant workers are all over. From a distance the work looks slow and lethargic. My grandparents crossed somewhere around El Paso years before my mother was born. She says they planted, picked, and packed just about everything that grows in the country. They went to every state, but it was pretty much the same wherever they went—industrial fields, cheap motels, dilapidated trailers, overcrowded vans, that kind of life.

When Tío Félix and Ana Flor went to visit my grandfather in Eagle Pass the year Carlos was killed, my grandfather told them not to bring my mom or me with them. When Tío Félix told my mom what my grandfather said, she just shrugged and went into the kitchen to make herself a cup of coffee. Sometimes I think my mom works two jobs so she can keep busy and not think of all the bad things in her life. She works and saves her money and acts all happy, but I can tell she's holding on to something that eats at her on the inside. I can see it in her eyes early in the morning when we're sitting in the little table in the kitchen and she turns away toward the back door like she wants to escape. Her eyes turn down, and she gets this faraway look, then her lips purse for a second as if she's remembered something terrible. But by the time she faces me again, she's got that placid smile plastered across her face like a mask.

I feel helpless about so many things—as if a current of electricity's running inside me, like I'm all wired up but can't release the energy. It presses against my chest and keeps me up at night thinking about all kinds of stupid shit. Like things I want to do, but there's always a wall that stops me. Like with Susi. Not just now and what's happened at Rayo's. It's from before. When Rambo kept her locked in the house like a bird in a cage, I wanted to help. But there was nothing I could do. When I'd bump into her at the Lone Star or walking home from the bus stop after school, she had this thing like an aura—a simmering anger like my mom's. I could never tell if she was happy or sad, if she would talk to me, smile, or scowl. Or just ignore me.

It's as if I know her, but I don't know her.

I make a list in my head of all the things that keep me awake: money, my mom, Tío Félix, school, college, Susi, Tiny, Magaña. These are things I have no control over, things I can't change. It must be how Carlos felt with the Buick, to have it there next to the house, waiting to be restored, but to be powerless because he didn't have the money to fix it or the know-how.

Stuff's always pulling at us from the outside. There's all this noise around us and we can't focus on what really matters. But now all the crap that used to clutter my brain at night seems small compared with what's happening now. None of it matters more than getting Susi out.

The Flying J Truck Stop in Combes is huge: one gas station for cars and one for trucks; a convenience store with showers and three restaurants; a CB radio sales and repair shop; and a truck wash.

Magaña drives around the parking lot, circles twice before pulling up to a spot in front of the convenience store. We sit with the car idling, look past the cigarette and beer posters on the window to a handful of men sitting in plastic booths eating burgers and tacos and shit. A gringo with a hipster haircut walks past and checks out our ride, gives us a nod. Magaña can't hide his pride. When the hipster's gone, Magaña kills the engine.

Then he pops open the glove compartment, grabs the pocketknife, and slides it into his back pocket. "Let's go."

We march into the store that's racks and racks of mud flaps, chrome parts, antennas, lights, tacky decorations, and junk to trick out trucks. We ask around for Pulga. A woman filling a coffeepot nods to the man standing behind the register. "Ask Jimmy. He's the manager."

Magaña cuts through the line at the register. "You Jimmy?"

The man's ringing up a bunch of snacks for a woman with two kids, blond short hair, look like twins. "That's my name," he says without looking up.

"You know where we can find Pulga?"

Jimmy nods to the side, eyes on the bags of chips and candies on the counter, making sure he's scanning everything right. "Feller does the custom work under that white tent yonder."

We walk out of the store and across the line of diesel pumps. There are seven semitrucks parked side by side along the large bays of the truck wash. At the end is a white tent like the ones they have at the art shows in Montrose. A shiny black Mack truck is parked beside the tent with a man leaning against the fender on the driver's side. He's older, tall, like, six feet—all bones like a skeleton, dark brown skin, and big round bug-eyes. His long bony fingers press down on a white pinstripe against the bodywork of the truck. He stops, steps back, and grins. "Chido vampiro, hijín. Get it right the first time 'cause that's the way you rock this gig."

I look at Magaña. "Dude's talking to himself."

"Amigo." Magaña places his right hand by his back pocket where he has the knife. "You Pulga?"

The dude steps away from the truck, looks us up and down, and gives us a nod.

"Our friend Huicho up in Diamond Park said you could help us out," Magaña says.

He looks behind us. "Where's your rig?'

"It's not that," Magaña says. "We need to find someone."

Pulga squints, his eyes move left and right, from Magaña to me and back again. "¿Qué pedo entonces?"

"Huicho said you could help us find this guy—a coyote."

"Huicho's dead, hijo."

"What're you talking about?"

Pulga kisses his thumb crossed over his index finger. "Lo descuartizaron. Cut him up into little pieces."

"That's bullshit." I look at Magaña. "We just saw him last night."

"His sister found him this morning stuffed in a fifty-five-gallon drum behind his house when she went out to feed the hogs." Pulga scratches the back of his ear, then looks at his fingers and wipes his hand on the side of his pants. He points at an open box in the shade close to where I stand. "Pass me the red tape, no, hijo?"

It takes me a moment. Huicho. It's not as if we really knew him. But, shit. I reach for the box on the ground. My hand trembles as I grab the tape.

"No," Pulga says, "the one next to it."

I toss it to him and he catches it with his arm like a football. Then he digs into his pocket and pulls out a utility knife, pushes the blade out. From the corner of my eye, I see Magaña dig his fingers into his back pocket.

Pulga uses the tip of the knife to start the tape, then retracts the blade. He snorts and spits a fat loogie, turns to the side of the truck, and starts the line of red tape along the top fender under the white pinstripe he just pressed on. "La pura neta, hijo," he says but stays focused on his work. "It's the truth. Canijo played the wrong game with the wrong people. I told him. I did. All the time I said he was fucking up. But no one listens anymore. And that's how this little game always ends."

It escapes my mouth like air. "Anaconda . . ."

Pulga freezes for a second, then keeps going, finishes adding the red line under the white one.

Magaña says, "Huicho said you could help us find him."

"Find who?"

"Anaconda."

Pulga grins. He's missing both his top front teeth. "No idea what you talking about, hijín."

"That ain't what Huicho said," Magaña says. "Anaconda killed my padrino. Raymundo Martínez."

Pulga cuts the end of the tape with his knife, tosses the roll back in the box, but misses. It rolls to my feet. I pick it up and place it in the box. "Ese pinche Rayo," he says real slow. "He had it coming too. Your padrino was no saint."

"But the cops are blaming our friend," I say. "She's in jail."

"Those two . . . eran bien cuates." He raises two fingers pressed together. "Anaconda brought the people across and Rayo kept them until the others came to get 'em."

"So why would he kill Rayo?" Magaña says.

"¿Quién sabe? But if I had to guess . . ." Pulga grins and rubs his thumb back and forth against his fingers like he's handling cash. "Feria—money. Or pussy. Anaconda's killed before. Many times. And he probably had Huicho killed 'cause he was talking to you two payasos."

I think of that last WhatsApp message. "Magaña. Maybe we should—"

He raises his hand to stop me and moves closer to Pulga. "Huicho told us you used to work for Anaconda."

The man smiles real wide.

"Do you know where he's hiding?"

Pulga laughs. "Anaconda don't hide." A nice blue Peterbilt's pulling up to the truck wash. He keeps his eye on it for a moment, then focuses on Magaña with those creepy bug-eyes. "Word is, he crossed back a few days ago."

"To Mexico?" I say.

"Where else?"

"You know where?"

He grins and presses his tongue over the hole where his teeth are missing. "That's his turf, hijo. You go down there, he'll kill you dead." Pulga shrugs and points at me. "He'll kill you." Then he points at Magaña. "And he'll kill you. Bien muertitos. La vida no vale nada pa' esos cabrones. Life ain't worth spit to them. Just look at how Huicho ended up. ¿Y pa' que?"

"Huicho said you hated Anaconda," I say.

"So what? Lots of people hate that hijo de puta. Shit. Lots of people want him dead too. And yet, there he is—alive and kicking and getting rich as fuck."

"So, help us," I say.

"Help you what?"

"Help us find him so we can take him to the cops."

Pulga laughs, spits to the side, and shakes his head. "Anaconda tiene gente en todos lados. His people keep an eye out for him. They're probably watching us right now. Same guys who did Huicho are out there waiting. Be patient. Your turn will come."

I glance at the blue Peterbilt, at the truckers walking to the store, a white Dodge Ram with a couple of farmers. It's all very normal. But Pulga's right. We can't do this. We can't just go to Mexico like that. It's not as if the Diamond Park police are gonna rush down there and arrest Anaconda anyway.

"Just tell us where in Mexico," Magaña says. "What's the name of the town?"

Pulga laughs and waves his arm as if he's sending us on our way. "Es un pueblito, shitty little place in the middle of the desert between Reynosa and Monterrey. Pero no se crean. Guadalupe Soto's Anaconda's town. He owns it and all the people in it. You go down there asking for him, they'll cut you up into little pieces and feed you to the pigs. Aunque dicen que no le hace como le hacen a uno si ya esta muerto."

"Huicho said you wanted to get back at Anaconda for what he did to your friend."

Pulga's expression falls. His whole face sags like a ball that's lost its air. "What are you talking about?"

"Some chick back in Mexico," Magaña says.

"The fuck you know about that?"

"Huicho told us," I say. "He said you wanted to get revenge."

"This is your chance," Magaña says. "'Cause we're gonna get this hijo de la chingada."

"She wasn't some chick," Pulga says real easy. "She was a woman—a girl. My sister Isabel." He crosses himself, kisses his thumb crossed over his index finger again. "La pobre."

"Help us," I say. "Help us help our friend. She doesn't deserve this . . . just like Isabel didn't deserve—"

"Didn't deserve what?" Pulga barks. Then he steps back and sits on the running board of the truck, bows his head. "I haven't been back there in years. And no way I'm going back."

"I get that," Magaña says. "But there has to be a way to catch this motherfucker."

"Catch him?" Pulga chuckles and shakes his head but keeps his eyes on his huaraches.

I tap Magaña on the arm and nod to the side. "Maybe he's right about going down there."

He ignores me and leans toward Pulga. "You sure he's in Guadalupe Soto?"

"I ain't sure of anything. But that's his town."

"You know where he lives, like, where in the town do we find him?" Magaña says and gives me a look.

Pulga shakes his head. "He could be anywhere."

"How do we know you're not setting us up?" I say.

"Ah, that's the shit, no?" Pulga raises his eyes and grins. "You have to take my word. That's how it works. Yo les digo que no vayan—I tell you not to go. But here you tell me you're going. What else do you want from me?"

We share a long, strange silence. I think of Susi and Rayo and Huicho. "Fine," I say, "thanks for your help."

We turn to go, but Pulga stops us. "If you're gonna cross," he says, "don't do it in Reynosa."

I look at Magaña, back at Pulga. "Why not?"

"That's his. He's got the border guards in his pocket. He'll know you're coming."

Magaña spits to the side and asks the question I'm too chicken to ask. "What happened to her?"

Pulga stands and rubs his bug-eyes like he's crying but he's not. Then he nods. "If you're stupid enough to go down to Guadalupe Soto, you'll find out."

PART III

25.

We sit in a booth at Whataburger on International Boulevard in Brownsville a dozen blocks from the bridge to Mexico.

"Maybe it's not such a good idea."

"What about la Susi?" Magaña says, chomping on his burger. "Think of her. It's the right thing to do. You told me that. Besides, we have the element of surprise. Anaconda ain't expecting shit."

I shake my head and pick at my fries. "I wish Tiny was here."

"Fuck Tiny."

"He knows Mexico."

"Tiny couldn't go back anyway. Didn't you see the Border Patrol station on our way in? And there's the bridge too. If Tiny leaves the country, he ain't getting back in unless Anaconda brings him on his back—"

"Okay, okay—I get it."

He grins like he does when he's being an ass. "You're Mexican, no?"

"But not Mexican from Mexico. And neither are you."

"But I've been. I know how to handle shit there."

"We don't even have passports."

"We don't need no stinking passports," he says. "People cross all the time. We'll make up a story. Only thing, there's a checkpoint's outside the border area about twenty miles into the country. But I'm sure we can find a way around it. Or we can bribe someone."

"Yeah, with what money?"

"It's Mexico. It doesn't take a lot. You just have to know how to play it. Trust me."

"I don't know." My stomach's a knot. Just looking at my burger makes me nauseous.

"Don't be such a pussy, pinche Flaco. Man up for once." He takes a big bite of his burger and points at me with it. "We'll cruise into Guadalupe Soto and ask around. Then we ambush the guy, drop him in the trunk, and race back."

"You make it sound so easy."

"Well, it's not. I know." He takes another bite—mustard dripping down the corner of his mouth—and talks with a mouthful. "But if we can figure out his movements, we'll be ahead of the game."

"*'Figure out his movements'*? How're we going to do that?"

"I don't know yet. But people in these little pueblos know everyone's business. We'll just have to be patient."

I want to do this thing. And I don't. It feels like when you're on the high diving board at the community pool and you know you want to jump. You have to. But you can't.

The thing that gets me is that going home would be worse. Eventually everything that happened in Diamond Park will come out. Everyone'll hate us.

Magaña sets down his burger and starts on the fries, big handfuls. Every table at the Whataburger has Mexicans, or Mexican Americans— brown people, whatever. No gringos. I think of the Mexicans Anaconda brings in, poor people from the southern states—Oaxaca and Guerrero, and even El Salvador and Guatemala and Honduras, places where the narcos and the cops and the military are killing whole families. If the Diamond Park cops actually did their jobs, we wouldn't even be here. Justice should be about catching the right person, sentencing the one who did the crime, not whoever's easier to grab. Like the people who come here looking for a safe place to live. They didn't commit a crime or anything, but ICE arrests them—not the bad guys. The shit's upside down.

"Okay, fine," I say and push my tray away. "Let's do this."

"¡Eso!" Magaña slaps me on the shoulder, then looks at my tray. "You gonna eat your burger, o qué?"

We drive with the top down along International Boulevard to the bridge. All along it's exchange houses, pawnshops, and gas stations. We pull over at the last gas station about three blocks before the bridge. Magaña tops off the gas. I walk over to the pay phone on the corner and dial Joe Cárdenas's cell phone number. A robotic operator tells me to deposit a buck twenty-five for three minutes.

I get change at the store and make the call but get Joe Cárdenas's voicemail. I try his office number. The secretary says he's indisposed. Makes it sound like he's in the toilet. I leave a message with her but she doesn't seem to understand what I'm talking about. "Just tell him . . . tell him the two guys he met at the restaurant in Diamond Park are crossing to Mexico, to a place called Guadalupe Soto to find Anaconda."

"Anaconda—like the snake?"

"Yes. Exactly." I give her my name and Magaña's name. "If he doesn't hear from us in a couple of days, it means we're in trouble."

"What?"

"Just tell him that." I don't know what else I can say. I mean, it's not like I can ask him to come rescue us or anything.

I hang up and stand there, my hand still holding the receiver. Magaña's done pumping gas. He moves the car near to where I stand and checks the pressure on the tires.

I drop five quarters into the phone and dial my mom's cell. It rings, then goes to voicemail. "Ma," I say. "It's me, Rafa. My phone died and I haven't been able to charge it but I . . . I wanted to tell you . . . that . . . so if you want to buy a house somewhere, that's cool by me. I think you deserve to do what you want. You don't need my approval. You work hard all the time. I think you should do what makes you happy." I pause for a second. Then I tell her the truth. "And I wanted to let you know Magaña and me are going into Mexico to a place called Guadalupe Soto to see if we can find this guy called Anaconda. We're trying to help Susi Taylor, who's in trouble kind of because of us. I think it's the right thing to do. If we find Anaconda, then Susi'll be okay. She's not kidnapped or anything, she's in jail in Diamond Park, and if we get this guy, then they'll let her out. Anyway, I just wanted to let you know I'm okay and that I love you. If we—"

A tone interrupts me. The robotic voice tells me I have thirty seconds left and to add another quarter.

"So when we get back," I say real quick, "I hope you and me can talk again like we did on Sunday, maybe go look at another house. And if you really want me to study medicine . . . maybe we can—"

The call cuts off. I hang up. I wipe the sweat from my forehead with my arm. Tears well up in my eyes but I hold them back just like the big fat knot in my throat.

Magaña's staring at me. I hold out the receiver. "You wanna call your mom?"

"Fuck that. Let's go."

I get in the car. A tricked-out Honda Civic a block away is playing rap real loud. Two Mexican girls in school uniforms, gray skirts and white blouses, run across the street. A moment later we're at the start of the bridge. The immigration officer who takes our money at the toll to cross the bridge looks even more Mexican than Tiny.

"This your car?" he says.

Magaña smiles big and proud. "Yessir, just bought it."

"Nice." He studies the Impala front and back. "Where you headed?"

"Just here . . . Matamoros."

He nods and we move forward. Magaña drives slow and easy across the bridge. There are no cars in our lane going to Mexico, but the traffic coming to the US is bumper-to-bumper across the entire bridge and back into Matamoros. The river's brownish green, the banks thick with bushes and small trees. I look back at the last of the USA. A hundred yards away or so I spot the sign for the University Inn Motel.

I turn back and stare at the front. I can tell Magaña saw me checking the place out. He's crossed here before. He knows the motel, the place where his aunt was raped, where his father killed that man. But he just points ahead, lifting his index finger from the hand that's resting on top of the steering wheel, and reads the sign out loud: "Bienvenidos a México."

We slow down and stop at one of the toll booths. The immigration officer's eating a sandwich. "¿Documentos?"

"Here's the thing, jefe," Magaña says in his very dramatic Mexican Spanish. "My mom's at the Seguro Social. They just called me this morning that she's dying. She ain't gonna make it another day. Pinches gringos wouldn't let her come over for treatment and you know how it is. I haven't seen her in I don't know how long and—"

"I need to see a passport or passport card, por favor."

"All I got's a driver's license. Please let us through. We're just going to the IMSS right here in Matamoros."

"I can't do that," the officer says, but his tone is just a little softer.

"Let me say goodbye to my poor mamacita," Magaña says, sounding like he's about to cry. "Look, I have just a few dollars, maybe you can get a beer after work or buy some flowers for your mother . . ."

The officer leans out of the booth and looks back at the US side, then at Magaña. "You know, los gringos won't let you back in without papers."

"I know, but it's my mom. I have to see her one last time," Magaña says and offers him three twenties folded twice. "Por favor, jefe."

The officer takes the cash. "I suppose . . . under such circumstances . . ."

Magaña winks at the man who presses a button, the gate goes up, and Magaña eases forward. We pass an area where a couple of cars are parked on the side. Half a dozen soldiers stand guard. A customs agent is searching someone's car. One of the soldiers raises his eyes, checks us out.

"I don't fucking believe it," I say as we drive onto the street. "No way."

"Mexicans," Magaña says proudly. "When it comes to our mothers we're real softies."

We pass a giant store called Garcia's and a bunch of street vendors on the sidewalk. Matamoros looks like Brownsville but instead of a bunch of exchange houses and pawnshops and big parking lots, there's pharmacies one after the other, dentist and doctor offices, more pharmacies, and a few bars, even an Irish pub. It's actually kind of nice, not as dirty as I thought it would be and the road's smooth, has narrow sidewalks with trees with the trunks painted white, one- and two-story buildings one next to the other, no parking lots or strip malls.

Magaña leans to the side like he's chilling. "Not so bad, eh?"

"So far, so good."

We follow the signs to Reynosa, go from this nice road with a median and little trees, to one with potholes and no sidewalk that runs alongside the railroad tracks. The buildings hide behind walls topped with barbed wire or broken glass. Graffiti everywhere. We pass a few houses on one side, shacks, like old places built of wood and corrugated steel, shit that wouldn't pass for a shed in H-Town. The farther we go, the more depressing it gets.

After a while the road gets decent again. But on both sides it's junkyard after junkyard, large industrial lots, sketchy-looking car-repair places. People walk on the side of the road as if in slow motion. Maybe this is the real Mexico—or at least the one you hear stories about.

The two-lane highway to Reynosa runs mostly parallel the Rio Grande, but we can't see the river. The dusty, smoggy air fades away. I put my hand out, pull the breeze in as the Impala climbs up to sixty. The countryside's flat and green and brown with small houses, corrals, goats, and skinny cows. Feels as if we've gone back in time, wooden electric poles, a man on a horse-drawn cart, kids watching a herd of goats, a restaurant with a hand-painted sign LOS AMIGOS—it's just a shack with plastic tables under a tree. Mexico doesn't feel dangerous, it just feels different, old and used. The people look regular, poor—but not like killers.

When I was little and we moved to Houston, I didn't know the secrets of the people in our neighborhood. We were kids and played in the streets and didn't know about the trouble the grownups had to deal with—rent, work, prejudice, immigration, and everything that comes with being poor and Mexican. But the neighborhood was like a pocket of Mexico. In those days a woman used to set up by the bus stop and sell tamales from a basket. After school and on the weekends a man would come around on a bike with a cooler in the front selling paletas and ice cream. Everyone spoke Spanish and looked Mexican, except for Rambo and the old man that lived in the house where Tiny moved into years later.

We didn't know who had papers and who didn't. We didn't think of poverty either. Back then, Julio and Tío Félix would have get-togethers at our house. The women would hang out in the kitchen or the living room and the men were all outside. Carlos and me would open beers for them and help Tío Félix fire up the grill. Someone had a boom box playing norteño. My mom was young and pretty. Guys would go inside and try to get her to dance or just come outside to the porch to talk like Magaña's mom always did. She was pretty too, had frizzy hair, and dressed real nice, and she always wore a ton of perfume. Sometimes she'd bring a friend from the dental hygienist school. She always seemed to enjoy herself. But not my mom. She stayed glued to Ana Flor and the married women who prepared the side dishes and complained about their husbands.

With Susi it was always tag or soccer. She was fast too. She ran the way people run in the movies, her whole body flowing like a wave, arms swinging in alternate rhythm with her legs, long trenzas bouncing left and right. It was like watching a kite in the air. Back then she used to wear these ratty black shoes that were like half sandals and half shoes. She said she hated them because they wouldn't allow her to run as fast as she really could. But her mother forced her to wear them because that's what she wore when she was little.

The street always had some kind of chalk marks for hopscotch or some other game we made up or just drawings. There was a basketball hoop on a wooden telephone pole and old shoes hanging from the electric wires. And always the smell of food cooking, like corn and meat and garlic, that was the smell of home.

I don't know when things started to change. The guy that used to go around selling fresh tortillas door to door stopped coming. Some of the families with kids moved out. Tío Félix stopped having get-togethers at the house. It was as if a switch was flicked and everyone stopped having fun.

Then Rambo went away to rehab. He came back looking real angry, face tight like a fist. My mom said he'd gotten help from the priest and some of the people from the church and kicked his habit. They called it the fellowship. Now he went to church or a meeting almost every day by himself.

One time Rambo went off on Susi because she was wearing pants and sneakers to church. That's how she always dressed. But not anymore. Rambo didn't like it. He said it was disrespectful to the priest and the people at the church—and even to Jesus himself.

Susi was like a stone. She just stood there outside the church like a statue while Rambo yelled at her, smacked her on the side of the face with an open hand.

She didn't cry. It was like she had a force field around her—like she internalized her power and simply took whatever her father dished out, just stared ahead like she didn't care, like she wasn't even there. That was the same look she had when she refused to get into Huicho's Volkswagen.

People said she was rebelling against her father because he was so strict. My mom even said Rambo was committing a grave fault, said you couldn't keep a poor girl inside like an animal. "One day she'll just snap," she said.

We bypass the city of Reynosa and follow the signs for Monterrey on Highway 40D. But about fifteen minutes out we come up to a traffic jam. Magaña slows down. Trucks on the left, cars to the right. Then I see the sign: CUSTOMS AND IMMIGRATION. There's a restaurant to the side and a convenience store—looks like a 7-Eleven—OXXO. Men and women and kids walk between the traffic selling candy and snacks from baskets and cold drinks from plastic buckets.

Magaña taps the steering wheel, looks left and right. "There it is."

"What's going on?"

"We're leaving the Free Zone. This is where we need our passports and paperwork for the car. It's like going into Mexico for real. They'll turn us around."

"Do we bribe them?"

"Yeah, 'cause we're loaded."

"You said—"

"I know," he says and looks back. "But we have to find a different way."

"What?"

He waves to the bus on his left and inches onto its lane, drives across the wide dirt median, and starts back toward Reynosa. A few hundred yards later he slows down, crosses the median and the southbound lane, and drives into a narrow road away from the highway.

"No, no, no," I say. "We're supposed to stay on the main highway. It's not safe."

"We'll be fine," he says and steers the Impala over the broken asphalt road, kicking up a cloud of dust around the shacks and small concrete houses that spread across the landscape like a graveyard.

26.

It isn't a town. It's more like a settlement, a place poor people squat, near where cars stop so they can make a few pesos and eke out a living. About half a mile from the highway we leave it all behind. Now it's just small plots with rows of plantings and empty fields of mezquite, huizache, and cacti.

"No way." I look back at where we came from. It's just dust and sky. "We don't even have a map."

Magaña ignores me. After a while the road changes from slightly paved to dirt. The Impala rattles and bounces all over the place—feels like it's going to fall apart. He slows it down. At twenty miles an hour the ride's tolerable. Finally, he looks at me, says, "We just need to head south."

"Sure, let me check my compass."

"Very funny, Flaco. The highway is to our left. That's all we need to know."

"What if we're going in circles?"

"We're not." He points at the road, a thin brown line that disappears into the horizon, where heat waves make the landscape dance so it looks like one of those impressionist paintings where all the individual brush strokes disappear when you blur your vision. "As soon as we come to where we can take a left, we'll head back to the highway."

I'm almost 100 percent sure we're driving too far west. And the longer we go, the closer we'll be to the middle of nowhere and the longer it'll take to get back on the highway. I lean toward Magaña and check the gauges. So far, so good. But I worry about the tires on this road. And we don't have water and it's hot as shit and we're driving straight into the sun. It means we're going west, not south.

The road and the landscape are totally desolate. I can understand how people can get killed and no one ever finds out. You die and maybe ten years later someone finds your bones. I think of all the stories I've heard about Mexico, of people shot up, hanging dead and naked under a bridge, dissolved in vats of acid, whole families left on the side of the road where no one will touch them except the vultures. I begin to pray in my head.

Just as I'm sure we're lost, we see a metal sign on the side of the road. It's rusted and riddled with bullet holes—LOS CHIVOS.

Magaña slaps me on the arm. "There you go. We can ask someone for directions back to the highway. ¿No que no, cabrón?"

But Los Chivos is dead. Magaña cruises real slow as we come in. All that's left of the town are a few dozen abandoned concrete and brick houses—vultures, dust, silence. Every building is a ruin, just walls, maybe a roof—no windows or doors, facades pockmarked by bullet holes.

"Whatever happened here," Magaña says like he knows what he's talking about, "must've happened a long time ago."

"Right."

"You can tell. No one's lived here in like forever, bro."

"Forever as in a month, or forever as in twenty years?"

"Years," he says. "Look at the weeds. And there's nothing. They've taken everything."

About twenty minutes after we pass Los Chivos, the landscape is mostly wild country, flat but with bigger mezquite brush and trees so that pretty soon the shrubs on the side of the road block our view of the countryside.

A dot like a mirage appears on the side of the road. As we get closer,

I look at Magaña and back at the road. It's a car, or a truck. Looks like people. I lean forward in my seat and squint.

"Chill," Magaña says and eases up on the gas.

A pickup's parked in the shade of a mezquite on the side of the road. A man in a brown suit and a white cowboy hat stands next to the truck. A woman in a dress like the ones Magaña's mom wears for work on Fridays, and two girls, maybe ten or eleven years old, wearing what look like miniature quince dresses, sit on rocks under the tree. The truck is a faded blue-and-white Chevy from the '70s.

As we get close, the man steps into the middle of the road and waves us down with his hat.

Magaña slows down.

"You stopping?"

"What do you think?"

"Maybe it's a trap."

"You watch too many movies, pinche Flaco."

Magaña pulls over. "Buenas, everything okay?"

"Es la troca," the man says. He's maybe in his sixties, has a sun-weathered face, gray hair, doesn't look rich or poor, but there's something about the way he handles himself, the way he moves that makes me think he's used to the desert and the dirt road, the sun, strangers driving up to talk to him in the middle of nowhere. His eyes are little black stones. He puts his hat back on. "It died. I think this time it's serious. Possibly the fuel pump."

Magaña looks at me.

"I can take a look," I say.

"No, no," he says and places his hand on top of the Impala's windshield, leans against it. "Ya hace harto rato que me da problemas. It's been giving me trouble for a while but I haven't had the time to attend to it. Now look at where it's left us."

The man gestures to the woman who's come around the side and is standing like a statue, holds a magazine over her brow to block the sun from her face. "We're on our way to a funeral in Tres Cruces. Perhaps you're headed that way?"

"Which way's that?" I say, which is a stupid thing to say because there's only two ways to go and our vehicles are pointing in the same direction.

"Aquí adelantito na' mas. Like twenty-five kilometers."

Magaña gives me that smart-ass smile. "And we can ask them for directions, que no?"

I step out of the car and pull the seat forward. The man gestures for the woman to get in. She ushers in the girls, then she nods at me and steps in. She's younger than the man by at least twenty years. She meets my gaze, then looks away. The man points to the back of the truck and waves for me to follow him. When I get there, he pulls the tailgate down. There's a shiny gray casket in the bed of the truck, nice polished brass poles and corners. Looks expensive.

"Magaña," I say. "I think we're gonna need your help over here."

He gets out of the car, stretches before coming around to where we stand, looks at the man, looks at the casket. Looks at me and back at the man.

"El difunto," the man says. "He must come with us."

"You got a real dead man in there?" Magaña says.

The man removes his hat and nods. "My hermano."

"You're kidding."

The man puts his hat back on. "We were on our way to the cemetery to bury my brother when the troca stalled."

Magaña shakes his head like he can't believe it. He gets the key from the ignition and pops open the trunk. When he comes back, he places his hand at the bottom of the casket and tests its weight. "It's heavy."

I give it a try. "Why don't you turn the car around? We can slide it into the trunk."

He does a three-point turn and backs up the Impala about a foot from the tailgate. We lift and slide the casket into the trunk. The moment it drops in, the Impala dips down like a lowrider. About a quarter of the casket sticks out of the trunk at an angle.

Magaña looks at the man and taps the top of the casket with the palm of his hand. "¿Está bien, no?"

The man nods and takes off his belt. It's real nice, engraved leather, has a big silver buckle. He pulls the trunk down on the casket and hands the belt to Magaña, who hands it to me. It's not long enough to tie the trunk to the back of the car, so I loop it around the side pole of the casket. When we're done, the old man gets in the back seat with the woman and the girls, and we're off again. Magaña keeps the Impala at a comfortable speed so the trunk won't bang against the top of the casket at every bump.

I turn in my seat and ask the old man if they're from Los Chivos.

"Ese pueblo," he says with a wave, "fue una tragedia. It's been dead a long time."

"What happened?"

"Some years back los Zetas came and took the town for themselves. Then the army took it back. They went back and forth like that for two years. Todos peleando por el miserable pueblo. Y al fín, they left it like you found it."

I want to ask him if everyone in the town was killed, but I'm afraid of the answer. Maybe the people just took off. Maybe they paid Anaconda to bring them across to Texas. I don't get how people can live like that, death waiting at every corner.

"Señor." Magaña glances at the old man in the rearview. "You know how to get back on the carretera?"

"To Reynosa?"

"Monterrey."

He points ahead. "Todo recto, until the crossroads where the Pepsi sign is. Then left, then the first right."

"Is it far?"

"Una hora más o menos."

I ask him if he knows the town of Guadalupe Soto.

"Never been," he says and points ahead. "It's on the way to Monterrey, no?"

"That's what we were told. Is it far?"

"Un poco."

"From the highway?"

"You have to turn off at the vulcanizadora where they fix tires. Then you go straight for maybe twenty minutes." After a moment he adds, "What's in Guadalupe Soto?"

"Amigos," I say and look at Magaña. "We're visiting."

"We're from Houston," he says.

The man nods. "I have family up there. They work construction. Do pretty well."

The Impala hits a pothole. The car bounces and the trunk slams against the casket. The man and woman turn to look. She's very serious. He smiles at me, adjusts his cowboy hat so it won't fly off.

Then Magaña slows down. "Flaco . . ."

There's two vehicles ahead.

"Aquí mismito es." The old man taps my shoulder. "Ya estamos. Tres Cruces."

The cemetery's small and crowded with wooden and stone crosses with mounds of earth and raised rectangular concrete tombs painted green and blue and pink faded by the desert sun. The property's enclosed with a barbed wire fence. The entrance has an ornate metal entry with an arch and iron gates, kind of like the entrance to a fancy ranch. The words spell out TRES CRUCES across the top. A black SUV is parked inside. It isn't until Magaña pulls up in front of the double-cab pickup outside the cemetery that I see the man leaning over the cab pointing a gun at us.

27.

Two men with assault rifles jump out of the truck bed and rush us, AK-47s, shiny and used, fingers on the trigger. I grab on to the armrest real hard like I'm falling, can't even start a prayer when the old man cries out, "No, no. ¡Soy yo, muchachos!" The old man pulls on my seat and leans forward. "Stop with your tonterías and help me get my brother out of the back. ¡Ándenle!"

The man on my side slings his rifle over his shoulder and opens my door like a valet.

The other one walks past Magaña's side and makes his way to the back of the Impala.

The old man taps my shoulder. "A ver, amigo, let me step out, pues."

I hop out of the car and pull the seat forward. I help the man out, then the woman. When she's out, she stands in front of me and fixes the lower part of her dress. For the first time since we stopped to pick them up she locks eyes with me and smiles. She's pretty, but not as young as I thought. She's Yolanda in fifteen years with a lot of makeup. She offers her hand. "Muchas gracias."

On the other side of the car Magaña's holding his seat forward for the two girls, who race into the cemetery, where a young man stands by the black SUV. He wears a black hat, cowboy boots, jeans, and a nice silk shirt that sparkles in the sun. When the girls reach him, he kneels and hugs them, one in each arm.

A priest in a black cassock steps out of the back of the SUV. He stands to the side and leafs through the pages of a Bible.

The two men with the rifles are struggling with the casket. I go help. One of them is rubbing the tip of his thumb against the lid of the casket where the trunk left a mark on the gray veneer. The old man is busy putting his belt back on.

"Pesa un chingo," I say to sort of break the ice.

The men look at me for a second. I look over the open trunk and gesture for Magaña to come help.

The two men take the front. Magaña and I take the back. We pull the casket out and carry it slowly to the gravesite that's on the other side of the SUV where the priest and the young man are waiting with the two girls. A gust of wind blows sweeping a wall of dust across the cemetery. We turn away. The girls cover their eyes with their hands.

A couple of graves past the hole, two old men with shovels sit on a raised tomb. They look poor, dark-skinned, skinny—remind me of the vultures we saw in Los Chivos.

The woman and the old man follow us to the gravesite. We lay the casket alongside the hole. The young man lets go of the girls' hands and walks past us and kisses the woman on the cheek. Then he kneels and kisses the hand of the old man. "Tío," he says, gets up and nods at us, but addresses the old man, "¿Y estos?"

The old man says something about his pickup. His nephew complains that he won't let him buy him a new truck. They laugh and the old man pats the young one on the shoulder and they go back to where the woman has joined the two girls so that now they're together like a family. But it's weird. No one seems sad. Kind of feels more like a family reunion.

The priest makes his way to the head of the casket and opens his Bible.

The wind gusts again, and everyone turns away from the dust. When it passes, the priest rubs his eyes and asks the young man if he's ready to begin.

He nods and glances at us.

I bow and tap Magaña on the arm so we can get the hell out. The nephew gestures with his hand. He wants us to stay.

I'm not sure what to do. But then the old man places his hand on the young man's arm, tells him to let us go. "They're on the way to Guadalupe Soto."

One of the two gravediggers squatting by the grave turns to the side and spits. Everyone stares at us as if they're waiting for something to happen—except for the two men with the rifles. They stand looking out at the road like soldiers.

The young man nods to the old man and shakes our hands. "Muchas gracias for helping my family, amigos. Que Dios los bendiga."

When we get to the Impala, the guy standing on the back of the pickup with the big machine gun goes, "Psst. How much for the car?"

Magaña smiles proudly. "It ain't for sale."

The man grins. "Everything's for sale, amigo."

We drive slowly around the pickup and continue on the dirt road. I look back. The gravediggers are wrapping a rope around the coffin to lower it into the hole.

We drive in silence for a while, five or ten minutes. The sun is strong, the breeze thin and delicate. I stare at the road, thanking God I'm still alive.

After what feels like forever, Magaña says, "Narcos."

"I don't know . . . maybe they just needed security."

"Yeah, right."

"But they were nice, no?"

"Check it out," he says and holds his hand up between the two of us. It's trembling.

The girls. Maybe they live with guns and see death every day. It makes me wonder how they'll grow up—princesses in quince dresses with armed escorts.

Tiny said Susi didn't want to have a quince. He said he met her one afternoon outside the Lone Star where she started going on about it, said her mother was obsessed with her quinceañera. "I swear to God, Tiny. You're so lucky you're not a girl. My mom's hounding me about my stupid quince like it's the most important thing in the universe."

Tiny said he told her she shouldn't make such a big deal about it. "It's tradition," he said.

"To hell with that," she said. "First of all, it's a waste of money. Money we don't even have. And you know what? I'm not going to be put on display like an object for everyone to admire. It's so superficial. It's like she's showing me off, selling me to the highest bidder or something. It's gross."

Tiny couldn't even get a word in.

"Do I even look like a princess to you?" she cried. "I'm not her. And I'm not Yolanda. And honestly, I'm not even Mexican." Then she paused and kind of made a face, then added, "Like not a hundred percent . . . you know what I mean."

That was when she was into wearing her hair loose, black T-shirts, ripped jeans, and black imitation Doc Martens she probably got at the flea market on Airline.

Tiny said she seemed so wound up and frustrated, he didn't know what to say. He said it scared him. But then she stopped ranting and said, "What's wrong with me, Tiny?"

———⌣———

Magaña slows down as we come to the highway. There are a few shacks at the junction, people selling snacks and cold drinks out of coolers. Magaña looks left and right, gets on the highway, then smiles at me. "Right on target, cabrón."

"Did Susi ever have her quince?"

"What?"

"Did she have it?"

"Really? Pinche Flaco. You're worrying about that right now?"

"I was just thinking . . ." I try and envision Susi all ladylike, her long hair, a tiara, the big fluffy dress. "Can you imagine her in one of those cake dresses?"

Magaña laughs. "And black combat boots."

He steps off the accelerator, slows down. There's a line of traffic ahead of us.

"What's up?"

"It ain't customs and immigration," he says. "That's back there."

We inch along. I pull myself up and look over the windshield. Both lanes are backed up at least twenty cars. At the end are two green military trucks and a Humvee. A bunch of soldiers walk around checking papers and searching cars.

28.

It's bumper to bumper. Everyone around us is stealing glances at each other, eyes blank with fear. It's as if they're trying to connect. I try to convince myself it's safe. It's the military. They're supposed to be on our side. But I know it's different in Mexico.

"What do you think they're looking for?" I say.

"I don't know, contraband, drugs, gringos."

"For real?"

"The fuck do I know?"

We get a little closer to the roadblock. The soldiers gesture for one of the cars in front of us to pull over on the shoulder. An officer—fat, boots unlaced, and no hat—chills on a camping chair under the shade of a mezquite while the soldiers run around and do all the work. Reminds me of Félix and his lawn crew.

Magaña looks at me, half smiles. "It's the Mexican version of ICE."

I laugh, but it's nerves. It's fear. That's how it comes out of me—a high-pitched chuckle I don't even recognize.

The soldiers wave a car through. We inch forward about a car space and stop. I lean to the side and glance at the gauges. The Impala's heating up.

"We're gonna need water."

Magaña peeks at the gauge. "We'll be fine."

I sit back and breathe deep. "They're probably looking for drugs, no?"

"You think?" The tension in his tone's like a firecracker. He leans forward, glances at the temperature gauge again. "I just hope they don't flag us down. We don't have papers to bring the car this far into the country."

We sit idling as the sun burns down on us, the dead air wrapping around us like a blanket. I feel myself melting into the vinyl. I wipe the sweat from my forehead, glance at the truck next to us. The passenger's staring at the soldiers, his eyes wide, his mouth half open like he can't believe what he sees. He turns and our eyes connect for a second, then he looks away quickly.

Another truck is waved through, and we move forward another space. The soldiers look small and thin, tiny heads under big metal helmets, baggy olive uniforms. They don't seem much older than Magaña and me. Makes me think of fate. Like, if life had been different, I could be one of them. And someone else could be me. And Magaña too. It's weird how one decision made by one person changes everything for everyone who comes later. Like my mom going to Chicago with the man who is my father. If she hadn't done that, I wouldn't exist. And Tiny. If his old man hadn't had the guts to leave his town in Guerrero and risk it all to come to the US, then what?

The soldiers order a car to pull over to the side. They surround it like a bunch of flies. One of them taps on the hatch, another barks an order, another gestures at the driver to get out.

A soldier stands like a statue between the two cars in front of us, rifle hanging on his shoulder. He's staring, checking out a girl in a car. Then he blinks and turns, points to the next car, and waves it forward.

The car the soldiers pulled over earlier has all the doors and the hatchback open. The people are pulling out all their stuff—duffel bags and plastic bags and boxes—and setting it all on the dirt. The soldiers go through everything, clothes and toys and food.

We're next in line. The temperature gauge is almost to the red. A soldier frowns at the man in the truck next to us, waves at it, and points to the shoulder. Then he steps up to the Impala on Magaña's side, seems to study the car for a moment. I hold my breath and stare ahead at the road. It's the only way I know to play innocent. Just like in Houston, mouth shut, eyes forward, become invisible.

He steps back and waves us past.

Magaña steps gently on the gas.

I sink back in my seat. But as we hit forty miles an hour, the Impala coughs and drops speed. The gauge is on the red.

"It's fine," Magaña says. "The wind'll cool it."

"No. It's overheating. You're gonna blow the engine."

He raises his eyes at the rearview and checks out the roadblock behind us. It's a couple hundred yards, maybe more. "Let's just get a little distance from those assholes," he says and steps on the gas. "Just in case."

"Really." A thin cloud of steam's rising from the front of the car, stinks of burned oil. "If you don't pull over, you're going to crack your engine and we'll be fucked for real."

Magaña frowns and pulls over on the shoulder, stops under the shade of a mezquite and turns off the ignition. The Impala shudders. The engine knocks and falls silent except for the light hiss of steam escaping what I hope is just the radiator cap and not a tear in a hose—or worse.

I step out of the car and walk away and around the tree as if I'm going somewhere, but I'm going nowhere. I'm like the engine, hot and stressed and angry. I'm an idiot for not thinking this through. I thought it would be cool to sit with Susi on the bus to Diamond Park, connect with her the way we sometimes do, like during the moments when she's not shutting herself off from the rest of the world.

I look at the sky and curse.

"Take it easy, bro." Magaña's out of the car, standing by the hood, hands resting at the sides of his waist. "We're okay."

"No! We're fucked. Did you see what happened back there?"

"It's cool." He grabs my arm. "They let us pass. We're good."

"Not that!" I tear away from him. "I mean the people at the cemetery. Those guys, the guys with the guns. They were narcos!"

"I know—"

"We could be dead."

"But we're not."

I roll my eyes, take another walk around the mezquite trying to release the pressure that's making it so damn hard for me to breathe. "We were so fucking lucky."

"That's what I'm saying." Magaña lets out this little whoop sound like he's celebrating. "We made it this far. We're gonna get this shit done, bro."

"Please . . ."

"Take it easy." He hangs his hands on his pant pockets. "We've come this far, no?"

"Barely!"

"Yeah, but we're here. This is for Susi, remember?"

The sound of her name takes the air out of me like a kick in the gut. I see her eyes locking with mine, the whole walk from the ambulance to the squad car like she's cursing me. I ruined her life.

But Magaña's right. We've made it this far. Maybe it'll work. Maybe it won't. I have to keep reminding myself that this is about integrity. We have to fix what we messed up—or at least try. For Susi and for her dad. And for Tiny too. If anything, I should be grateful to Magaña for sticking with me on this. I would've never done this on my own—or with Tiny. I can say whatever I want about Magaña, but he's good at this shit.

"I'm okay," I say and walk slowly to the Impala. A big-ass semi rumbles past on the highway, kicking a cloud of dust in its wake.

"How long you think we have to wait?" he says.

I open the hood. Steam's no longer coming out the front of the car. But I know it's hot. It'll take forever for the car to cool off on its own. I can't see a break in a hose. No steam. Nothing from the radiator. I check the oil. It's low. Burned most of it—or leaked it. But we're good. Carlos told me once that when a car's low on oil it doesn't necessarily mean it's empty. A car like the Impala might take five or six quarts. If the dipstick's on empty, one or two quarts might bring it back to the full mark. I'm hoping he was right.

I tap the radiator cap. Magaña looks over my shoulder. "Don't open it."

"I know." I turn and lean my butt against the car, cross my arms. Magaña does the same. Another semi races past.

"Fuckers drive fast," he says.

"I would too around here."

"You hungry?"

I laugh like it's a joke—hungry. If we turned around and started back, we probably wouldn't make it. I run my Nike back and forth on the ground like I'm scratching the earth. "You have any regrets?"

"What, like in life?"

I nod.

"Fuck that."

"I'm just saying."

"We're not dying, bro."

"The whole trip I've been thinking about stuff."

"Well, don't."

"I'm serious."

"You thinking too much, cabrón." He taps the side of his head with the palm of his hand. "Shit just makes you doubt yourself. You have to be in the moment. Believe in yourself and what we're doing now in this moment as it happens."

"You sound like a TED talk."

"Whatever," he says, his tone sharp like maybe I hit a nerve. "You ever notice how everyone's always shitting on us? Even the teachers, always telling us about all the shit we're doing wrong, what fuckups we are. All they ever do is threaten us with the miserable futures we're facing 'cause we're not sitting quietly in class, or 'cause we didn't turn in a homework assignment." He makes a voice and adds, "You better straighten up, Antonio, or you're going to end up working at a gas station for minimum wage."

"It's more than that."

"Yeah, it's more. It's a hell of a lot more. It's how the clerks keep checking us out when we walk into Walmart . . . or how . . . or how . . . how Félix said that one time how you might get a job at Chuy's Auto Body. That's what's expected of us. Shit. No one ever says, 'Hey, you ever consider being a lawyer 'cause you're pretty sharp with the tongue,' or anything like that. We, you and me—and Tiny—we need to shoot for more than what they expect from us."

I hate to admit it but it's true. That's how it is for us most of the time. Worse for him. And worse for Tiny because he doesn't speak the best English. But he tries. Cabrón holds his own real well. I look down and trace the pattern the pebbles make—so many different shades of brown. I take a few steps and crouch, gather a few of the darker rocks, make a circle with them.

"Yeah, exactly." Magaña steps away from the car, comes around to the other side, and stands in front of where I'm making a design with the rocks. "The fuck's that?" he says.

I stand and look down at the repeating pattern. A series of rocks set in circles that interloop like the Olympic logo but different. If I blur my eyes, it looks like a tunnel. "Rocks," I say.

"Bullshit."

I look at him and smile. "It's just a little mark. A tattoo on the Mexican desert that says we were here."

He stares at me like I'm crazy. Then he pokes me on the chest with his index finger. "You know, when we were sitting in the restaurant with Joe Cárdenas, I realized he's not such a big deal. He's got the billboard and the late-night commercials on Spanish TV. But he's like the rest of us, just some cabrón happens to be a lawyer. I figured something out then. We gotta do better, bro. I'm gonna do better. I'm gonna go to college and become a lawyer, help out la Raza. We need that."

"Sounds like a plan."

"Don't patronize me like that. I know I might not get into college right now 'cause of my grades, but up until that moment, I didn't know what I wanted to do. It's like I've been treading water all my life. And honestly, it made me anxious as shit 'cause everyone's always, like, 'What're you gonna do when you graduate?' and 'Have you considered the army?' Well, fuck it. I had no idea what to do until that moment in the restaurant. Why would I even wanna go to some expensive-ass college when I don't even know what I wanna be?"

"I get it, man—"

"You realize fucking Tiny had no option 'cause he was illegal. He was fucked from the start, and he still got good grades. Cabrón's smart as shit. He's the smartest of us and he can't do a fucking thing with it 'cause he ain't got the papers. That's a waste, bro. A total waste."

I never heard Magaña talk like that. Only thing he was ever passionate about was cars and chicks.

"You always had art, Flaco. You got the talent and you've stuck with it. Remember when we were little and you used to draw the comics, the X-Men and the guys from Star Wars and Spider-Man? And look"—he points at the rocks—"you just made art with nothing but rocks. Who the fuck does that?"

I smile. I cut my teeth copying superheroes. Now I'm painting with rocks. I guess I've come a long way.

He pokes my chest again. "You're gonna be famous, cabrón. You're gonna come up with your own comic—a brown superhero, some kind of Super Vato or some shit like that—and it's gonna be gold."

"Now who's patronizing who?"

"I'm serious. When we met Joe Cárdenas, I figured it all out. That's when I knew we had to come find Anaconda. It's like some shit clicked in my head and I figured everything out."

He steps back and spits on the ground, spreads his arms out. "That was when I figured that, for once, I could be the good guy. It's so fucking clear. We're gonna catch this hijo de puta and get Susi released from jail. And when we get back I'm gonna go to HCC. I'm gonna bring my grades up, then transfer to U of H or maybe even Rice. I'm gonna go to law school, bro. Watch me. I'm gonna be a lawyer."

"Yeah, why the fuck not?" I say it, but I don't believe it. We're just two pendejos talking shit in this stretch of desert road in the middle of nowhere Mexico, surrounded by dirty cops and narcos. The only thing I believe in right now is God.

"Think positive," he says and smacks my arm. Then his tone changes. "Let's open the radiator."

I move aside. He uses his foot to flick the valve. On the fourth try it hisses but no steam spits up.

He looks at me. Takes his T-shirt off and throws it on the cap, turns it, and pulls it off.

I peek in. Bone dry. "We're fucked."

He looks in, makes a turn where he stands like he's looking for something, then stops. He puts his T-shirt back on, unzips his pants, and pees in the radiator just like that. When he's done, he nods at me.

I take my turn. He gives me a big smile like he's saved the day. But our pee doesn't fill it up. We're not gonna get very far like this. No way. The car needs coolant and water, and the engine needs oil.

Still, Magaña puts the cap back on and closes the hood. When we get back on the road, we keep our eyes on the temperature gauge. We go one, two, three miles. The needle rises but stays just above the center. Perfect.

I lean back on my seat and sigh. The sun is getting close to the horizon to our right. The landscape's warm and inviting like a trap. "Maybe you're right," I say. "Maybe it'll work out. Someone might help us out and we'll get Susi out and you'll become a lawyer."

"But not just any lawyer," he says with one of those classic Magaña smiles. "I'm gonna be big."

"Yeah." I laugh. "You're gonna be big-time."

"Bigger than Joe Cárdenas."

29.

We're on the highway for almost an hour when we see the vulcanizadora the old man told us about. The place is shuttered—a tin shack with a hand-painted sign, stacks of old tires, and a couple of junked, rusted cars.

Magaña slows the car hard and turns left. We cruise slowly down the narrow asphalt road.

Magaña takes in the landscape. "Looks like Texas, que no?"

"Like the hill country with no hills."

About five minutes in, the road gets worse, starts with a few potholes, then long stretches of dirt and rock. Then asphalt again. We pass a few people walking toward the highway, three older couples carrying plastic mesh bags loaded with stuff. They look like the Raza on the Expreso, men with cowboy hats and boots or huaraches, women in long woven dresses and rebozos.

Magaña pulls over by a couple of old men carrying firewood on their backs. "Buenas," he calls out all friendly. "Is this the way to Guadalupe Soto?"

The men set their loads on the ground. One of them steps forward and points at the road with his arm. "Recto. Todo recto. Straight ahead. Ya falta poco."

Magaña nods and drives off slowly. I'm pretty sure he's doing it so the Impala won't kick up dust on the men. The old Magaña wouldn't even think about that. Maybe this trip has changed him. Or Joe Cárdenas or the idea of being a lawyer or just cruising in the open desert, seeing how people live, the poverty—the danger.

This moment, here on this road, and before when we met those people at the funeral, is like an out-of-body experience. I don't know if it's lack of sleep or this current of fear that won't leave me alone, but the whole day's been like something that doesn't exist—like it's not really happening.

And now, with the late-afternoon light changing, getting warm and sharp, it seems even more like a dream. I lean my head to the side and let the wind blow through my hair while I stare at the sunset in the rearview mirror until it's just a thin red line like blood. I don't even want to imagine this road at night. Ahead of us, the lights of Guadalupe Soto glow like an omen.

⌄

We pass a few small shacks of corrugated steel and cardboard, barbed-wire fences. Magaña slows down. It's just small ranchos. Goats and pigs and a few skinny cows. The air smells of burning charcoal and manure.

As we get closer to the town, we pass a few concrete and brick houses built right up to the road. We pass a junkyard. A Pentecostal church. A bar, an auto repair shop. A man on a bicycle. Two pickup trucks parked in front of a restaurant. Banda music blaring from speakers.

After a few blocks, the road improves. There's a sidewalk on one side. The houses stand one next to the other surrounded by short stone walls, scrawny trees in the yards, streetlights on the corners. A skinny brown dog crosses the road. Magaña pulls over just past a taquería across the street from a small store with a blue awning—the Mexican version of a convenience store.

"What's up?"

"I don't know," he says. "Anaconda probably knows we have the Impala. The plaza's gotta be just a few blocks."

"What, you wanna walk?"

He doesn't answer, just stares ahead at a water delivery truck pulling up to the corner. A man swings down from the back, rings a doorbell and whistles.

"No. No way," I say. "You heard Pulga. This is Anaconda's town. He'll find us before we find him."

"I get it. But if we walk we can talk to people. We can ask around—"

"Oh, perfect. We can tell everyone we're here to take Anaconda back to the States so he can get the chair."

"It's an injection," he says. "But yeah, kind of."

"Dude—" I think of Susi sitting in jail. Her dead father. She probably doesn't even know he's dead. I get out of the car and follow Magaña across the street toward the town square. At the next block the sidewalk narrows. We pass a group of teenagers leaning over the open hood of a pickup truck, a young couple talking in front of a door.

I elbow Magaña. "You brought the knife, right?"

30.

We stop on the corner across the plaza. It has just a few small trees and an iron gazebo at the center. The church is across from us. Magaña touches his back pocket, feels for the knife. "I have an idea . . . Anaconda's a coyote, right? What if we ask around for a coyote like we're customers."

"What if he recognizes us?"

"Bro, we're, like, the last people he's thinking of, especially if we're looking for someone to cross us over."

"He'll recognize us for sure."

"No, he won't," he says with a shrug and taps my shoulder. "Shit, he might even take us over. Imagine if he walks us into Brownsville just like that?"

I have no idea what else we can do. I'm thinking maybe we'll never see Anaconda and we'll just go home. But if we do find him and he takes us over like Magaña says, we can alert the cops. They'll bust him. At least back in the States the cops'll be on our side . . . I think . . . I hope.

"So where do we find a coyote?" I say.

"In a bar."

"Dude, we're minors—"

"It's Mexico. That shit doesn't matter."

"Maybe there's like a feed store or a hardware store where workers gather, like in the parking lot of the Fiesta—"

"Please. We're ambitious young men from Chiapas looking to go over and work hard to help our families."

"I get that. But you don't just walk into a bar and ask for a coyote. No way."

He looks across the street. "I have an idea. But let me do the talking. Your Spanish'll give us away."

"What're you talking about?"

"You have an accent. They'll tell right away you ain't native."

"Hey, I got an A in Spanish—"

"So? You don't sound Mexican from Mexico." He starts across the street to the plaza. There's a few old people and children. A man selling nieves pushes his cart past us. At the far corner a man's playing the guitar for a couple sitting on a bench. Two stray dogs are humping in the grassy area near the gazebo.

"Now what?"

Magaña nods to the other side of the plaza. "Shoeshine."

"We're wearing sneakers."

"Shoeshine guys are like barbers; they hear all the gossip."

We walk past the gazebo to a group of boys sitting on a bench, checking out a lucha magazine, shoeshine boxes at their feet. They're about eleven or twelve. One is older, maybe fifteen. They look real poor, wear dirty hand-me-down clothes and huaraches.

"Whassup, amigos," Magaña says all cocky.

The boys glance up from the magazine, then down at our shoes.

"Mi hermano y yo, we're looking to cross over pa'l norte. They told us to go to Guadalupe Soto and ask around, said there was someone here who, ya saben, pues . . . someone to . . . help us out with that."

"A coyote?" a boy wearing an old DeWalt baseball cap says.

Magaña nods.

"Not around here," the boy says. "Not that I know of."

By the way they look at us, I can tell they're trying to figure out who we are, maybe whether we're legit or if we're carrying cash.

The older boy points at Magaña's sneakers. "Where'd you get them?"

Magaña looks at his shoes. Adidas. "Puebla," he says, probably because that's where his mother's family's from.

"I didn't know they sold those here," the boy says.

"Got them used," Magaña says real quick, "from the nuns at a shelter."

The boy nods, keeps his eyes on the shoes like he wants them.

"Pues aquí ni madres," the boy with the DeWalt cap says, "we don't know of any coyotes or anything like that."

Magaña grins and scratches the back of his head. "Híjole, all the way from Chiapas, and now there's no one here." He looks at me. "I suppose we just keep going to Reynosa, no?"

The older boy shrugs. "People go just like that. No le hace."

"'Cause we'd pay, no?" Magaña says. "We got the money, con eso no hay pedo."

The boys look at one another and shake their heads no. After a weird few seconds of silence, the older boy grabs his shoeshine box and slings it over his shoulder. "Ya pues, vamos a trabajar, muchachos."

They all take their boxes and walk away. Then they huddle for a moment on the other side of the gazebo before going their separate ways.

Magaña shoves his hands in his pockets.

I look at him. "What now?"

"I'm not sure, but those guys know exactly what's going on."

"It sure didn't sound like it."

"Whatever." He takes a deep breath and looks around. "I'm starving. You?"

"I could go for a taco."

"Or five." He taps me on the chest with the back of his hand.

We cross the street and start in the direction opposite where we came from. A block later we find a little taquería. The whole front is open. A cook's shaving meat off a big spindle of meat kind of like the way they make gyros for tacos al pastor. Another man's cooking behind the counter. We order. Magaña pays with a twenty-dollar bill. The cashier looks at the money up against the light for a couple of seconds, then brings out a small calculator and does a division, gives him change in pesos. We take a seat way in the back at one of the metal tables with the Carta Blanca logo.

Magaña nods. "Cool place, no?"

The walls are bright orange. There's a poster of a waterfall and one of San Luis Potosí. Two families with kids sit near the entrance. Smells like charcoal and onions and salt.

"What're we gonna do now?"

He smiles. "Eat."

"I'm serious."

"Shit, bro. Why don't you figure something out? My brain hurts from doing all the thinking."

The tacos come in corn tortillas with grilled onions and cilantro and a quarter slice of lime. There's salsa on the table. We dig in.

Magaña nods, speaks with a mouthful. "Good, no?"

"Tiny was right. Tastes better in Mexico. Like, way better."

We eat like pigs. End up ordering seconds of carnitas and al pastor and lengua. When we're done, I lean back on the chair and stretch my legs. I feel like my stomach's gonna burst. All I want is to find a bed and crash, just lie flat on my back and close my eyes and zonk out for two or three days. "Maybe we should find a place to spend the night. And then tomorrow—"

A man with a red face and a cowboy hat at the front of the taquería locks eyes with me.

I kick Magaña under the table. "Don't turn around."

"What?"

"Some guy's coming over."

Magaña turns around.

"You got your knife?"

The man makes his way to our table, tips his hat up. "Buenas." His face is deep red, not like he's blushing but red like raw skin, almost purple. "I heard you're looking for someone to take you to the other side."

Magaña glances at me, then nods at the cowboy. "Sí, señor. My brother and me."

"Where you from?" he says.

"Chiapas."

"¿No me digan?" He pulls out a chair, turns it around, and sits straddling it, arms crossed over the backrest. "What part?"

"From there," Magaña says, his Spanish sounding like a bad imitation of la India María. "Un pueblito. Santa Ana."

He nods. "You know where you're headed?"

"Pues to the other side."

"But what part?" he says. "You got people there, familia?"

"A cousin," Magaña says quickly. "In Houston."

"That's good. He's got work for you there?"

Magaña nods again.

The cowboy looks at me. "And you?"

"He doesn't talk much," Magaña says and taps the side of his head. "Has a problem. He's . . . medio lento."

The man with the red face studies me for a second, then smiles. "I have a nephew like that. Kind of makes you love them more, no?"

Magaña nods. "It's not their fault."

"No. Absolutely not." He looks over the empty plates, the paper napkins, and the empty bottles. "I won't lie to you, muchachos. It's getting harder and harder to cross. Hay migra por todos lados. It makes it expensive, and there's no guarantee you won't get caught. We cross in Reynosa. When we make it over, we take you to a house and wait. It might take a day or a week. When we know it's safe, we deliver you right at your cousin's door in Houston."

"Where's the house?" Magaña asks.

"Don't worry about that."

"'Ta bien, pues. And so . . . how much?"

"Three grand each—and in dollars." The man with the red face reaches across the table and takes a toothpick from the little container next to the salt shaker, puts it in his mouth. "Half up front and half when we get to the safe house. Your cousin paying for you?"

Magaña nods.

"Vientos. He can wire the money then."

Magaña looks at me and back at the man with the red face and nods.

"'Ta bien entonces." The man leans forward and whispers, "There'll be a white Bimbo truck parked in the empty lot by the junkyard at the entrance of town."

"Bimbo like the bread?"

The man nods. "Looks just like one of their trucks. Be there tonight by eleven. And tell your cousin to be ready. We'll send him a WhatsApp from the truck so he can transfer la feria."

Magaña nods, offers his hand. "Gracias."

"They call me Rojo," he says and stands, looks at me, back at Magaña. "Don't be late or we leave without you and we're not doing another run for at least two weeks."

I watch him leave. "You think maybe he's with Anaconda?"

"No idea."

The clock on the wall says it's 9:20. "I guess we're gonna meet this Bimbo truck and hope Anaconda's there."

"I guess."

"And then what?"

"I don't know," he says, and does exactly what Rojo did, takes a toothpick from the little jar on the table, places it on the side of his mouth, and gives me that devil's grin.

31.

We buy four bottles of water at the taquería and go check on the Impala. It sits where we left it, untouched. I guess there's nothing to steal, no stereo, tires, cool rims—just an old car with no top. I open the hood and we pour the water in the radiator.

"So how're we gonna do this?"

Magaña shuts the hood and dusts his hands against the sides of his pants. "I think we should leave it here. Just in case."

"In case of what?"

"In case Anaconda's there. He might not recognize us but he'll recognize the car for sure. Besides, we can't drive up to the junkyard in a car. That'd be weird, no?"

"This is getting way complicated," I say. "If Anaconda's there, we're gonna have to figure something out—either go along, or dip."

"We'll be fine," he says like it's nothing, and we start walking toward the end of town.

The evening has cooled off quite a bit. Feels nice. The air has a funky texture to it—a light grit, not dust, but something sour and organic. Makes me think of the country, like when we were driving to Huicho's chicken farm in Diamond Park.

I ate way too much. My stomach feels like it's got rocks in it. We go about seven blocks and the sidewalk ends. Dogs bark from behind a fence, sets off all the other dogs. Magaña's getting nervous with all the barking, moves close to me, keeps looking back.

"¡Oigan!" a boy calls from across the street, walks quickly to where we are. He's one of the shoeshine boys, about thirteen years old, short and stocky. He nods at Magaña. "You still looking for a coyote?"

Magaña looks at me, then at the boy. "We just talked to this guy Rojo."

"No, no. You don't wanna go with him. Ese hijo de la chingada está con los narcos. He'll force you to carry for him."

"Carry what?" I say.

"What do you think, güey?" He points to a space between the next two houses, kind of an alley but too narrow for a car. "I got a guy you can trust." He crosses his thumb and index finger like a tiny cross and kisses it. Then he walks to the opening between the two houses.

We follow slowly. "What's the guy's name?" Magaña asks.

The boy turns around. "His name?"

The blow hits me from behind, nails me just below the head. I see a flash. Next thing I'm on my knees. When I look up, the older boy from the plaza is out of the alley throwing punches at Magaña, arms swinging like a machine. They drop to the ground together and roll on the dirt.

The other boy jumps in, both fuckers nailing Magaña with fists and kicks.

I push myself up to stand, but someone jumps on my back, drops me face flat on the ground.

I get kicked on the thigh, punched in the face. Pain shoots up my side, the back of my head, my face. I free my arm from under me and throw a punch blindly—one-two-three. A boy steps back. I pull myself up and stand, bring my guard up.

The boy's about five feet away from me, fists up, eyes wide and scared.

Magaña calls out, "Flaco!" He's still on the ground, curled into a ball, while the other two pummel him with kicks.

I run to them, grab the younger one from behind, pull him off Magaña, throw him to the ground. The boy that first attacked me jumps on my back, tries to get a full nelson on me. I turn and hook him hard on the stomach, follow with a bunch of fast jabs—one-two-three-four—as hard as I can. They connect to his face, shoulder, head. He backs up, trips, and falls.

When I turn, Magaña's back on his feet, charging the older boy. He tackles him to the ground and starts with the punches in big wide arcs—left-right-left.

The younger boy jumps on my back, grabs me by the neck. I run backward and slam him against a wall. His grip slackens. I elbow him in the stomach, and he drops to his knees. I throw a hard right to his head. He drops, curls up like a fetus on the ground, and I kick him with all have.

I see the other boy coming from the side and turn to face him. He stops, looks at Magaña, who has his knife out, ready to charge.

The older boy's gone.

Magaña lunges forward and swings his knife, cuts the boy on the arm.

The kid backs up, covers the cut with his hand.

Magaña draws his arm back for the kill.

"No!" I cry.

He freezes. The boy does a quick half turn and takes off, disappears into the alley. Magaña's about to take off after him when I yell, "Stop! Leave it alone. They're gone."

He stares at me like I'm one of them, teeth clenched, eyes wide, the knife firm in his hand—blood on the blade.

"Let's go," I say, my voice trembling. "Let's get the fuck outta here."

I'm thinking of the whole plan, of Mexico and everything we were doing. We go. Forget Anaconda. Forget everything.

But Magaña shudders real quick like he's waking from a dream. He looks around, then calmly wipes the blade against the side of his pants and folds the knife. "You're right. Fuck. I almost lost it there, cabrón. You okay?"

I nod. "You?"

"Could've been worse."

I touch my cheek. "You got a pretty serious scrape." The left side of his cheek is all red and swollen, but no blood.

"A little battle scar," he says, full of bravado, as if we weren't almost killed. I'm still trembling. I taste blood on my lip.

Magaña starts walking toward town. When I don't follow, he turns, spreads his arms out. "You coming or what?"

My whole body feels tight, tired. My stomach's all queasy.

"What," he says, "we're not doing this now?"

I want to say no. I want to turn and walk in the opposite direction, get the hell out of town. But I just lower my head and follow.

Each step seems to weigh more and more. But I keep going. Every now and then we look back in case of the shoeshine boys. Magaña keeps the folded knife in his hand.

When we finally come to a tall chain-link fence with a landscape of junked cars and mountains of scrap metal, we stop.

Magaña grins at me and puts the knife in his pocket.

I look back. The road's deserted, just a couple of food stands in the next block. "Let's go," I say. "This isn't working out. It's going from bad to worse. We should just get back in the car and go."

"No fucking way."

"So we're just gonna walk into another trap? What if Rojo's just another thief? What if he *is* a narco?"

"If we stop now, it's all been for nothing." He turns, hangs his fingers on the chain-link fence and peers into the junkyard. "We need to do this," he whispers. "We need to save Susi."

"Magaña . . ."

"I'm serious, Flaco. This is it."

I look around hoping to find something—a way out of this mess— but there's only darkness and the whole world pressing against us. And it's all my fault.

"Fuck it," I say and start marching up the road. Magaña follows. When we get closer to the entrance, we can make out the outline of the Bimbo truck parked between an old single-wide trailer and a mound of scrap metal. A crowd's gathered in a tight group around the truck. The place stinks of stale tortillas, open sewer, and dog shit.

Magaña grabs my arm. "Remember to keep your mouth shut. You're slow in the head."

"I know."

"We can't get the cash so he won't take us."

"So?"

"So nothing. Let's just try and take it as far as we can and see if we can find out about Anaconda. At least those assholes didn't take my keys. There's no way I'm leaving the Impala behind."

We walk slowly to where the truck's parked and join the crowd, mostly young men, half a dozen women, and a few little kids. Raza just like in the Expreso, but these guys look tired and hungry and scared.

The back of the truck's open. Rojo and another man stand inside, stare down at their phones. After a moment, Rojo looks up and gestures with his phone at the group. "A ver, compas. There's very little room. It's gonna be tight. Only essentials. One person, one bag. When we make it to Reynosa, we'll give you the opportunity to eat and drink before we cross."

The Raza shuffles. Some of the men kneel and take things out of their bags. A woman sets down her big purse and moves the contents into her backpack.

"Cuando estén listos," Rojo says, "come up one at a time. We'll check the transfer. Make sure to move all the way inside to make room for the others, entienden?"

Everyone pushes forward, crowding the back of the truck. Two men help a woman climb up. A boy about ten hops in after her.

The woman tells Rojo her name. The other man taps the screen of his smartphone and nods.

"'Ta bien. Pásenle." Rojo gestures for her to go inside. "Hasta dentro. You too, chamaco. All the way to the end."

A man climbs up. They follow like this, one person a time. Rojo and the other man don't bother helping anyone. They just check the phone and bark orders. Everyone obeys like sheep. Magaña and I stay at the end of the line. Everyone stinks of sweat and old clothes. I figure they've probably been traveling for days. Ahead of us, a man nods to another as they approach the back of the truck. It's like they know the drill—been there, done that.

I tilt my head toward Magaña and whisper, "No Anaconda."

Two young men climb up together and are checked in. They move to the back of the truck and another man climbs up. Rojo stops him. "No, no. Momento, Esteban. We haven't heard shit from your brother, eh?"

"Sí, señor," Esteban says and removes his cap, holds it with both hands level with his stomach, bows his head. "When I talked to him, he told me he would send it by tonight."

"No se haga pendejo," Rojo barks. "It is tonight."

"Sí, sí—I know, but he said—"

"I don't give a shit what he said. We talked about this in San Luis. El que no paga no pasa."

"Pero, señor, Rojo, por favor. I told him and he said he would take care of it. He's good for it. You have my word."

The man standing next to Rojo whispers something. Rojo nods and waves his index finger in Esteban's face. "If we don't get the transfer by the time we get to Reynosa, you're going to pay one way or another, entiendes?"

Esteban nods politely and shuffles in, disappears inside the dark truck. Then Rojo leans over and tells the man to message someone named Pelón. "Tell him we have three mules, maybe four."

Magaña climbs in, then gives me a hand up. My legs are like Jell-O, my stomach's doing somersaults. I clench my teeth and take a deep breath.

"Los Chiapanecos, ¿no?" Rojo says.

Magaña nods.

Just then a pair of headlights turn off the road and into the junkyard. A big pickup speeds up to the back of the truck. A man steps out, leaves the truck running, headlights blinding us. He pushes his cowboy hat up just a bit and glances at his wristwatch. "What's the holdup, Rojo?"

"No holdup, patrón. We're just making accounts y ya agarramos camino."

The man looks up—Anaconda.

Magaña covers his eyes with his hand. I turn away, look into the truck. Everyone's packed in like cattle, sitting on the floor, shoulder to shoulder, bags between their legs.

"¿Cuántos son?" Anaconda doesn't bother with us. We're just product. He could be moving sacks of shit.

"Thirty-six. Twenty-eight from Ortega, six that we got in San Luis, and two from here."

"'Ta bien pues," Anaconda says and turns to the other man. "And you, tocayo, what's new?"

"Nada, puro jale."

"Send me a WhatsApp when you hit the road. González said you're clear all the way to Reynosa." He glances at his watch. "Better hurry."

"Sí, señor."

"I'll be at Las Maravillas. Send me the accounting when you're on the road." He adjusts his hat and gets back in the truck. Takes off. Fucker never even looked our way.

Magaña leans toward me, whispers, "Did you get all that?"

"Chiapas!" Rojo barks. "Did your cousin come through, o qué?"

"I don't . . . ," Magaña mumbles. "He hasn't . . . no, señor."

My stomach turns and turns. I don't know if it's the tacos or the fear or the people in the truck that remind me of the stash house, the mattresses, the stink, and the blood. A wave of nausea squeezes my gut. I step past

Magaña and lean over the edge of the truck, stick out my head in case I puke.

Magaña puts his arm around my shoulder. "What's wrong?"

I shake my head. A baby's crying inside the truck. It's all turning in my head, my stomach.

"¿Entonces qué?" Rojo says. "We gotta move, muchachos."

"I think he's sick," Magaña says and shoves me off the truck.

I drop to my knees. He jumps after me, leans over me, whispers, "Be sick. Puke."

I grab my stomach and moan, but nothing comes out. I can't.

"I don't know what's wrong with him," Magaña cries.

Rojo hops off the truck. "Look for me in two weeks if you get your shit together." He waves at his partner. "Vámonos, Paco."

Paco rolls down the door of the truck, locks it. He tosses the keys to Rojo and makes his way around to the front of the truck. Rojo gets in the driver's side and starts the truck, makes a fast U-turn, and leaves us in a cloud of dust. We watch it leave the junkyard, turn left and down the road until the lights disappear.

Magaña stands and pats my back. "Nice work, pinche Flaco. I'm impressed."

"About what?"

"Your moves, cabrón. That shit was genius."

I stand and dust off the knees of my jeans. "What moves? I was gonna be sick for real."

"Don't fuck around."

We start walking toward the road. "So what now?"

"Didn't you hear Anaconda? We go find that place, Las Maravillas."

32.

We walk back to town and into a tiny store on the corner near where we parked the Impala. The place is crowded with products stacked all the way to the ceiling. There's hardly any room to move. An old man sits behind a counter watching a soccer match on a small black-and-white television.

Magaña goes to the drink cooler and peeks in. I stay by the counter and ask the man where Las Maravillas is.

He looks at me suspiciously. "Aren't you a little young for that action, hijo?"

"It's my birthday."

Magaña joins me and sets a bottle of water on the counter.

The man nods at the water. "Son quince."

"Y Las Maravillas?" I say.

Two little kids run into the store followed by an older woman. The man greets each of them by name, smiles. Then he looks at me. "Two blocks that way and turn left. It's another three blocks after that."

Magaña pays for the water. When we step out, he drinks it and tosses the empty on the sidewalk. "Sounds like a fun place, que no?"

"You think it's a whorehouse?"

"I hope so."

"You got a one-track mind, cabrón."

"Don't you?"

We come to the end of the block and turn up the street. We hear the music before we see Las Maravillas, a cantina or bar or whatever kind of place. The entrance has a crude painting of a woman wearing a skimpy dress and a tiny bikini top and high heels on each side. The way in is through a black curtain that's slightly pulled to the side. Inside it glows red like it's on fire.

Magaña nods to the side. "Check it out."

"I see it." Anaconda's red pickup is parked three cars down. "What do you think?"

"He's probably getting it on with some chick. Or drinking. That would be better."

"Pulga said the dude owns the town, probably owns this place."

We stand across the street. Banda or cumbia or a mix of the two blares out of the place.

Magaña points to the paintings at the entrance. "You could do much better."

"That's not saying much."

"The artist probably had no experience with women."

"Or maybe just doesn't know how to paint."

We stare at the entrance for a moment. Then he says, "You should go in."

"You serious?"

"Say you're looking for your father or something."

"Yeah, that would go over real well."

"¿Entonces qué?"

"Let's wait for him to come out. Maybe he'll be hammered."

"Seriously?"

"Yeah. Then we jump him."

"Pinche Flaco. One moment you're all chicken, now you say we should jump the thug in the middle of the street on his home turf."

"It's just an idea."

"No, no," he says and slaps me on the back. "I like it. It's got balls. You surprise me."

"You said it—the element of surprise. If I go in there, we lose it."

"We don't know that for sure."

"True. But it could be the other way around." I'm sure as hell not going in there on my own. "Besides, even if we knock him out or whatever, how're we gonna get him back to Texas?"

Magaña's silent, parks his ass on the edge of the sidewalk.

I join him. We stare the front of the cantina. "If we jump him by his truck," I say, "we can shove him inside and drive it back over the border."

"I'm not leaving the Impala."

Two men come around the corner and walk into Las Maravillas. After a while the music changes. Norteño—a lot like Tejano music—lots of accordion and pain.

When my mom and I got off the Greyhound in Houston, we sat on the sidewalk with, like, four bags and two big boxes—everything we owned in the world. It wasn't hot yet but it was humid. I could feel the difference in my lungs from the dry cold of Chicago. She'd cried the whole ride south. I didn't understand that she was heartbroken. I thought she was just sad because we left the place where we lived, which wasn't much, but it was home.

Thing is, Chicago was tied to the man. She didn't tell me that and I didn't get it then. But I could feel it—Chicago was a broken dream.

We sat quietly waiting for her brother Félix to pick us up. It was dawn and still dark, and we were alone in the middle of a strange city. The sound of trucks came and went from the freeway overpass. But between all of it was the distant sound of Tejano music coming from a car or some after-hours bar. The accordion worked real heavy on me, tugged at my little four-year-old heart that didn't know what to make of any of it other than knowing things were different and that my mom was hurting real bad. I wanted to impress her by saying something clever, disrupt the moment, maybe make things better. "I can breathe easier here," I said.

She looked at me, her tears reflecting the lights of the shops across the road. For a moment I thought what I'd said had backfired, that I was making things worse. But she took my hand and squeezed it real hard and said, "Me too, mi amor. Me too."

I was being literal. I had no idea of the metaphor. But to her, breathing easier meant we were finally free of the man who was my father. She was heartbroken but she was free.

I can't remember what happened after that, except that that moment became my first memory of Texas.

Now I wonder whether this will be my memory of Mexico. Magaña biting his fingernails, his eyes locked on the entrance to Las Maravillas, my stomach a knot, head buzzing, my whole body aching.

Anaconda could stay there all night, and I'm exhausted. All my energy's been spent. To sit here and wait is just gonna make things harder. We need to finish this. I stand and step out on the street. "I'll go. I'll go in and ask for him. I'll tell him to come outside. Then we jump him."

"No mames."

"You said he probably wouldn't recognize us."

"Come on, Flaco—"

"We have to. We have to do it for Susi."

"The fuck's wrong with you, bro?"

"Someone'll help us." I look up and down the street but it's deserted except for a drunk sleeping it off on the stoop of a house on the next block. "There's two of us. We'll kick his ass."

"No we won't."

"Why not?"

He nods behind me. "'Cause he's right there."

Anaconda wobbles out of Las Maravillas with a woman under his arm, faces glued together in a kiss. They waver all over the sidewalk and make their way past Anaconda's pickup and across the street without looking.

Magaña and I follow, keep half a block away. They go down another block and turn the corner. When we get there, we see them walk into a house.

The streetlight on the corner's out. A dog barks across the street. The house is in the middle of the block, looks like all the others—one-story concrete, windows with metal bars, a short wall around it, and a metal gate. Inside, a clean white Nissan's parked in the driveway.

"We should wait," Magaña says and thrusts his hips forward and back.

"Who gives a shit about that?"

"He'll be tired."

"Or sober."

"Good point."

"¿Entonces?"

Magaña studies the house for a moment, then looks at me. "I don't know."

"I wish we could call the cops."

"Fuckers are probably in his pocket."

"I mean the cops from Diamond Park."

He rolls his eyes. "Fuck it, we should go in—"

"And then what?"

"Knock him over the head with something."

"You think that really works?"

"I saw a couple of gabachos from the halfway house get in a real fist-fight. One of them knocked the other one out with a punch to the head. Bam!" He fake punches the side of his head above the ear. "Right here. Dropped him instantly."

I look past him at the house. "How're we gonna get in?"

He walks slowly to the wall, runs his hand over the top. It's only like five or six feet high. "The back door." He leans forward and laces his hands together, offering me a step up.

I walk past him and jump, pull myself up and turn, sit on the wall. He does the same. Then we turn and jump inside.

The curtains are drawn on the windows, but I have this creepy feeling Anaconda's watching us from the inside, waiting for the right moment to nail us. Magaña nods to where the Nissan's parked. There's a path that disappears to the side of the house.

I grab his arm. "Hold on a sec." I peek through a window. It's dark inside. I walk up to the front door and try the knob real slow. It's unlocked. I smile at Magaña and give him a thumbs-up.

The living room's dim. The light's coming from the hallway to our right. There's a couple of fancy-looking couches, a big flat-screen TV, a bureau with a statue of the Virgen, veladoras, and two small framed photographs, portraits of young men.

Ahead of us is a dining room with a round table and tall chairs. The floor's white tile and the walls pink, reminds me of a bathroom, even smells of Pine-Sol and cigarette smoke.

Magaña nods toward the hallway.

"The fuck are we gonna do?" I whisper so low I think he doesn't hear me because he keeps making his way across the living room. "Magaña . . ."

He gestures with his hand for me to follow, moves past the couch. "We need something to hit him with."

I spread my arms. "Like what?"

He looks around, points to a ceramic vase a little bigger than a football at the center of the coffee table. He's closer but he doesn't take it. Instead, he goes to the hallway and peeks left and right. Then he glances back at me and points to the vase, gestures for me to come.

I grab it. It's heavy. I make my way to where he stands.

"¿Pero qué te pasa, mi amor," a woman's voice complains. "Ay, mi baby, don't fall asleep."

Magaña grins and takes the vase from me, whispers, "I'll hit Ana-conda, you take the woman."

"Take her how?"

"Just hold her down or something. We'll tie her up."

"Fuck that."

He offers me the vase. "You wanna knock out Anaconda?"

"No way."

We move forward real slow. The door to the bedroom's half open. I can see the corner of the bed. Anaconda's naked legs sprawled out on it.

On the other side of the bed the woman's sitting up looking into something—maybe his wallet. She's young, pretty with long black hair, a lot of makeup—and totally naked. I stare at her breasts for a second, then I look at Magaña, staring at me with that devil's grin. "You ready?"

I'm not—never will be.

He holds the vase in one hand and runs in.

The woman jumps up and screams. Magaña raises the vase over his head and brings it down hard on Anaconda's face. The vase bounces and falls to the floor next to the bed, doesn't even crack. Anaconda doesn't flinch. He's out—or dead.

"¿Qué—chingada madre?" the woman yells. "What are you doing? Sálganse de aquí. Get the hell out of my house! ¡Rateros!"

I come around the bed to her side of the room. She's screaming, shuffling, tits bouncing all over.

"Shut her up!" Magaña yells.

I grab her arms. She screams and struggles. She's strong as fuck, gets loose, and steps back. I see her arm come around in slow motion. I pull back, but not fast enough. Her fist connects with the side of my face. My knees buckle and I fall back on a bureau with a bunch of perfume bottles.

I struggle to stand. Just as I get my footing, I get another fist clear to my left temple. I hear Magaña's voice from far away: ". . . Shut her up, Flaco!"

The room's tilting under my feet.

The woman turns away, goes through a pair of pants on the chair, a belt, like she's getting dressed, but she isn't. I don't get it. I turn to Magaña. He's all fuzzy and out of focus. I squint. His eyes grow wide, he points to the other side of the room.

When I turn, the woman comes into focus. She's holding a big-ass silver automatic pistol with both hands—aimed straight at my face.

I close my eyes and wait for the sound, the bullet—death.

"A ver, cabrones, hijos de su chingada madre." Her voice is firm like a cop's. "The hell do you want here, eh? Come into my house like that?"

A wave of dizziness grabs me. My legs melt. I reach for the bureau to steady myself.

"No, no!" she cries and waves the gun. "Hands up. Up, cabrón." She points at Magaña. "You too. Manos bien arriba, pinches putos."

We do what she says. She keeps moving the gun between Magaña and me, wipes the sweat from her forehead. "What do you want? Who sent you?"

"No one," Magaña says, his voice cracking. "We—we just—that—what happens—we—"

"We came for him," I say real quick and nod at the bed. "Our friend's in trouble because of him."

The woman grins. "You even know who that is, pendejo?"

"Anaconda?"

She shakes her head. "Ese cabrón's untouchable in these parts. No way you're getting away with this. You're dead men. Entienden? Muertos."

"We have no beef with you," Magaña says. His tone is back to normal, no attitude, just Magaña. "We just want him."

She steps to the side, placing herself at an angle so Magaña and me are in the same line of sight. "Pull your pants down," she says. "Both of you. Pull them down."

"Our pants?" Magaña says and looks at me, his hands still up in the air.

"That's what I said. And your underwear. Ándenle. Down to your ankles. Now!"

Magaña unbuttons his pants and lowers his pants and underwear. Then he puts his hands back up real slow like he's not sure if that's what he's supposed to do.

"You too, cabrón," She barks and points the gun at my crotch. "Down to your ankles!"

I do what she says.

"Now, tell me. Who the hell sent you? El Gori? Luis? Chayo? Who?"

"We don't work for anyone," Magaña says. "We just need him to get our friend out of trouble."

The woman takes a step closer to Magaña and points the gun at his crotch. "The truth. Right now—don't be talking no chingaderas."

Magaña's hands tremble, his face contorts like he's about to cry. He opens his mouth but nothing comes out.

"I'm not fucking around!" she cries.

"It's the truth," I say. It comes out of me real fast like I'm praying as I fall to my death. "Anaconda was up in Texas and he killed his godfather and they arrested our friend thinking she did it but she didn't and we didn't know what to do so we came here to take him back to the States so they'll let our friend go."

"¿Qué?"

"Anaconda killed—"

"Ya, I heard you. Pero que pedo? Are you crazy or stupid or what?" she says and waves the gun at the bed where Anaconda lies unconscious. "Este hijo de puta runs the town. You'll never get out of Guadalupe Soto alive. Estan jodidos."

"We will if you let us go," I say.

"We have a car." Magaña points down at his pants. "Is it okay?"

The woman nods and backs up, sits on the chair, but keeps the gun pointed at Magaña.

I pull my pants up as well. "We'll put him in the trunk and drive straight back to Diamond Park."

"And what?" She laughs and wipes her nose with the back of her wrist. "You just going to cross the border asi como si nada?"

I nod.

The woman seems to think about it, nods at Magaña. "What happened to your padrino?"

"He stabbed him."

"No mames." She chuckles and sets the gun on her lap, keeps her hand beside it. "You two pendejos have no idea where you are, eh? We live that shit every day—ten times over. No, no—mil veces. We're killing each other like animals y a todos les vale madres."

I think of Tiny and the tattoo he wanted: México Lindo y Querido. Of how he always said Mexico was in his heart forever but that he would never come back, that it broke his heart.

"I'm sorry." It slips out of me like tears because I mean it for real. I was sorry for so many things, Susi and Tiny and Rambo and now this poor naked woman—and for Mexico.

"'Ta bien, pues," she says calmly. "Take him. Get this trash out of my house. I won't stop you. El marrano este never pays me anyway. Like everything else, he just uses and uses and that's it—throws you away like trash. That's all we are to him."

"For real?" Magaña says.

She nods. "But you better hurry before he wakes up."

Magaña looks at me, a huge smile plastered across his face. "I'll get the car."

"No, no." The woman grabs the gun, points it at him "You're not going anywhere, güero. Qué, you think I'm stupid?"

"But—"

"How do I know you're not going for help?"

"'Cause I'm not." Magaña stands at the threshold, one foot out of the room. "I swear. It's just a car, an old Impala. It's parked on that street as you come into town where there's a tiendita with blue awning."

"It's the truth," I say.

The woman looks at me and I don't know. Maybe I've got that kind of honest face or something because she gestures at Magaña with the gun. He doesn't even bother to look at me as he takes off.

33.

As soon as Magaña runs out of the house, the woman stands. She sets the gun down on the bureau and gestures with her hand for me to turn around. "You mind?"

I turn away and stare at Anaconda lying on the bed—legs and arms spread out, eyes closed, blood on his face and pillow. His chest rises with every breath. At least he's not dead.

"A ver," she says and I turn around. She put on a pink robe with white fluff around the top. She tosses me a necktie. "You better tie him up real good before he wakes up or we'll all end up descuartizados."

I cross Anaconda's hands one over the other and loop the necktie three times around his wrists. His face is like a tomato. His nose and forehead are swollen. Blood's slowly coming out of his nose. With each breath it bubbles around his nostrils. His hair's caked with it, but it doesn't look like it's still bleeding. It's just what's there, red soaking slowly into the pink sheets.

I double knot the tie as tight as I can, then I pull the leather belt with the big silver buckle from Anaconda's pants and use it to tie his feet at the ankles. The whole time the woman just stands there, watching, says nothing.

Anaconda doesn't look as big and mean as he did at Rayo's. Maybe because he's passed out. Or naked. In another world he could be my neighbor or one of Félix's buddies hanging out at Julio's or something. I wonder how a person becomes a criminal. Money. Okay, that part is obvious. But everybody wants money. I guess Rayo made out pretty well hiding the migrants. He sure didn't seem like a rich guy though. But what do I know? Maybe he had a big mansion somewhere in Diamond Park.

"Entonces," the woman says. "You boys are really doing this, eh?"

I nod and sit at the foot of the bed.

She sits on the chair and crosses her legs. For the first time I notice her for real—like a person. She reminds me of Yolanda—pretty—but not super pretty like Magaña's Daniela Castro lookalike, but still. I could see someone paying to have sex with her.

"So what happened?" she says.

"What?"

"To your friend. How did this hijo de la chingada set him up for the blame?"

"She. My friend. She's a she." I give her the details of how Anaconda stabbed Rayo and ran away and how the cops arrested Susi.

"Don't the cops over there need evidence to take her in?"

"She had Rayo's blood on her . . . and her prints were on the knife."

She grins and recrosses her legs. "And you don't believe she could do something like that 'cause she's a woman?"

"She's sixteen."

"No te creas," she says. "She might be capable of more than you think, güero. Ever think of that?"

No. Or maybe I did but—Susi would never hurt anyone. She's a good person—as good as they come—like Tiny and Carlos.

It's weird how we all start out in the same place. Except maybe Magaña. That cabrón has always had this angry streak in him. Like he's evil, but not always. It's more like an entitlement, like he's always fighting for his place in the world. He doesn't shy away from shit. Honestly, though, I kind of envy that. I wish a part of me could be like that. Not 100 percent like

Magaña but just a little. Sometimes, I hate it that I'm too shy—too damn nice. Maybe I should've told Susi how I feel about her. But I'm not even sure how that is.

Maybe Susi thinks I don't care about her. Maybe that was why she gave me that look when the cops put her in the squad car. She didn't look at Magaña or Tiny. She looked at me.

"Whatever happens," the woman says, "I hope I never have to see this one again. He's like a pinche virus. Guadalupe Soto used to be a nice enough place until he showed up. Cabrón ain't even from here."

"Where's he from?"

"Del otro lado," she says and walks to the side of the bed, looks down at Anaconda like she's trying to make up her mind about something. "Es mas gringo que el pinche McDonald's. People like him come here because it's an easy ride to the border. El hijo de puta paid off the mayor and the cops—got rich but left a trail of bodies along the way. The shit people will do for money."

Ironic. She's selling her body. Carlos might have been right about some people who have sex for money—that they're sad creatures—but not everyone's like that. This woman doesn't seem sad—she seems tough. Maybe that's the thing. We're all just trying to survive, always looking for something better. Like the people stuffed inside that Bimbo truck.

Tiny said that when he was little and they came to the States, his family worked the fields—even him. They traveled from town to town and worked all day—even weekends.

The sound of the Impala's engine breaks the silence. The squeak of the brakes, then the dog across the street starts barking again. The car door closes and a few seconds later Magaña runs into the house. His face is red, sweaty, eyes wide with excitement—or panic. He looks at me, at the woman, back at me, at Anaconda and back at me. "Cool. You tied him up."

He walks past me to the foot of the bed, looks at the woman sitting on the chair with her legs crossed, like all she needs is a glass of wine instead of that pistol, and says, "Thank you."

In all the years I've known Magaña I don't think I've ever heard him say those two words.

"Better hurry up before he wakes up or one of his lieutenants comes looking for him," the woman says.

"Órale, Flaco." Magaña grabs the belt at Anaconda's feet. "Come on, bro. Let's go."

I take Anaconda by the shoulders but we can barely move him.

"Fuck it." Magaña waves me over. "Help me here. We'll just drag his ass."

We grab the belt at the ankles and pull. Anaconda drops on the floor with a flat thud, doesn't flinch or make a noise. The woman watches us drag him out by his feet across the living room, leaving a streak of blood on the white tile. We stop at the door. Magaña steps out and reaches in across the threshold. The dog across the street keeps barking and barking.

I take Anaconda's hands and we carry him inches above the ground out and down the steps on the asphalt, stop at the gate. The street's deserted, dead quiet except for the dog. We half carry, half drag him to the back of the Impala.

The woman leans against the threshold at the front of the house, the pistol in one hand. We crouch and grab Anaconda by the armpits, lift him, and set him half inside the trunk. I hold him in place. Magaña takes a deep breath and wipes his nose with his arm. "You smell like my Language Arts teacher."

I glance at the woman. She just stands there like she's watching a couple of kids playing in the street—except for the silver pistol at her side.

We raise Anaconda's legs and roll him into the trunk, tuck his feet in. Magaña slams the trunk shut, then stops. "We need something for his mouth."

I look at the house and back at Magaña.

"Ask her for something."

"You ask her."

He looks past me. "Señorita, do you have, like, a handkerchief or something we can use to . . . you know . . . gag him?"

The woman shuffles back in the house. Magaña gets in the car. A moment later she comes back out and hands me a T-shirt.

When I take it from her, she looks me in the eyes and it's like she could be anybody—Ana Flor, my mom, Susi.

"What's your name?" I say.

"Valentina," she says and smiles for the first time.

"Gracias, Valentina."

She nods and stares at me like she's memorizing my face, kind of scares me.

"What's going to happen to you?" I say.

She shrugs. "Solo Dios sabe, güero." Only. God. Knows.

Magaña's in the driver's seat, has the engine running. "Let's go!"

I jump in. The Impala pulls forward real fast, takes a hard right. The engine howls as we pick up speed. We pass Las Maravillas, the stores, the houses, the junkyard—a straight shot to the highway.

"We fucking got him!" Magaña cries, his eyes shooting in all directions—the road, me, the rearview. A moment later he smiles. Then he starts laughing like he's high. "We fucking made it!"

But we haven't. Not yet.

We have Anaconda in the trunk. Magaña speeds, the car rattles and bounces all over the place on the shitty road.

"Take it easy on the car," I say.

"Don't jinx it, cabrón."

The night's pitch-black. The headlights illuminate ten or fifteen yards ahead. All we can see is that small space of broken asphalt. And the stars, more than I've ever seen in my life. For the first time I get what Susi told me once about the universe, that it has no end, that we're nothing by comparison.

But I don't really believe that. Susi and Tiny and Magaña and me, we're more than nothing. We matter. We're part of the world and the world is part of the universe. True, what happens to us might not change anything out there, but that doesn't mean we're insignificant. Our lives, this moment matter. Saving Susi matters. Everything matters.

I look at my hands, the T-shirt. I show it to Magaña. "We have to gag him."

"What, now?"

"Dude . . ."

When we get to the vulcanizadora at the junction with the highway to Reynosa, he pulls over.

I look back. Darkness. In all directions—darkness.

We get out and walk to the back of the car. Magaña flicks open his knife. "Just in case."

"You think he's awake?"

"I don't know. You tied him up good, no?"

I nod and bunch up the shirt. Magaña slides the key in and turns it. The trunk pops open. Anaconda's zonked out, body twisted uncomfortably—just like we left him. I reach in and force the T-shirt in his bloody mouth, feed it to him until I can't put any more in.

I step back and Magaña shuts the trunk. He smiles at me as he folds the knife. "Piece of fucking cake."

"Yeah. Tres pinches leches."

We get back in the car. Magaña takes it up to seventy. The wind feels good, cool and dry. I close my eyes. It's gotta be, like, three in the morning. We're so close and yet so far. We just need to cross over. I hope we can make it all the way to Diamond Park. Can't wait to see the detective's face when we show up with Anaconda. And Susi. She's gonna freak.

The adrenaline in me eases away. Sleep comes gently. I dream that I'm somewhere that looks like the San Jacinto Monument. Susi sits on a stone bench a few feet from where I am. I keep walking toward her, but I can't seem to get any closer. Every time I open my mouth to tell her not to move, to wait, the sound of an airplane drowns my voice. Then Tiny shows up. He's pissed at me. "Why'd you do it, pinche Flaco? Nos chingaste a todos," he says.

"No," I say. "I didn't know. It was Magaña. It's his car."

"Flaco . . . Flaco," he says it again and again like I can't hear him. "Flaco!"

"Flaco . . . It's Magaña."

I open my eyes. Lights. A ton of bright lights across the road in the distance. Cars lined up. "What is it?"

"Probably that roadblock."

"What do you think?"

"They let us pass before," he says.

"Maybe there's another way?"

He shakes his head. "Too dark. We're gonna have to wing it."

We pull up behind another car. Everything's at a standstill. But the line's not long. We can hear the soldiers yelling and giving orders, metal jingling, car doors opening and closing. This time it's the military—and the police.

I look back, no lights. At least no one from Guadalupe Soto's after us. Not yet.

We inch forward—four cars away. A generator's chugging and rumbling, feeding the lights on rickety stands. Stinks like diesel fumes. Cops and soldiers are searching every single car.

We pull forward. Three cars away.

A cop waves at the driver, points to a space where a car they just searched took off. They're taking everything out of a truck. The driver stands by the side, arms crossed, watching.

We pull up. One car away.

The policeman points to the median. The car ahead of us pulls up there. Two soldiers walk over and talk to the driver. The trunk pops up. I look at Magaña. "We're fucked."

The cop who seems to be in charge walks up to our car on my side, leans in—smiles. It takes me a moment to recognize the old man from the funeral. "You smell like my wife," he says. Then he taps my shoulder and nods at Magaña. "¿Y qué tal? You made it to Guadalupe Soto?"

"Sí, señor," Magaña says.

"Found what you were looking for?"

We nod.

"¿Y ya van de regreso?"

I bite my lip.

"Sí, señor."

The old man taps my shoulder again and waves, gesturing for us to move along. "Buen viaje, muchachos." Then he points to the soldier ahead of us and barks, "Cabo, let these ones through."

The soldier moves out of the way. Magaña steps gently on the gas. I wave. The old man nods, still smiling, as if he knows we're up to no good but is paying back the favor.

When we're back up to speed on the highway, Magaña exhales. "I can't fucking believe it."

"No good deed goes unpunished."

After a moment, he says, "The fuck does that even mean?"

"It's a saying."

"Yeah, but it doesn't make any sense."

I think about it. A good deed punished. He's right. It doesn't. I laugh and laugh, can't stop. Magaña too, both of us laugh hysterically like we're high or crazy—or both.

Then I hear a noise. "What was that?"

At first Magaña doesn't answer. A moment later it happens again—a thump knocking against the back of the car.

"I think Anaconda's awake."

34.

I look back. The trunk is down, locked. "There's no way he can get out, right?"

Magaña doesn't answer. The knocking goes on for a while. Then it's quiet again. It starts again and stops. For a long time it's just the rumbling of the big block engine and the wind cutting over the open convertible. Then it starts all over again—*knock-knock*—like the devil's at our door.

I imagine Anaconda getting loose, somehow jimmying the latch, the big trunk popping open.

Magaña focuses on the road, hands tight on the steering wheel. I lean to the side and check the gauges. The temperature gauge is fine for now. But we're low on fuel, less than a quarter tank. "We're gonna need gas."

"We're fine."

"No, we're not. We used three-quarters since Brownsville. There's no fucking way—"

"You see a gas station?"

"No but—"

"Then shut it. We'll get gas when we cross over."

I sit back, try and exhale the tension. We won't make to Brownsville on a quarter tank—but you never know.

It feels like forever until we can make out the reddish glow of the lights of Reynosa in the distance. I check the gas gauge again. It's between a quarter tank and empty. I glance at Magaña, but he ignores me, stares at the road, eyes wide, alert.

I envision Susi walking out of that sheriff's office. I think of the different ways I can apologize. I can say I'm sorry a thousand times, but how will she know it's from the heart? And what about Magaña, will he apologize or gloat?

At home, my mom and Tío Félix and Ana Flor must be freaking out because of the message I left on my mom's phone. She's probably awake right now, hasn't slept all night. Maybe they lit some candles, went to see Magaña's mom, who knows nothing of what we're up to. Maybe they'll argue. I can almost see them sitting in the kitchen, drinking Nescafé and telling stories, trying to figure out what the fuck's going on, my mom crossing herself and praying to the Virgen for the safety of her only son.

We take the loop and bypass Reynosa, follow the signs for Matamoros so that pretty soon we're speeding along that narrow two-lane highway that runs parallel the river. The sky in front of us is getting lighter. The stars are beginning to fade. I can smell the river, thick and organic like something alive and hungry.

The knocking in the back comes and goes, but it's less frequent, weaker. I'm not even paying attention anymore. I just sit with my eyes staring at the coming of dawn, my head buzzing from lack of sleep.

As we come into Matamoros, the light of dawn gives shape to buildings and bushes and trees. Everything's still, quiet like a cemetery.

"We're gonna have to play this right," Magaña says, his voice deep and sharp. "We have to get to the other side no matter what."

As we come up to the street with the row of pharmacies, I realize all it would take is one Mexican border cop getting curious, asking for papers, checking the trunk. If they find Anaconda, we're screwed.

We come up to the bridge with its friendly sign: FELIZ VIAJE.

Five cars in line. We pull up behind a pickup. One car's waved through.

The Mexican immigration officer takes the toll money, hands over the change, and the car goes through, just like that.

It's not even six a.m. and there's a long line of Raza walking across the bridge, probably going to their jobs on the American side.

The next car goes through. Then the pickup. We pull up to the booth. The officer checks us out. He looks tired. Maybe he's been working all night, just wants to go home to his wife and kids, sleep for three days. That's what I want, sleep.

He steps out of the booth and taps on the hood of the car, looks the Impala up and down, asks if it's our car.

Magaña nods. "Sí, señor."

"How long were you in Mexico?"

"Just one night."

"In Matamoros?"

Magaña nods.

The officer glances at me. I look away. He taps the hood again. "¿Visitando familia?"

We both nod at the same time.

The officer steps back in his booth and smiles at Magaña. "My father used to have a car like this. But it wasn't convertible. Nice car."

Magaña offers him the money for the toll.

There's a loud knock in the back—*toc*.

The officer glances at the trunk, then at Magaña. He steps out of the booth again. Another knock.

He walks back real slow and points to the side where another car is parked. "A ver, a ver, joven. Hágame el favor. Pull up over there."

I stare ahead at the bridge. The US side is so close. So. Close. There's just a couple of cars. Customs and Border Patrol officers hang out like they're waiting for us. An officer leads a black dog around the pickup that was in front of us.

From my peripheral vision I see the Mexican immigration officer signal someone to our right. Two soldiers stand by in the place where he wants us to pull over.

The devil's grin grows across Magaña's face. He inches the car forward. The moment we come to the middle of the lane, he floors it. The engine roars, the tires screech. Someone yells. The car leaps ahead, slams against the curb. The front right tire blows and the car sinks down on my side. I grab on to the dash, my shoulder slams against the door. The Raza on the pedestrian pass stop and stare. Magaña turns the wheel in one direction, then the other as the car fishtails. He gains control and straightens the car, but it's losing speed fast. The rim grinds against the asphalt, raising a stink of burned rubber.

The officers on the US side all freeze at the same time. Then they scatter. A Border Patrol officer moves as if in slow motion—reaches for the gun at his belt, holds it up, aims at us. Two police officers on the southbound lane run to the northbound lane and take cover behind a concrete barricade.

Magaña swerves just as we come to the US side. We hit the median before the booth. The car leaps to the right and stops sideways across the lane.

In seconds we're surrounded by a dozen officers, guns drawn, cussing and screaming, "Hands up. Out of the car. Now!"

"On the ground. On the ground!"

"On the fucking ground. Hands where I can see them!"

I step out and drop to my knees, hands up. Someone grabs my wrist, pulls my arm back hard, pushes me down, face to the ground. He digs a knee against the middle of my back, his whole weight pressing against my lungs. I feel the handcuffs strap around my wrists, the side of my face flat against the asphalt. I look at the rim of the front tire, strings of steel and rubber hanging around it. And all I can think of is how well those ratty old tires stood up to the trip.

They leave me cuffed, facedown on the ground. I can't see Magaña.

But I hear the officers talking at the same time. A dog's sniffing around the car. Someone says I smell like a prostitute. A guy laughs. The trunk slams shut. Then I hear Anaconda coughing and cussing.

An officer picks me up, helps me to my feet. Magaña's on the other side of the car, hands cuffed at the back. I don't see Anaconda.

A group of, like, ten cops leads us into the Customs and Border Protection building. The air-conditioning is freezing cold, smells of paper. They put us in separate rooms, just like in Diamond Park.

I sit in a hard metal chair. The room's plain, no desk or file cabinets or computers or posters or pictures. Looks like a closet with a few plastic hardback chairs, a camera in the top-right corner of the ceiling. An officer takes my wallet, my license, walks out of the room, shuts the door. Three others enter, take the plastic chairs, and proceed to grill me about what happened—start from the beginning.

I tell them everything. That Anaconda killed Raymundo Martínez in Diamond Park and the cops there are holding Susi Taylor as a suspect so Magaña and I went down to Mexico to get the guy and bring him to justice. I tell them everything, every detail—except about Tiny.

At one point, two cops come in with a man in a navy-blue suit and tie who looks like a lawyer, all groomed, clean shaven, wears glasses.

When I'm done with my story, I ask, "Are we under arrest?"

They laugh.

"Not today, you're not," the man in the suit says. "But Francisco Salas Rubio sure as hell is."

"Who's that?"

"El Anaconda," he says, then flips open his wallet, FBI in big block letters just like in the movies. "Rubio's been a wanted man for half a decade."

I sit back, but an officer pulls me forward, leans over my shoulder, and takes the cuffs off. Another officer hands me my wallet and asks if I'd like some coffee or a Coke or water.

I take a deep breath. Then it all comes out of me like a song: *Safe. We're safe, safe, safe.* For the first time in I don't know how long, I can breathe. I take it in long and deep. The tightness around my shoulders and neck dissipates with every breath. I look at the officer. "You got any Dr Pepper?"

They laugh. "We can handle that," one of the Border Patrol guys says and walks out.

"Where's Magaña?"

"He's using the restroom," an officer says. "You all need to call your folks and let them know you're safe."

One of the customs guys comes into the room with a can of Dr Pepper. I pop it open and drink half of it in one long gulp. The taste is a million memories at once: my mom, Ana Flor, Susi, Tiny, Carlos, and they're all good, even the ones with Félix—even when he was being an asshole. I see myself running to the Lone Star to buy a candy bar. It's early evening in summer and we've just had dinner. The sun is still out and the air feels warm and moist and I can hear Tuerto barking and the old lady gossiping over the fence and the laughter of a boy pushing his friend on a Big Wheel with no handlebars and Susi's calling from the yard, "What's up, Flaco?"

One by one the officers leave the room, go back to work doing whatever it is they do, and pretty soon it's just me sitting alone in the hard chair in the air-conditioned office.

I close my eyes and think of Tiny, wish he had been with us for this, wish I could tell him what happened. He'd freak. I can almost see him laughing, saying no way, that it was impossible, asking all kinds of questions, his eyes all round and wide, his goofy laugh, his excitement, asking me what kind of tacos I ate, telling me, "Didn't I tell you, güey, they're better, no?"

Yes, the tacos were way better. And yes, we did it. We got Anaconda. But he'll never know.

The door opens and startles me back to reality. Magaña waltzes in like he's the king of the world, a can of orange Fanta in his hand. He holds it up and sings, "We're heroes, cabrón. Real heroes!"

I stand and we high-five each other. "We are," I say with a smile so big it hurts my face. "I can't believe we pulled it off. It's crazy."

"I can," he says, all smug like he always is, as if we do this kind of shit every day. "Come on. The cops say we're good to go."

"What about the Impala?"

"They towed it to the pound," he says like it's nothing and walks out of the room. I follow him down the hallway. A Border Patrol officer smiles at us as he passes. A cop nods at Magaña and points to the side—the exit.

When we get out, we stop at the end of the customs building on the corner of International Boulevard. Everything looks bigger and wider and cleaner—even the little park on the corner.

"So what's the plan?"

Magaña rubs his hands together and smiles. "Food."

"What about the car?"

"I'm gonna have my cousin pick it up and take it to a shop."

"How we getting home?"

He waves a piece of paper. "Expreso, bro. How do you think?"

"Where'd you get those?"

"The FBI dude," he says, and we start the four-block walk to the station. "'Cause that's how they treat real American heroes."

At the corner a lady has a little tamal stand, just a couple buckets and an umbrella. We scrounge up all our change and a few pesos and buy a couple tamales each, chicken with green sauce.

When we get on the bus, Magaña starts like he always does. He goes on and on about how we saved Susi, how we nailed a criminal—a criminal whose stature Magaña has already upgraded from wanted to the FBI's Ten Most Wanted. His exaggerations build up pretty damn fast.

The bus pulls out. I look out the window at the bridge to Mexico. Border Patrol officers are marching a line of about a dozen Mexicans down the road and leading them onto a white bus, the kind with steel mesh on the windows. Illegals. I wonder if it's the people in the Bimbo truck from

Guadalupe Soto. What does it matter? They're all the same, Raza just trying to get ahead in life. I know Anaconda was a bad guy, but is helping people cross over such a bad thing? If they're illegal, then who's legal? Tiny wasn't illegal. There was nothing about the dude that put him on the other side of the law. As a matter of fact, I can think of a ton of bolillos who should be illegal. Tiny didn't deserve to disappear like he did. Shit's unfair.

". . . Diamond Park?" Magaña says as he ends his monologue. His face is tight with anticipation, as if he's going to a party.

"What?"

"Pick up Susi, no?"

"For real?"

"Yeah, bro. We'll get her out of jail and bring her home," he says. "We're heroes."

It sounds good to me. I imagine us in the lobby of the police station, Susi walking out—no, Susi running up to me—and thanking me for saving her. But a moment later the logistics become clear. "She's a minor. The cops said they have to release her to her parents."

"Rambo's dead, remember?"

"She has a mother," I say. "Besides, we're broke. We'd be stuck in Diamond Park forever."

Magaña looks away for a moment. "Maybe you're right."

I tell myself it'll work out, but I'm afraid this isn't the end. For some reason, shit can get hung up on a technicality or something. The cops in Brownsville have to talk to the cops in Diamond Park and tell them what went down; there's paperwork; Susi's mom has to get down there but she never leaves the house. We can't do much more but we can't just leave her like that. "We should call Joe Cárdenas when we get home," I say, "make sure he knows what's going on."

"Sounds like a plan," he says, all pumped up. "And now what?"

I recline my seat all the way back and close my eyes. "Sleep."

35.

The Expreso makes it into Houston in the late afternoon. When I finally get home, the first thing I see is my mom sitting in the living room, her old wood bead rosary in her hand. And just as I imagined, there're a few extra candles burning at the feet of the Virgen. She sees me walk in and her face contorts real slow as if she can't decide whether to smile or cry. Then she runs to me, screaming, "Rafael! Dios mío, but where have you been? Why didn't you call me back? Qué susto me diste."

She says all this as we hug. She kisses my cheeks and runs her hands all over my face like a blind person trying to figure out what I look like.

"It's a long story."

"I've been worried sick." She sobs and hugs me again. "Your message—"

"I know. And I'm sorry. But it's all good now. I'm back."

Ana Flor marches out of the kitchen and crosses herself. "Rafael, pero válgame. Thank God. Are you hungry, mijo?" She doesn't wait for me to answer and goes right back into the kitchen, straps on her apron, and starts warming up leftovers and tortillas.

Félix waddles out of his bedroom and leans against the threshold, looks like he's tied one on, eyes red and puffy like he's been passed out for the last couple hours. "Mira na' mas. Just look what the cat dragged in."

"I'm sorry I didn't call. My—"

"I told them you'd be fine," he says and scratches his stomach like an ape. "But these women don't listen to reason, they just weep and pray and think the worst."

"Félix, por favor," Ana Flor calls from the kitchen. "Why don't you make yourself useful and go back to bed?"

Félix nods at me, then looks at my mom. "You happy now, Fernanda?"

She glares at Félix, then looks at me. "I called everyone I knew. And the police. I was getting ready to go look for you." She pulls me to a chair at the dining room table. She sits beside me and won't let go of my hand, won't stop looking at me, won't stop crying, smiling, crossing herself.

Félix walks over and ruffles my hair. "It's true. She was putting together a search party. The whole neighborhood was ready to go to Mexico and kick some narco ass." He gives me a pat on the back. "Glad to see you're back safe." Then he goes back into his room and shuts the door.

A few minutes later Ana Flor comes out with a bowl of stew and a cloth with warm tortillas. They watch me eat in silence, no questions. After I'm about halfway done with the meal, I tell them what happened, sparing them some of the details like Susi and the blood and Rambo and how Huicho ended up. When I'm done with the story, Ana Flor reaches across the table and places her hand on my arm and says, "Mr. Taylor passed away. They found him down there in that town. They said it was an overdose."

I nod and bite my tongue. I stare down at my empty plate and think of everything that happened, one thing after another, rolling down on us like an avalanche. And all we did was go get a stupid car.

"Mr. Taylor's service is the day after tomorrow," my mother says real gently and taps my hand. "You should get some sleep, mi amor. We can talk more in the morning."

When I go to bed, I finally plug in my phone to charge. I listen to my messages. It's just my mom. At first, she sounds concerned and even angry. But then her voice starts changing. By the fourth message she sounds scared. She speaks real fast. Her tone's shrill like I've never heard before. Her panic comes through in the words she mispronounces as she pleads and begs Jesus to bring her news of me. And then the messages are just desperate, raw cries for help. It's as if her vocal cords have been torn away, exposing her broken heart.

I can see her sitting in the kitchen at night, the phone in her hand, alone with her anguish. Like Susi and Tiny and Rambo and Huicho and everyone else. The tightness in my throat contracts like a fist and swells until it's impossible to hold it down. It claws at my insides so hard I have to bury my face in the pillow and let it all out into the silence of my room.

⌄

Being home feels weird, like I'm here but not here. Like I'm floating in space. The sounds that used to be so familiar—the lady sweeping her porch, Tuerto barking next door, the trucks on the road, Félix going on and on about nothing—they're all accentuated over a deep silence that won't leave me. I don't know what it is, but it's always there—like a ringing in the ears except there's no ring—just this empty, dead silence.

⌄

The afternoon of Rambo's service I sit between Ana Flor and my mom, who's taken the whole day off. Each one holds one of my hands, won't loosen their grip even after our hands get all sweaty.

Félix went to work. Tiny and his family are gone. And Magaña's not here either. But Susi's here. She's out of jail, out of Diamond Park, and sitting in the front row between her mother and Yolanda. The whole time they just stare at the casket. The people of the neighborhood go one by one up to the dead man, the addict who broke and killed himself with an overdose of heroin.

I don't go up. My mom goes and Ana Flor goes, but I stay in my place just like Rambo used to sit at mass on Sundays—a fucking rock—with my back straight and my eyes ahead, looking at Jesus on the cross and wondering whether he's had a hand in any of the shit that went down.

Thing is, Rambo tried so fucking hard. Dude fought and fought against the need for heroin until I invited Susi to come to Diamond Park. Yes, if Magaña hadn't been a dick, maybe none of this would've happened. But it did. And even as the priest goes on about how we're all God's children and we're all forgiven in His eyes and Rambo is now in that new place next to Him, the guilt and the anger I hold inside won't leave me. I keep clenching my jaw. My thoughts drift through all the details of the last few days as if searching for something that'll release the pressure, looking for an answer to a question that doesn't even exist.

When the service ends and I stand behind my mom waiting for people to pass so we can get out, Yolanda and Susi walk by. Susi looks ahead, avoiding everyone's glance, turning herself invisible.

I reach past my mom and touch her arm. "Susi," I say quickly. "I'm sorry."

She ignores me and walks past with her back straight, head held high and her eyes forward like she's in a trance, a robot just like Rambo. Other people reach out. Yolanda nods and smiles and says thanks. But not Susi. She just walks like a soldier out of the church, makes me wonder if she's fucked up, traumatized by all the shit that happened.

It's not as if I expected a thanks or a smile or anything. I just wanted her to know, to acknowledge that I knew I fucked up and that I was sorry. I guess it's what people talk about when they say they're looking for closure. Like this isn't over until somehow Susi looks me in the eye and tells me it's okay or that she gets it—even if it's not in those exact words.

Later, we have a miserable early dinner at home with Tío Félix, who goes on and on about Rambo as if he knew the dude. I'm suffocating. I gotta get the hell out of the house and breathe. But when I reach the door, my mom stops me.

"Where you going, mi amor?"

"Just out," I say, my jaw clenched, tension running through me like an electric wire to the doorknob. I have no idea what I'm doing anymore, where I'm going or anything. I just need space. I need to breathe.

"Gonna light one up with your buddies?" Félix says.

I shake my head, not because I'm denying what he said, but because he doesn't know shit and doesn't deserve an explanation. I glance at my mom. "I'm going to the Lone Star to get a Dr Pepper."

The minute I'm out the door, Tuerto comes to the fence barking. I stick my fingers through the chain link to quiet him down. Above the Lone Star, the lights on the big Joe Cárdenas billboard are warming up. It's still early and the sky's got this clean, pale color, like the sky in the Mexican desert.

I wait for the mail lady to drive past. Then I cross the street, go into the Lone Star. When I walk out, Magaña's walking up the road from the bus stop. We meet on the corner across from the Taylor house.

"How was the service?" he says in his usual tone, makes it sound like he's being condescending, but I know he's not.

I shrug and we start toward my house. After a while he says, "So much for being heroes, que no?"

"Does the neighborhood feel strange to you?"

"The fuck you talking about?" he says all happy. "Same place, same people."

"I don't know, there's this strange vibe."

"The hell you smoking, pinche Flaco." He kicks at the fence where Tuerto's barking. The mail lady's on her way back and pulls up to the house as we get there. She hands me the mail.

Magaña nods to the corner where Tiny's house sits empty. "Kind of weird not seeing the van there, que no?"

"And Tiny's dad working on it."

"And the kids playing in the street." He turns to me and holds up a joint. "You wanna spark one up real quick?"

We walk over to Tiny's house and sit on the front steps. Magaña lights up and takes a long toke, stretches his arm out in front of him, and examines the joint like it's something special. "My cousin picked up the Impala from the pound and had it towed to a shop down there, but they said it might take a while. It's got a busted axle. And he has to find a replacement rear quarter panel."

I take a drag off the joint and pass it back. "Gonna cost some bucks, no?"

"Probably," he says. "But I just dropped an application at the AutoZone. Juan el Gordo says the pay's not great but you get a pretty decent discount."

"Yeah, but they don't sell body panels for '59 Impalas."

"True." He laughs. "But I'm sure I can find one in a junkyard. I'm gonna do what you said and keep it original."

"It performed real well, no?"

He nods at the stack of mail in my hand. "You gonna open that, o qué?"

The letter on top of the stack of junk mail is addressed to me, Rafael Herrera. It's from the California Institute of the Arts.

"I don't know."

"What the hell?" He takes a drag and offers the joint to me.

I shake my head. "It really doesn't matter either way."

"The fuck you talking about? That's your future right there, bro."

I smile and tap my chest with the side of my fist. "My future's in here, cabrón."

"Pinche Flaco. Just open the fucking letter."

I bite my lower lip and look down the street at the empty lot where the Buick used to be.

Magaña does the same. "But if you got in, you'll go, right?"

I shrug. "There's the tuition. And then there's my mom."

"Fuck that. You're going for sure." He takes another drag off the joint and rubs it out against the step and puts it in his breast pocket. "You're going even if it means I have to sell the Impala to pay for it."

"Yeah, right."

"I'm serious." He stands to face me and taps his heart with the side of his fist. "I will. I want you to go, Flaco. You got the talent for sure, and you work your ass off. You deserve that shit more than anyone I know."

I can see it in his eyes. I can tell. He's for real.

"I gotta dip," he says and steps back. "Let me know when you're gonna open it. I wanna be there. And don't worry about your mom. We're all family here, bro. We'll take good care of her."

With that he turns and skips off toward the Joe Cárdenas billboard. I look down at the letter and back at the empty lot. Houston. It's pretty much all I've ever known. Carlos didn't have this chance. His only way out was to join the army, get the fuck out. It was a gamble and he lost.

"Flaco?"

Susi's standing on the sidewalk, her hand on the gate to the house. Behind her, the sky's a deep blue, the first few stars struggling against the lights of the city.

"I'm sorry." The words come out of my mouth automatically like a recording. "I didn't know any of this was going to happen. Magaña—I—"

"It's cool."

"No, it's not. Cárdenas said . . . We thought if we found Anaconda—"

"I know." She laughs and comes in and sits on the step next to me. "I can't believe you did that."

"We did it for you."

"You guys are crazy."

That's all she said about it. And that's the thing I now know about Susi: She's nice and she's also tough. I didn't get it until now. All those times when I thought she was being weird, she was just figuring herself out. Now she knows.

She leans against me real friendly and nods at the letter in my hand. "You got in?"

"Don't know." I show her the envelope, but she doesn't look at it.

"I—I was really happy that you came with us . . . until that happened," I say. "I didn't know those guys. I didn't know anything. And Magaña. I swear. I . . ."

She tilts her head to the side and lays her hand on my wrist. Feels warm, almost electric, and all the weird feelings I've been stuck with since we got back from Diamond Park evaporate, just go away real slow, like smoke in a breeze.

"Don't do that," she says. "It was my choice. I'm the one who wanted to go. And what happened had nothing to do with you. Why do guys always think girls need to be saved?"

"You were in jail." My voice cracks when I say it. I don't fucking get it. I would've been freaking out, sitting in a cell in Diamond Park on murder charges. But then, the more I think about it, the more I understand. Like Valentina said, maybe Susi's capable of more than I think.

"I wasn't under arrest, dummy. My dad had to come get me," she says this real quick and then her tone drops to a whisper. "I guess you know how that turned out."

Her dad. Yeah, I know how it turned out. But it could have been worse for her. I try to go over everything I remember from that first day and after, when Magaña and I went back to Diamond Park and everything Cárdenas said. But all I see is Susi with a shirt covered in blood, her hands in handcuffs, and her angry dark eyes looking at me like she's ready to kill me.

My tongue's tied real tight in my throat. This is the closest I've ever been to her—or anyone. It's just like it was with Carlos and Tiny. I just don't know what to say. So we sit there in silence for a while until I finally say, "I'm glad you got home okay."

"Me too."

I think of her locked in that cell and how shitty that had to be. "Was there a window in your cell?"

"What?"

"Magaña and I were talking about that when we went back to try and get you out."

"You guys are weird, for real."

I laugh. I guess we are. "So when did you get home?"

"Tuesday. My mom and Yolanda picked me up with my uncle Eufemio, but we had to deal with my dad . . . you know . . ."

I clench my jaw. I don't know if I want to scream or laugh or what. Tuesday. That was the day Magaña and I crossed into Mexico.

"I've been angry for a real long time," she says suddenly. "Like really, really angry at everyone, at my parents and the world and everything— even God."

"You're smart, Susi." It comes out of me real soft and tender so that I almost don't recognize my own voice. "Maybe you understand things the rest of us don't. Maybe that's what makes you angry. Like if you're really, really smart, maybe you see everything for what it is, no? That shit would make me angry too."

"Maybe . . ." She says it in a way that feels as if she's going to say something else but doesn't.

I want to ask her what happened. I want to tell her we're friends. That she can let me in. That she can trust me. This whole thing . . . it could've been cut so short. But I know the reason she's here talking to me and telling me this is so I understand that what happened is not my fault and that she's okay—more than okay. So I bite my tongue. I might not understand everything she's telling me, but I understand how she feels inside because we all feel like sometimes other people see us as weak or helpless or as less than. Like the way Magaña always feels he has to help me. But it's okay to be who we are. Valentina said it. Maybe we're all capable of more than what others think.

"It sucks that Tiny had to leave," I say, sort of moving the conversation along because I'm trying to avoid the question I'm dying to ask.

She nods and stands. "I wanted to say goodbye. My mom's taking us to her sister's in Uvalde for the rest of the school year and maybe the summer."

I have to ask.

"She feels like she's under the microscope here." She squints, crinkles her nose. "You know, with all the gossip and stuff."

"That neighborhood chisme," I say.

I have to ask.

She walks out the gate. I follow her and we stand close together in the same square of concrete sidewalk. I can smell the soap in her hair, makes me think of youth, of the neighborhood and the time before Diamond Park.

"I know it sounds weird, but I'm gonna miss you, Flaco."

"Susi," I say at last. "Did you . . . ?"

"Flaco—"

"I'm sorry. I just . . . you know . . ." But I can't. I can't spell it out. I can't say it out loud because she's giving me that Susi Taylor look, powerful and all-knowing, yet mysterious. She holds me like that for what seems like forever, telling me I already know the answer. Then she leans forward and kisses me on the lips. Just a quick friendly peck with a little more love than you'd expect and says, "Just do me a favor and don't believe all the chisme, okay?"

And just like that she turns and walks away. Classic Susi.

There's so much I want to say to her—that I was sure of so many things, that she needed me, that only I could save her, and that I was wrong to be so sure and about so many other things, and that we're a lot alike. That we're a hell of a lot more on the inside than what people see. But I think she knows this—and a lot more.

I don't go after her. Instead, I go back and sit on the step and look at the place where the Buick used to be. I can almost see Magaña and Tiny and me squeezed together in the front seat. We're all there—even Carlos and Susi and Yolanda and Huicho and Valentina. The Buick's all pimped out and badass-looking. I see it kind of like Diego Rivera's mural in the National Palace in Mexico City with all the important people in our history—Miguel Hidalgo and Benito Juárez and Zapata and Pancho Villa—but bigger, bigger than the Joe Cárdenas billboard and with a giant Mexican flag in the background and all of us looking real proud because we are.

I don't tell my mom about the letter from Cal Arts. I kiss her good night and go to bed. And still my mind turns like it's caught in a wheel, turning and turning and turning with all kinds of thoughts about Susi and Diamond Park and going to California and how Magaña offered to sell his car. And I believe he would. Fucker talks a lot of shit but that was for real.

I keep telling myself I'm lucky. My mom's love. I get it. I get the hurt she must've felt when she thought I might not come back. And Ana Flor and even Félix too. They all care in their own way—even Félix. He puts up this big badass front, but he cares. And he does what he can. That's just how he is. I know that now. And I'm lucky for Susi's friendship and maybe even her respect. Shit. That's for real. And Magaña. All these years of friendship and I always had my doubts about him—not anymore.

I close my eyes and think of California, of the ocean and the mountains. Texas and California used to be part of Mexico. They should have pretty good Mexican food there. Probably a lot of fish tacos and maybe even some pretty good barbacoa.

My phone buzzes with a WhatsApp message. I don't recognize the number, says, *Whaz up, cabrón?*

I answer, *Nothing.*

You get Susi out?

I look at the number, but I don't recognize it. I don't even know the 611 area code. The first thing that comes into my mind is Anaconda. Or Rojo. One of his people. I sit up and tap a message: *Who is this?*

Tiny. Who else?

For real?

En serio. We're in Bakersfield.

Where's that?

California.

ACKNOWLEDGMENTS

I'm forever grateful to my wife Lorraine for her undying support and to my kids, Chloe, Finn and Alexia for their inspiration and wonder. I love you guys.

I'm deeply indebted to my editor, Andrew Karre, for his detailed and tireless work in making *Diamond Park* what it is today. To Anne Heausler for her fine eye and to the team at Dutton, thank you. A hearty abrazo to my stupendous agent, Isabelle Bleecker, and to my readers, Alvaro Saar Rios and Sarah Cortez, whom I forced to suffer through an early draft of the manuscript, thank you. And as always, I'd like to give a shout out to my lovely friends the Byrds in El Paso, especially Lee, who suggested I develop a short story into a novel—¡mil gracias!

I would also like to express my sincere gratitude to the Sarasota County Artist Alliance Ringling Towers Grant for the financial support it provided during my revision process.

RESOURCES

If you, like Susi, are experiencing suicidal thoughts, please know that there is help. Go to suicidepreventionlifeline.org or call 800-273-8255.